OR
WHATEVERHAPPENED
TO
RICHARDBEYMER?

A NOVEL

To Nada
A little something to read
while the 'guys' are playing
cards — WRITER George
AKA - George OOPS

Loving and grateful appreciation to my dear (Dr.) Pamela Paradowski, for making all the hours, days, weeks, months and years of editing here in the mental institution—known affectionately as the planet earth—such a creative joy.

To James Moore, musician-poet extraordinaire and fellow inmate, who insisted on obsessively checking, rechecking and re-rechecking my spelling and grammatical punctuation to make sure the reader would not find out how hopelessly negligent I am in these areas.

The underlying cause of all shame is the deep and unshakable suspicion that I am an impostor.

Jed McKenna, Author of *Spiritual Enlightenment*
The damnedest thing

PREFACE

A WARNING TO THE READER

Although a preface is usually an opening statement written by the author to introduce his or her novel, in this case, Noel Vera, Film Critic at Large, gives a far better impression of these pages than I ever could, allowing the reader to make up their mind if they want to venture into them...or not.

It's a strange, strange, strange book: for a few pages you marvel at the outlandishness, the outrageousness, and you wonder if Beymer can keep up the intensity; he can, but you (or at least I) can't--after those first few pages I have to put it down and try to continue with the rest of my day, shivering from the chill of having just stepped in from way out there, drinking in out of a need of reassurance the relative normalcy. That's probably why it took me the better part of a year to read this.

Problem is, you don't quite stop reading--it sits there, in the corner, daring you to pick it up again. Sometimes I catch it staring at me (damn those eyes). When I'm not looking, I'm sure it's pushing itself off a stack, clambering quietly up another; sometimes I imagine it's riffling its pages, just to provoke me. It's difficult trying to concentrate when you're this paranoid about a novel.

It's a film script, something I wish I'd have thought of first (or at least, come out with a book in this format first), and that's only natural; Beymer's a Hollywood actor, or started out that way. I remember him from West Side Story, easily (and I believe Beymer himself would agree and he does) the blandest, least interesting aspect of that movie. He's grown far more fascinating since, what with his participation as Benjamin Horne in David Lynch's breakthrough series Twin Peaks and with the production of this book.

Don't get me wrong--this is not an easy read, but there are parts in here that are worth the pain. Erotic fabulist bizarre slapstick I'd be pained to try compare with what I've read or seen elsewhere, medical procedures that segue way into action set-pieces both on the molecular and astronomical and fantasy level, bits of business and acts of copulation I'd wish to have scrubbed from my mind and other things far too disgusting and disturbing to mention. This is one sick dude, and I'm glad he's around--but also glad he's only one of a small handful.

He imagines his death--he imagines several deaths, in fact, some spectacular, others gruesome, but that's not the worst (or best) thing about his book at all. No, the best (worst) thing about the book is this, that behind all the surrealism, the metaphysical slapstick, the Vonnegut comedy, the twists and turns and transitions that feel so much like Bunuel, Cronenberg, Lynch and MAD Magazine, you do sense something: an indefinable sadness, a sense of a man wondering, questing, struggling to find out just who he is. There's a whisper of pathos behind this book, the bewilderment of a man who enjoyed enormous success right there at the beginning, then learned that success may not be all there is to life--that there's so much more strange and wonderful and terrible things happening to you in life that at any stage you might feel small, vulnerable, even irrelevant. Eventually it does become readable, because Beymer for all his faults speaks to us about our anxieties, our insecurities regarding who we really are and where do we really stand. Eventually it's readable (if in small doses, along a long period of time) because we recognize ourselves in his predicament, losers who get enough of a taste of success to want to stay in the game, and are forever running around in circles, trying to get a taste of that long-vanished drug ever since.

That George Oops (wonder about that name--does Beymer consider himself an accident? Perhaps considers all of us some random quirk of fate?), he's like an everyman, investigator, trying to drill deep into the sea of self-indulgence to discover the truth about life and love and everything, his spacesuit a metaphor or evocation of Don Quixote's tin armor suit, wielding his typewriter for a lance (instead of a deadly spear we hear the rat-tat-tat of sharp words), sitting on his mule of a hospital trolley and charging forward to tilt not windmills, but nurses, starlets, next-door neighbors.

It's often overly intense, and just as often considerably self-indulgent (despite opinions otherwise). But it's ultimately moving, a one-of-a-kind experience, and not something I'd want to forego (that said, it's probably not something I'd like to read again, at least not for a while). And now that I have hopefully done justice to the experience of reading Beymer's novel, biography, experiment, what-have-you, I hope the damned book will sit quiet in its corner, and stop making eyes at me. I need to think.

To which Beymer replied, "No, you need to **stop** thinking... you've been warned."

SETTING THE SCENE

In regards to the subtitle, *Whatever Happened to Richard Beymer?*, before you conclude the author is a completely self-absorbed, self-promoting, egocentric, bag of wind, hear me out.

First, let me set the scene. It's the late 60's, early 70's. The film *West Side Story* (that Natalie Wood and I starred in) and my 15 minutes of fame have come and gone. The Beatles have broken up. Ronald Reagan has given up doing commercials for 20 Mule Team Borax laundry booster and become Governor of California. Jimi Hendrix has OD'd on heroin, followed a couple of weeks later by Janis Joplin, and within a year Jim Morrison *breaks on through to the other side.*

America, in its infinite wisdom, makes Richard Millhouse Nixon president of the United States, an office from which he will be forced to resign due to a little burglary he gets involved in. Kubrick has released his masterpiece *2001* and blown our collective cinematic mind. Trying to figure out how to abandon Vietnam so America doesn't look like it got its ass kicked, the powers that be cleverly decide to sneak out under cover of the slogan "Peace with Dignity."

Presidential hopeful Robert Kennedy follows behind a mule cart along with 50,000 other mourners, in a funeral procession bearing the murdered body of Martin Luther King. Kennedy is himself assassinated four months later, officially ending any dream of Camelot. Bob Dylan is still on the pop charts. Gas is 35 cents a gallon. Movies are a buck twenty-five. The Twin Towers are nearing completion. Indian gurus are flocking to the U.S. with their ancient Vedic wisdom to complete the picture show of *being here now* that some of us experienced in the *acid coming attractions.* And finally, we've landed on the moon. And for the first time in human history we are able to look back at ourselves from POINT OF VIEW of an INFINITELY WIDE Kodak Moment and see, if there were any doubt, the insignificance of our collective existence.

And me? I'm going through it stoned. I'm now in phase three of Timothy Leary's "tune in, turn on and drop out." Unemployed. Broke. Career in the toilet. Making 16mm underground films with my wind-up Bolex. Eating rice and veggies. Letting my barbershop haircut grow to my shoulders. Exploring *love and peace* in the day and *sex, drugs and rock 'n' roll* in the night. Reading books about God realization and thinking enlightenment is just a few months of meditation away.

I'm living with an actress and filming our life together as we *trip* through our psychedelic love affair. We see the world through *the news with Walter Cronkite* who reminds us nightly—though not intentionally—that *Nothing is real, and nothing to get hung about.* We're taking black-and-white Polaroids and waiting sixty seconds to see our naked images and, like John and Yoko, we're getting comfortable with what we see.

We're cohabitating in this one room garret on the top floor of a three-story dwelling that Jack London built in Hollywood at the turn of the century. There's a little shed on the roof. I turn it into an editing studio-slash-futon bedroom that we get to by pulling down a ladder and climbing up through a hole in the ceiling—forty bucks a month. The only connection I still have with Hollywood is what little I can see of the Paramount studio lot from my roof. All is well though, in fact, *weller* than it's ever been in my life.

It was somewhere in here that Richard Lamparski called. Who's Richard Lamparski you may well ask? He's the author of a series of books entitled, "Whatever Happened to. . . ?" He tracks down the once-famous and not so-famous celebrities in show biz and fills you in on their fall from grace. You getting the picture?

Now when Richard Lamparski called and asked if I would be in his book, it was clear that I had officially been accepted in the *has been hall of fame.* In other words, no one in Hollywood any longer cared who, where, or even if I existed. So I say, "Sure, why not? Come over. Let's talk."

I don't know what I was thinking. Maybe I thought that some producer would see the piece and say, "Yeah, him, that guy from *West Side Story* . . . what's-his-name. Let's give him the lead in our next major multimillion dollar motion picture."

Dreams of fame die hard.

So I do the interview and I get my page in the book with a picture between Frankie Avalon and Spanky McFarland. And there you have it, the final nail in the coffin of my short but "I"-opening career.

Then, just when I'm getting the hang of this love and peace business—a rude awakening. My girlfriend is introduced to this major rock star backstage after his concert, fucks him, and leaves the next day on his world tour. I find out watching TV that night. There she is with the rock star on the entertainment news waving to the crowd as they board his private jet.

I try to maintain but I go into a major tailspin crashing headlong into an abyss of self-pity. I'm trying to stay alive at this depth but there's not much oxygen down here. I don't know—maybe it's days later, maybe weeks, maybe months—I'm laid out on my futon obsessively going over my ever-increasing list of *what could have beens* when I catch a glimpse of the Lamkparski book.

There I am, just another "whatever happened to. . .?" I was supposed to become a star, direct, produce, date models and movie actresses, be on the cover of magazines at the check-out stand, jet around the world, be nominated for Academy Awards, be on the late night talk shows hawking my latest film, back presidential candidates, rub elbows with the elite . . . be a *somebody*. But instead, I'm wallowing here in my self-indulgent paralysis, rock bottom in obscurity.

Without really thinking, I find myself scribbling on a piece of paper: "Whatever Happened To—dot, dot, dot?" Maybe this was a way to pull myself out of the doldrums. Maybe, if I went back over my life, wrote it down scene by scene, like a movie, I could figure out where the story fell apart and my destiny abandoned me.

Instead of going back and starting at the beginning with birth and all, I decided to begin where I was—stuck in my head—and work backwards from there.

What was immediately apparent was, I had been living my life backwards all along, inasmuch as my life had been nothing more than a continual search for proof to justify the clutter of my past so I could avoid the present. What could be a better definition of insanity than that?

So for the next twenty years, I continued to write my backwards' screenplay, rummaging around in ever and ever increasingly subtler crevices of my beleaguered psyche for clues to what happened to me.

CUT TO: YEARS LATER: Hollywood is so far in the past it isn't even on the radar screen. In the intervening years, I've switched from film to a small hand-held video camera; the convenience of this new technology allowing me to record everyone and everything in my life twenty-four seven—which I did obsessively to the consternation of some friends who, rather than being willing participants to the constant filming of my life, chose to walk away in disgust and anger, sometimes even attempting to smash my camera on exiting to make their point. I've got everything of whatever happened to me on my shelves in *intimate* detail. Where most people write a journal or a diary of their life, I've videotaped mine—UP CLOSE and ZOOMED IN. I've got the uncensored version of *Sex, Lies and Videotape*. I've got all the *good stuff* before Hollywood cuts it out.

CUT TO: Somewhere in THE MID-90's. PANORAMIC-SHOT. Moving up the PERUVIAN AMAZON RIVER. Me and a few other mind-expanding adventurers are going to meet up with a shaman who lives deep in the jungle. He will guide us through a mind-altering ritual, which consists of ingesting the sacred ayahuasca plant, then laying back and surrendering to the clues, that hopefully, the universe will regurgitate.

CUT TO: DEEP IN THE JUNGLE. I'm naked, covered in mud, stoned out of my mind, running around on all fours like some monkey man, having reverted back to a time prior to walking erect.

CUT TO: POINT OF VIEW THROUGH MY SONY MINI DV VIDEO CAMERA that I have strapped to my monkey hand, recording the whole adventure. I turn the camera on myself and catch a glimpse of my evolutionary descent in the LCD screen.

"Fuck!?" [Refer to cover photo.]

So Richard Lamparski, all these years later, here's the answer to your question: "Whatever Happened to Richard Beymer?" Nothing! He never existed. He's an image in mind, not my mind —Thee mind . . . a fictitious character made up to star in the movie of my so-called life.

So, to fill in the blanks, here's a copy of my novel that was inspired by your question, which over the intervening years I have shortened, for economy's sake, to simply—'who am I?'

With gratitude,
R. B.

P.S. By the way, Richard Lamparski, whatever happened to you?

". . . I know . . . I know . . . but if IT could . . . if. For the sake of argument, say IT could. IT would appear as light reflected on a flawless screen, projected through a never-ending "real" of mind-stuff, endlessly contrived plots of imprisoned selves chattering away at twenty-four frames a second, which we have falsely identified as ourselves, sitting here in the darkened theater of our minds, conjuring the next twist and turn in the movie we refer to as our lives." George Oops

THE BACK STORY

The thing to keep in mind while reading these pages is, this isn't so much the work of a writer as it is of a collector. I go up and down the alleys of my mind, and others', rummaging through whatever has been thrown out; recycling dreams, thoughts, secrets, fantasies, doodles, other people's good ideas, overheard conversations, and whatever else I can salvage from the psychic dumpster.

In reality, I'm a junk collector with an eye for thrown out, discarded, assumed useless things, things that I might rearrange into meanings, not of their original intention, but of my alienated point of view.

Anyone with perception will realize soon enough, I suspect, that these are only words, and my real screenplay remains hidden in the silence between what I say and don't say, shrouded in words that I use to lie about, hint about, talk around about, about this and that and the other, to throw myself—and anyone else who happens to be within earshot—off track.

Inevitably though, the silence I try to maintain gives way to questions of: Who am I? Where am I?—And of course, the big one—Am I at all? Which in turn opens Pandora's beautifully, irresistible, infinite toy box and the whole thing comes spewing out all over again—the chaos, the confusion, the endless choices, the apparent appearance of the existence of things and so on and so forth, and I am back here again for the umpteen-billionth time trying to talk my way out of it.

These pages then, are an accumulation of some of my failed attempts at being silent.

Basically, this is research material for a screenplay to be edited and programmed into a video communiqué and eventually fed via inner space link-up to the Mother Ship, for an ultimate computer readout, regarding all categories of Self-inquiry, and/or self-deception in relation to existence both imagined and real. In response, I hope to receive back the latest correction of my trajectory along with the estimated time of my departure.

For years there was no problem. Twice a day, for about an hour morning and evening, I would rummage through whatever had been thrown out the days and weeks before: erasing, rearranging, cutting and pasting and integrating these latest finds into the array of junk already strewn across my cluttered apartment floor—much of it dating back decades.

The clues that I had logged over the years suggested that whatever it was I was in search of was deceptively obvious and irreconcilably linked to the one in search—that is, me—or rather "I," from which "me" is an obvious contrivance to maintain the deception to which I've grown accustomed.

To this end I focused all my energy. My search was for the commonality that would unify this disparate display of nonsense that I had gone to such lengths to collect. I was looking for the *beforeness* to Now—the ultimate concept that would explain *in a single breath or half-breath* everything from the *big bang* to *Spanky and the Gang*. I was looking for a single utterance, so flawless, so complete, so compelling that even the most doubting of Thomases would have to bow to the truth of it.

For years I followed this routine religiously. Then one day a glitch. For no apparent reason that I could detect, I started losing it—my mind, that is. I couldn't find it anywhere. In fact, I was barely a rumor of my former existence. Hearsay was the only proof of my whereabouts. Finally, all those years of probing the intricacies of duality had paid off. For some inexplicable reason, I had come untethered from the persuasive images of doubt that had plagued my existence for as far back as I can remember.

It wasn't long after that I started forgetting names, dates, people, places, appointments, where I left my keys, where I parked my car, what day it was, what I had said just a few minutes before. And more times than I care to remember, I forgot to take the lens cap off my karma . . . I mean, camera, accounting for the lengthy scenes of narration over black that permeate this screenplay.

Which reminds me—so it doesn't become an issue later—I would like to say a few words about this narration business. My feeling is that it should be in the first person, in *his* voice, superimposed and fading back and forth with *her* voice, giving the impression of the obsession her earlier image made on his imagination.

Perhaps he's remembering a previous life, or a version of himself in a parallel universe, a dream perhaps, or something he saw in an old Forties movie on TV late at night while eating Sarah Lee banana cake, stoned, recovering from amyl nitrates in a stinking hot New York apartment on the Lower East Side above a Chinese laundry lying next to Marie, naked, asleep, exuding rivulets of his lustful deposit from between the crack of her Botticelli ass.

The writer has long ago forgotten (or refuses to acknowledge) where the initial impulse arose for his screenplay out of fear of being exposed for the fraud he suspects himself to be. Consequently he has convinced himself, like most screenwriters, that what is on these pages is his uniquely original idea.

The thing is, there is no telling at this point what's real or imagined, nor is it necessary to know. So don't make the mistake of trying to figure what the hell is going on at this point. Even the author is struggling with this dilemma.

What's relevant will be made clear in due course when death appears inevitable. But for now, just carry on and let what doesn't make sense slide, which is exactly what it did—my mind that is—so much so, that I began doubting my own existence. I became obsessed with finding some sort of confirmation that I was who I appeared to be. Out of desperation I started stopping people on the street and asking them if they remembered me from the *good ol' days* or some flick I was in, and if so, would they please direct me back to the Mother Ship. Consequently, I ended up here—in dar loony bin.

I tried to explain to the mutants who run this nuthouse that I wasn't from here. Their vacant stares left no doubt they questioned my sanity.

"Doubt!" I railed, repeatedly slamming my fists against my head. "Yes, I have doubts...I have doubts just about everything...everything there is to have doubts about, I have. But, of one thing I am sure, without a doubt...I am NOT from here...this planet, solar system, galaxy or universe, for that matter."

No response!

"Look," I said, changing to a more friendly buddy-buddy approach, "you seem to be a reasonable bunch. Believe me when I say, I had absolutely nothing *whatsoever* to do with ending up here. I was forced to make an emergency landing. If I had a choice, which I didn't, but if I did, I would have circumvented this place as far as humanly possible."

All the while I'm trying to convince these lunkheads that I didn't want to be here, I'm thinking to myself, the outrageous goings-on on this planet have a definite appeal to my hedonistic nature and I would give anything to hang out here for awhile and...fucking go for it. But I didn't let on.

The thing was, I instinctively knew that if I went for it, and by that I mean, actually landed here, became like a regular person, you know...got involved in the whole *Homo sapiens* thing and let's say...went to Hollywood and got in the movies, that given my obsessive nature, the chances of my ever extracting myself from the fascination of my own image up there on the screen and returning to the Mother Ship would be next to impossible.

I pleaded on my knees with these dimwits, my arms stretched to the heavens, tears streaming down my cheeks. "I beg you, just let me make some repairs, work out a design problem or two, take a few souvenir Polaroids and I'll be outta here, gone, vapor trails. I promise, I won't tell anybody I saw what was going on here."

They started grumbling amongst themselves. Maybe I was getting through. I decided to hit them with the heavy stuff. "What you see before you is an illusion," I bellowed, "a projection, a transmission from a reflection emanating from your imagination. I'm the result of some peculiarity, some miscalculation in perfection's scheme of things and *zap!* this digital cosmic dream blew into existence, full blown, exhibiting all the appearance of *reality* and bringing me along with it. But believe me, I'm here to tell you, I had no choice in the matter. I was just along for the ride. I *am*...that's all I know. And I told them so.

More blank stares.

I gave it one last shot. "You, me, all of it...it's all an illusion as far as the 'I' can see. We're all just devices, objects, shadows on the cave wall, projections in the scheme of things, the dream of things. It's all the Do of the Tao. I do nothing, create nothing, decide nothing, am nothing, contribute nil. I have no real existence, consequently, no will, no choice, no permanence, any more than a dream, a mirage or a shadow. All there is, is karma, and as you can see, I have a shitload, the weight of which forced me to make this emergency landing. Look, all I want to do is jettison some of this crap that I've collected over the eons so I'll be light enough to lift off and get the hell outta here."

Well, that did it. I was immediately outfitted in a snuggly-fitting canvas jacket with extra long sleeves that tied in the back and escorted posthaste to the space that I now occupy—a windowless accommodation with wall-to-wall padding.

It is from here that I'm documenting the plight of my journey—which I'm disguising as a Hollywood screenplay—in the hope that it will be made into a major motion picture and someone in some audience somewhere will recognize in the character I'm playing, the *real me*, for the inner dimensional space/time priority courier that I am, come to my aid, and help me escape the gravity of the situation.

I should have known I was in for it by the way they gutted me from the wreckage. On impact the designated escape hatch collapsed into nothing more than a slit. Certainly there was no escaping through it. I mean, in a pinch, maybe, just maybe, I could get a couple fingers through, maybe even three or four, but head and shoulders? Forget it! No way was I going to pass through this opening without some serious consequences—as in major damage to mind and body.

So there I am, panicking, running through my options, which had dwindled to none, when I hear this low, rumbling, gurgling sound. At first I thought it was something I ate. Within a few seconds, it crescendos into a deafening mix of discordant harmonics, a cacophony of shrieking voices causing the whole spaceship to come unglued.

Well, I figure this is it, right? This must be death coming at me, right? The shaking, quaking, losing control, everything going black. What else could it be? I'd read the *Tibetan Book of the Dead*. I'd gone through the Sixties, taken acid, died, been reborn countless times. I knew about these things. The first *Bardo* was on its way nonstop from hell. "Relax," I told myself. "It's just me in disguise trying to scare the shit out of myself to see if I'll fall for the old 'don't-look-now-but-you-don't-have-a-body' trick."

So I'm bracing myself for the onslaught of images, right? I'm telling myself, just relax, nothing is real...it's all in your head... surrender . . . take it as it comes . . . don't give it any more attention than any other thought. Then, just as I'm beginning to calm down, I hear these desperate distant echoing voices calling from . . . I don't know . . . the other side of the universe, sounding like they were being amplified through some cosmic, digital reverb unit and they're screaming at me to, "HOLD ON, KEEP BREATHING" and "PUSH HARDER." Now the breathing made sense. If I could keep breathing I would stay conscious, but push…push what harder, and where?

There was no doubt about it, I was in serious trouble, a fact made abundantly clear when the walls started undulating like I'm in a rubber room. I figured I was either dreaming or that tab of acid I took thirty years ago had finally kicked in.

Before I can determine what the hell is happening to me, these giant hands squeeze in through the escape hatch, grab me by the head, and start pulling. The more I resist the harder they pull until I'm flying down this tunnel. I mean, in a matter of seconds I've gone from zero to warp speed, passing photons as if standing still and accelerating exponentially until my velocity precedes my appearance to keep up with myself.

Something blows past me. I think I recognize it. Yes! It's my mind. I recognize the doubt. Then . . . something up ahead approaching faster than the speed of light. By the time I'm able to make out what it is, it's too late. I'm already on an unavoidable collision course with the end of time, an instant of light in an otherwise infinite space of nothing.

Now when I say nothing, I don't mean nothing as in something that isn't there, but rather *Nothingness*, as in before nothing ever was—OH! SHIT! I barely have time to assume the crash position when I'm launched out of this black hole. I mean, I explode onto the scene. Before I can catch my breath, one of my rescuers yanks me up by the heels and starts slapping me around. I have no idea why, especially after they had gone to such lengths to extricate me. Whatever the reason, I'm too weak to fight back. I gulp in a big dose of whatever it is they're inhaling on this planet and burst out crying. I mean, a grown man crying like a baby. I don't know what happened. I must have hyperventilated or something. Anyway, I lost it, most embarrassing, fainted, right there on the spot, out, blotto— FADED TO BLACK.

· · ·

When I finally did come around, so much time had passed I couldn't remember anything of the crash. It turned out that I was in worse shape than I thought. I had no control of my bladder or bowels, couldn't manage my arms or legs, had lost all my hair and teeth, couldn't speak the language, my brain felt like mush, and to top it all off, I suffered from a terminal case of amnesia. Consequently, I couldn't remember who I was or where I was from. I had to be taught how to walk, talk, eat, tie my shoes, blow my nose, and wipe my ass—most humiliating.

My convalescence seemed to go on forever. I never really did get the hang of certain things, like spelling, math, small talk, asserting myself, work and social amenities. However, conjuring images that apparently weren't there came easy, as did art, music, acting (although many critics would disagree) procrastinating, wondering, wandering, sex and of course, making movies, in other words, all the right-brain stuff—or is it left-brain? My assigned caretakers were these hardworking, naive, good-hearted, Midwestern, middle class, puritanical, meat-and-potato, cigarette-smoking, sexually-repressed, God-fearing, all-American, good-looking newlyweds.

They seemed thrilled with the prospect of showing me the ropes. They wasted no time in fabricating a whole identity for me—a past, a future, a list of likes, dislikes, opinions, beliefs, desires, judgments, fears, limitations, fixations, obsessions, expectations—in other words, what to think, say, and do in any given situation. Just follow the script, and as long as I didn't go off improvising and asking a lot of embarrassing questions, I could have a hell of a good time here and never have to reveal who I really am. I just had to remember, when I saw myself coming, to look the other way.

This domestication went on for quite a few years and all the while the recurring glimmer of *something else* persisted, an intangible *non-thing* that increasingly visited my imagination, of which I am still in search—and the identity of which I suspect, ultimately, I AM!

SCENE I

HOW TO MAKE PERFECT MOVIES
with your Bell and Howell 16mm Home Movie Camera

FADE UP: THE PRESENT. NEW YORK CITY. INTERIOR. SMALL CLUTTERED STUDIO APARTMENT. LOWER EASTSIDE. THREE-STORY WALK-UP.

The sacred Shiva chant on the stereo mixes tastefully with the oohhs and aahhs and occasional outbursts of the woman fucking in the next apartment. It's late, maybe two in the morning.

SOUND OVER: SOMEONE MUMBLING ALONG AS HE TYPES.

The CAMERA PANS THE ROOM in search of the mumbler, moving past an impressive array of video cameras, sound and computer editing gear stacked on a table along a brick wall on which is scrawled the words: LET IT SETTLE ITSELF in huge red-dripping, painted letters.

On the opposite wall, from one end of the room to the other, are shelves stacked from floor to ceiling with videotapes. The dates on them suggest some were shot five, ten, as many as thirty years before.

MOVING DOWN TO THE FLOOR, THE CAMERA GLIDES OVER PILES OF BOOKS with titles like: *How to Know God, Tantric Sex, I Am That, Magic Mushroom Growers Guide, Experimental Cinema, Aliens Among Us, How to Make Perfect Movies.*

Moving on, THE CAMERA PASSES OVER a curious accumulation of assorted objects littered across the floor—a phony beard, a banged-up space helmet, a wig of dreadlocks draped over a lava lamp undulating its red phallic sludge, and piled in a heap on a floor-futon, a beat-up silver spacesuit and oxygen backpack. This is one of those ridiculous Hollywood B movie spacesuit contraptions that Flash Gordon might have worn in one of his science fiction space adventure Saturday matinee serial movies back in the 50's, when you got two feature films, a short, at least ten cartoons, coming attractions and a bag of popcorn for forty-five cents—and if you were lucky, a stolen kiss from Mary Olmstead in the back row.

Finally, we discover the mumbler, Writer George—late forties, sitting in the eerie glow of his computer, hunched over the keyboard, naked, silhouetted in the purple pulsating light from the neon sign across the street.

He sits facing the brick wall separating him and the couple fucking in the next apartment. The slut's sexual forays over the months have definitely had an influence on Writer George's unraveling psyche as she's slithered her way more and more into his never-ending screenplay.

But tonight he can't let his mind go there. He's got to stay focused. It looks as if the end of his screenplay is actually in sight this time. There's only one little problem—the writer's block he's been bogged down in for the last week—due, in no small part, to his erotic fantasies of the slut in the next apartment. A succession of cold showers has become his first line of defense.

Dripping wet, Writer George returns to his computer, scarfs down some cold Thai takeout, smashes in some earplugs and immerses himself back into his screenplay.

In an attempt to break his writer's block, Writer George decides to go for a more supernatural approach. He lightly rests his fingers on the keyboard as if invoking the spirits of the Ouija, closes his eyes, and waits for guidance from the *other side*.

Almost immediately, quite apart from any prompting from himself, Writer George finds his fingers typing: E-T-Y. He hasn't thought of Ety for years. Her image comes streaming back, accompanied by the memory of a video he shot of her at least twenty years earlier. Excited with the possibility that this is the guidance he's been looking for, Writer George makes a fast sweep of his video-packed shelves, finds the tape in question, shoves it in the VCR and pushes play.

CUT TO: TV MONITOR. ETY. INTERIOR BEDROOM. NIGHT.

Ety sits on her bed up against the wall. The only light comes from the nightstand. She's a poet. Beautiful Semitic face. Tight outdoor body. Cigarette in one hand, pen in the other, her handwritten pages propped on her pulled-up knees.

The LOW ANGLE of the video suggests that George is situated on the floor at the foot of Ety's bed recording her. She talks to George through his camera and, although a bit self-conscious, it's apparent that Ety is thoroughly enjoying George's attention.

ETY: I told you that I wanted to crucify you.

GEORGE: Crucify me!

ETY: Yes ... I had the thought the other day that I wanted to crucify you for some purpose. It was very religious though. When I start writing something, I start at the end. The first sentence is the end of the story... like here. (She points to her pages.) He was crucified ... then the story begins ... how he came to be crucified.

Writer George stops the video and considers Ety's writing method might be helpful to get his creative juices flowing again. He decides to give her last-scene-first approach a try. George types:

CUT TO: THE LAST SCENE.

And we do . . .

CUT TO: INTERIOR. MENTAL INSTITUTION. CLOSE-UP ON THE LITTLE PEEP HOLE IN ONE OF THE CELL DOORS.

All we can see on the other side is the mouth of someone screaming. The screamer is SPACEMAN GEORGE, Writer George's insane alter ego.

> SPACEMAN GEORGE: I'm losing my mind . . . I
> can't remember who I am . . . Tell me. Am I
> right? Am I losing my mind? I need a choice chip.
> Tell the doctor I need a choice chip.

CUT TO: MENTAL INSTITUTION. CORRIDOR. UPSIDE-DOWN MOVING SHOT FROM SPACEMAN GEORGE'S POINT OF VIEW.

Two Gestapo-type, muscle-bound orderlies are dragging him by his feet down a corridor lined with crazies even more off their rockers than Spaceman George. They applaud and yell and spit and piss and punch and splatter Spaceman George with their dinner as he's pulled along.

> SPACEMAN GEORGE: (screaming) NO! Please
> don't fry my brains. I'm not crazy like the rest of
> these wackos. For God's sake, tell the doctor I've
> got to have a choice chip.

CUT TO: THE LITTLE GREEN ROOM at the end of the hall. The door flies open and Spaceman George is hustled in and slammed into a high-backed wooden-carved chair rigged with arm straps and leg clamps, looking like something salvaged from a Gothic torture chamber.

For the first time, we have a good look at Spaceman George. This is one crazed Homo sapien—dreadlocks, straggly beard, dressed in a filthy silver spacesuit, bound in a straitjacket and dripping in spaghetti, mashed potatoes, piss and banana cream pie.

To complete the meal, DR. JULIA J. OLSON leans into the shot—a masochist's wet dream. This aging dominatrix obviously loves her work. She's a large Ukrainian brute of a woman with breasts like bowling balls. Thick glasses make her eyes appear to pop out of her head, and her makeup looks as if it were applied with a blowtorch.

With fiendish delight, Dr. Julia J. fits Spaceman George with an over-sized metal helmet, known to the inmates as the discombobulator. It looks like a banged-up World War I German Wehrmacht Combat helmet, with protruding wires that the good doctor attaches to an ominous-looking black box.

> SPACEMAN GEORGE: NO! Shit, not the
> discombobulator. You're going to fry my brains,
> right?

> DR. OLSON: Trust me here, George. Once
> you've been uncombobulated, you're going to feel
> so much better. Think of it as a minor rewrite.

> SPACEMAN GEORGE: But I like the way the
> script is coming along. I'm almost finished. In fact,

this is the last scene. Besides this isn't my right hat size.

DR. OLSON: (as she tightens the chin strap) I don't know, I think it rather suits you. Now George, what's this business of you insisting life is an illusion?

SPACEMAN GEORGE: No, that's not exactly what I said. What I said was, 'Life is but a dream.' You know, 'row, row, row your boat, gently down the stream . . . merrily, merrily, merrily, merrily . . . life is but a . . . '

DR. OLSON: Now George, we can't have you going around spreading all these nasty rumors that nothing is what it appears to be, now can we? That would really upset the ol' applecart.

SPACEMAN GEORGE: Okay . . . okay. I'll drop the whole alien thing. I'm from here . . . born and raised in Iowa. I didn't see anything.

DR. OLSON: Now George, don't you think it's a little late for that?

SPACEMAN GEORGE: Please, I can't go without knowing. Not after all we've been through. Please, one last choice chip.

DR. OLSON: All right, George, for ol' time's sake, but this is it. What are your choices?

SPACEMAN GEORGE: (desperately trying to organize his thoughts) Okay, my choices are . . . am I who I appear to be to others, the same as to myself or…see, I'm getting all confused. I used to know this. Okay, now I got it. If I am who I appear to be as if I am to others . . . OH, SHIT!

DR. OLSON: George, I understand and I choose . . . neither.

SPACEMAN GEORGE: No, don't bail on me at a time like this. You said anytime I needed a choice chip, *you* would choose.

DR. OLSON: And I'm telling you . . . I choose . . . neither.

SPACEMAN GEORGE: Neither? What kind of choice is that?

DR. OLSON: You see, it works like this, George. There's this and that and neither. Neither, being the obvious choice for not choosing . . . a constant option.

Before Spaceman George has a chance to debate the issue, Dr. Olson wedges a stick between his teeth, and with maniacal delight, throws the switch.

ZAP! . . . The voltage surges through Spaceman George sending him into uncontrolled spasms, jerking and twists.

DR. OLSON: So how's that for an illusion, hey Georgie?

George's eyes appear to almost pop out of his head. Smoke and sparks shoot out from under the discombobulator. He clamps down on the stick so hard that it snaps in two. As the pieces fly out of his mouth, he releases a horrific scream.

END LAST SCENE—FIRST

IOWA. FORTY YEARS EARLIER.

Echoes of Spaceman George's scream can still be heard.

HIGH, PANORAMIC, POSTCARD VIEW OF ENDLESS FIELDS OF CORN BACKLIT BY THE SETTING SUN.

The last of Spaceman George's scream DISSOLVES away into the SCREECHING OF A RED-TAILED HAWK that glides into the frame on a summer current. The bird circles for a moment then flies off in the direction of the '47 Ford, moving along a dusty dirt road.

> YOUNG GEORGE: (VOICEOVER) Who is me?

> FATHER: (VOICEOVER) What are you talking about, boy? You're you, George . . . my son. What a silly question.

> YOUNG GEORGE: (VOICEOVER) That's my name, but who am I . . . really, I mean?

> FATHER: (VOICEOVER) That's who you are . . . really.

Over the following dialogue, the CAMERA MOVES DOWN in a lazy circling descent, ending eventually framed on the windshield of the Ford and its two occupants—Young George and his father.

George's father is in his late twenties. He's a tall, dark, good-looking, mustached, fit, C-average, Iowa country boy, who, as the high school quarterback, no doubt had his pick of any of the fine young country girls, of which Young George's mother was definitely the finest with her movie star looks.

Young George has been endowed with the good looks of his parents. He's a lanky nine-year-old with a reticent, friendly demeanor. Although Young George doesn't know it, he's secreting a raging chaos that—as we will see later—is destined to erupt. But for now, there's no trace of this eventuality and life is quite mellow in its postwar exhaustion.

Young George is leaning out the window of the Ford squinting one-eyed through his makeshift camera—a cardboard tube, made from a roll of toilet paper.

> YOUNG GEORGE: But sometimes when I look through my camera, I'm not here.

> FATHER: Yeah, then where do you think you are?

> YOUNG GEORGE: I don't know . . . somewhere else.

> FATHER: And where's that?

> YOUNG GEORGE: It's not a real place that you can see or anything. It's somewhere else . . . back here.

> FATHER: Back here, where?

YOUNG GEORGE: Back ... of what I see, where everything goes. Where it ends in back of my camera.

FATHER: It's not a real camera, George. It's a cardboard tube from a roll of toilet paper.

YOUNG GEORGE: That's what everybody thinks.

FATHER: George, you're letting your imagination run away with you. That kind of crazy talk runs on your mother's side of the family. You're getting to be a young man now. You got to stop talking like this or people will think you got a screw loose. It's embarrassing. You understand me, boy? You remember your Aunt Pinky, talking all that craziness about seeing flying saucers and strange creatures from other planets come to visit her in the middle of night?

YOUNG GEORGE: But I saw them. They gave me this camera.

FATHER: George, you keep talking like this and you'll end up in the loony bin like your Aunt Pinky. You want to get some place in this life you can't let people know what you're really thinking and feeling. Best you just keep your mind on herding the sheep.

YOUNG GEORGE: But we don't have any sheep.

FATHER: Yeah, well, if we did.

YOUNG GEORGE: Uncle Leroy told Billy that in front of the neighbors he shouldn't talk about politics, God, or masturbation.

FATHER: (speechless for a moment) Yeah, well, Billy's older than you.

YOUNG GEORGE: Isn't that what Grandma does when she sits in the rocker in the afternoon . . . masturbation?

FATHER: No, George, that's meditation what Grandma does.

YOUNG GEORGE: What's meditation?

FATHER: Well . . . I'm not rightly sure. Grandma says she talks to God.

YOUNG GEORGE: Really? Can anybody talk to God?

FATHER: I suppose anyone can talk to God but there's no guarantee He'll answer.

The CAMERA MOVES into Young George as he ponders this possibility.

YOUNG GEORGE: (to himself) I would like that. I would like to talk to God.

CUT TO: INTERIOR. GEORGE'S GRANDPARENTS' FARMHOUSE. ATTIC. CLOSE-UP ON THE OPEN PAGE OF A NATIONAL GEOGRAPHIC MAGAZINE. VINTAGE 1945.

The photograph is of a Hindu sage, sitting in meditation: legs crossed, back straight, hands folded, eyes closed. The caption reads:

> The yogi is practicing the ancient art of meditation, an inner quest that takes him deeper and deeper inside, purportedly to a more real Self that waits to receive him. Then, whatever is to be done is supposedly done by *something else* that the yogi, as a person, has nothing to do with.

The camera moves off the magazine and tilts up to Young George who, like the yogi, sits with legs crossed, eyes closed, back straight. Over this scene we hear Writer George, YEARS LATER—IN THE PRESENT—mumbling along as he types his never-ending screenplay.

WRITER GEORGE: (VOICEOVER) The thought of going crazy like Aunt Pinky was terrifying. I decided to take Dad's advice and keep my *real* thoughts to myself. All I had to do was pretend I was who I appeared to be. I decided to create a character, a whole other person, just like actors do in the movies. That way no one would suspect what I was really up to. For public consumption I would be this normal, everyday, courteous, kind, charming, controlling, self-righteous, inhibited, non-committal, womanizing, god-fearing, uptight, typical garden-variety, dysfunctional, all-American, co-dependent male. How difficult could that be?

I decided to call my character Richard—my middle name. Richard would be the shell, he'd take the brunt, leaving George free to explore the netherworlds of madness, mayhem, meditation, and of course . . . making movies.

In no time at all I was working this acting trick for all it was worth. Actually, I became quite good at it. You might even say, an expert. As a consequence of the level of skill I attained over the years, I actually convinced myself I was who I pretended to be. I had, in effect, totally forgotten who I really was.

Now, with no apparent intervention from my pesky mind, I could get down to the serious business of exploring the more perverted nooks and crannies of this seductive little planet.

As a result of my self-deception, the somewhere-else place dwindled to nothing more than a faint childhood memory . . . and then gone.

For years life followed its predictable, well-worn, ego-gratifying course until, one day, in my mid-twenties, inspired by a drug-induced painting frenzy, the *somewhere-else place* resurfaced. Right there between brush strokes it oozed out from under my light cadmium yellow. I recognized it by its familiar trademark—the absence of the presence of anything recognizable.

It was here, laid out in a cold sweat under my easel where I had fallen in the middle of my freshly painted psychedelic self-portrait that I realized my life, as I had come to know it, was about to slip into the void and there was absolutely nothing I could do about it but take the *trip*, which I did, reluctantly however, holding on for dear life, which was the first thing to go, of course—my dear life, that is.

In its place a wondrous fiction swirled about me, a panoramic chaos of celestial imaginings that extended out past the limit of reason, orbiting somewhere in limbo between the bounded shapes and shifting void of my unraveling perceptions, and witnessed, not from my vantage point, but rather from those who have crossed over and no longer observe from a *me-and-thee* point of view.

My descent was going extremely well, very pleasant actually, nothing like I expected and not at all like the horror stories I had heard of earlier explorers in these distant realms. All indications were I was going to have a picture-perfect death.

Then, all of a sudden, only inches from touchdown, all was thwarted by an overwhelming feeling of remorse. Maybe I hadn't done enough. Maybe the important thing had been missed. Maybe the time allotted me had been misused—that I had sacrificed the details for the effect— that it had all been about my inability to resist not knowing—that I had forsaken the blessing of anonymity for the vanity of being a *somebody*.

This blatant realization left me in such a fuzzy state that the precise moment of impact went unnoticed. I only remember waking wadded in a twisted heap—*somewhere else*. In the meantime, a million turns of the universe had come and gone in my absence and the world was already preparing to forget the majesty of my brief appearance.

When I surfaced from my *trip* some eight hours later, my alien status had been reestablished beyond question. My only dilemma was how long I would keep up the pretense of being a *someone*, in lieu of the fact that I not only wasn't who I thought I was, but was absolutely not the 'who' others saw me as either.

This led me to speculate that if I am not the 'who' I think I am, then you are not the 'who' you think you are either. It then followed, at least in my twisted mind, that my 'who' to you is just another 'I' convinced it's a 'me', as, in turn, my 'I' is similarly convinced, leaving the actuality of both our existences up for grabs.

After my revelation, the *somewhere-else place* revealed itself more and more. It would appear and disappear without warning, catching me off-guard each time. All I knew was *It* happened—whatever *It* was. *It* appeared, or rather didn't appear, as the presence of nothingness, a gap, a brief moment out of time and space unaccounted for. I felt it most intensely just prior to falling asleep when drifting in that in-between place, not yet asleep, but no longer awake.

To see if I could catch this elusive *moment*, I secretly carried a mini tape recorder around with me all the time, the microphone hidden up my sleeve. I also bugged the phone and recorded all my conversations. Later I switched to a video camera. Sometimes I recorded my whole day that I might, by chance, capture this fleeting moment . . . this *something other*, of which I was in search, and hopefully on slow-motion replay, would be revealed, its existence confirmed and my sanity no longer in question.

I became convinced that lodged somewhere in these ancestral mumblings was hidden a sign, a hint, a clue, possibly camouflaged in the form of a genetic code and if deciphered could unlock a reality beyond the range of human detection but well within the parameters of being. That is to say, a code, hidden, perhaps in the recesses of the molecular structure, which holds the key to what is real and what appears to be . . . but isn't.

It came to me that if this code could be broken and the information integrated into the human circuitry, it could awaken those ancient powers lying dormant for millennia, eventually facilitating a *lift off* from this temporal existence, allowing one—this one—to soar unrestricted to the womb of the one True Mother who waits in creation's constant labor for the return of her doubting child.

I first happened on this notion in a manuscript I found in a dream I had.

THE DREAM

NEW YORK CITY. MORNING RUSH HOUR. HIGH WIDE-ANGLE. The camera SLOWLY ZOOMS down into a crowd, looking like ants emerging from the subway.

I'm eventually singled out, not as me, Writer George, but disguised as my alter ego, SPACEMAN GEORGE— bearded, dreadlocks, decked out in a grimy, silver spacesuit from a bad 60's sci-fi flick I had done, and pushing a shopping cart piled with discarded, assumed useless junk.

The passer-byers haven't a clue I'm here. That's the beauty of my scheme. The wannabesomebodies scrape by me as if I'm invisible, all gussied up in their latest corporate, look-alike, matching mindsets.

I've taken on the perfect disguise—a bagman, a crazy, a nobody, a nothing, a total failure, the kind of loser-guy that those in search of being a *somebody* avoid at all costs—and they do, stumbling over themselves to detour around me. Consequently, I'm hidden in plain sight with an unobstructed view of the human race.

From my wall-less fortification, I take aim at these self-infatuated, evolutionary marathoners with my mini DV spy cam that I have cleverly hidden in the hollow of a cardboard tube from a roll of toilet paper—a trick I learned as a kid.

So there's absolutely no doubt I am totally wacko, I squint one-eyed through my pretend camera acting as if I'm relaying landing instructions to incoming UFO's.

The truth of the matter is, I'm on a mission of the utmost secrecy. I can't reveal all at this time, but what I can say is, I was dispatched here from the Pleiades, a galaxy some four-hundred-thousand light years away, with instructions to compile a video diary of daily life on this planet, an update, if you will, of human progress, so that an evaluation can be made if it is worthwhile to continue this experiment in evolution given the insatiable thirst humans have developed for inflicting pain and suffering on themselves and others of their species.

The original plan was that by now present-day Homo sapiens would have evolved into loving, joyous, wise, compassionate beings, extolling all the virtues of the gods that had created them. But obviously something had run amuck.

This is why I was enlisted to document, as intimately as possible, what the hell is exactly going on here (without revealing myself, of course) and relay my findings back to the Mother Ship.

I find I get my best evidence in those dark and foreboding places in my mind's "I". It's here, in the illusionary underworld scrounging around for clues as to what's really going on behind all the play-acting, that I stumble onto Maya—the greatest diva of them all—ablaze in the spotlight, naked, unveiled for the bitch that she is, performing her one-woman, insane, death-defying, extravaganza "reality" show, the likes of which I have only seen in dreams, nightmares, madhouses, the evening news and, of course . . . the movies.

Her lure is intoxicating. It's all I can do to remain conscious long enough to rip off a few seconds of video with my spycam, then I'm out of here before I end up like the rest of her mindless devotees.

I follow the exit signs through a maze of underground passageways eventually emerging out of a manhole in Lower Manhattan, looking up the skirt of a woman in mid-leap as she hurls herself over my camera and runs across the street through the rush-hour traffic.

'My God, I thought I had lost her.' It's the woman I've been following for weeks, an actress who is suspected of killing her director/boyfriend. I'd been hired to gather video evidence to be used against her in a murder trial. It's a sleazy job, I know, but I'm an out-of-work actor and I need the gig.

I catch up with her reflection in a store window and follow her through the crowd. She doesn't give the slightest indication she knows I'm just a few steps behind her. I knock into someone or someone knocks into me. The picture goes haywire.

When I finally regain control of the camera, I'm astonished to find that I am no longer in New York City but in Paris, in a video I shot some ten years earlier, walking and talking with my filmmaker friend Mark.

[NOTE: As a consequence of his obsession to videotape his life, George is constantly having **VIDEO FLASHBACKS**, scattered recollections of videos he's shot, sometimes years earlier, that surface out of some obscure connection relating to the convoluted way in which George's synapses and receptors fire off.] For example:

CUT TO: VIDEO FLASHBACK

PARIS STREET. DAY. MOVING HAND HELD SHOT. MARK.

Mark and I are maneuvering through the backstreets of Saint German de Pre, dodging cars, bicycles, and semi-curious Parisians with an attitude. Mark is yelling over the traffic.

> MARK: So, as I was saying, the people behind you are totally intrigued by this process. You see, we have this tradition . . . that somehow or other if you are on a screen then you've got to be somebody. And you're not somebody unless you're this something, flat image . . . which is going to be made even flatter in a second if you don't get out of the way of this car.

END VIDEO FLASHBACK

I stumble. When I regain control I'm back in New York. The Actress I was following comes into focus out of the blur of a passing car window. She brushes by me and hurries through the crowd just managing to catch a bus at the end of the block. In her haste, she drops some pages bound in a red cover. They skid into the gutter. The bus pulls away. I follow it through my zoom lens ending in a CLOSE-UP of the Actress pounding on the back window, pointing, trying to make me aware of whatever it was she dropped.

I WIDEN OUT and TILT DOWN to a film script. The title on the red cover reads *THE SILENT WATCHER.* The pages flutter open from the passing traffic. They're scrawled in an unreadable language, a lot of curly-cues, flips, and extended jagged lines but somehow I understand—it's like that in dreams.

I ZOOM IN CLOSER on the pages. They begin with a description of these travelers from another dimension— Time Priority Couriers, as they are referred to—magicians of infinite magic who transcend the self-reflection of their own being, creating universes within universes whenever and wherever the whim hits them.

The *piece de resistance* of their magical repertoire is being able to be at any one place before they've arrived without having ever left where they never were, and doing this entirely without mirrors, false bottoms or marked cards.

Described as reclusive types, these cosmic pranksters hang out in the underground, apparently doing their best work *out of sight*, thereby preserving the integrity of their misdirection.

It seems that one of their favorite hangouts is in the molecular structure of certain nocturnal pearl assent fungi that flourish in the light of the moon, germinating in the dung of undulant animals. Here, nestled in the DNA, these mind-altering mischief-makers have waited patiently for countless millennia for their potential human audience to evolve that they might *trip* them up as they make their way from the trees to terra firma.

These *mind-fuckers*, as they are sometimes referred to, figured it was inevitable, that by scattering themselves on the evolutionary path of these insatiably curious human prototypes, that they would one day be ingested by them, causing a blast of memory-release so potent, so mind-boggling, so filled with celestial imaginings, that these unsuspecting tree dwellers would have no choice but to evolve into the likeness of their cosmic benefactors.

The initial signs of transformation were increased visual perception, prolonged sexual gratification, walking erect, the ability to bring images into the present by naming them, art, inner sight, knowledge of the stars and all things past and future, mastery over the senses, the ability to witness life without being involved, an awareness of Self, and, of course—making movies.

So, according to plan, these potential humanoids were unable to resist the temptation to dine on the *fruit of the gods*, consequently undermining their resistance to accept what they didn't know they knew they knew all along, and which we, their distant offspring, are just beginning to suspect, that we are the gods we keep searching the heavens for. FADE TO BLACK:

END DREAM

FADE UP: CLOSE. 16MM. BLACK AND WHITE. HOME MOVIE FOOTAGE. A bronze pendulum slices through the black. It swings back and forth behind a glass-enclosed case reflecting Young George (age ten) squinting one-eyed through his BELL & HOWELL HOME MOVIE CAMERA that has replaced his toilet-roll camera. For illumination, Young George has a flashlight taped to the top of it.

WRITER GEORGE: (VOICEOVER in the PRESENT, mumbling along as he types) And my film begins like this. But for the lack of funds I would be shooting it right now. Instead, I must be content to use these white pages for a screen and on them substitute language for a camera along with angles, sound, acting, costumes, lights, action and all the rest of the moviemaking magic to somehow convey the transparency of imagination, where . . .

My film begins with a clock being wound, a clock much taller than me, like the grandfather clock at my grandparents' house, the one at the bottom of the stairs, at the top of which was a long dark corridor that led to the attic. It was here in the darkness where all the monsters and demons waited for me, grunting their obscene incantations in a mindless orgy of my anticipated slaughter.

Everywhere there was anywhere there was darkness, they were there, my dearest enemies, grotesque creatures, lining my only escape route, punctually waiting to catch me off-guard just that once that they might enlist me into their hideous ranks if—by the time the clock struck the final hour—I hadn't made it the length of the corridor to the safety of the attic and slammed the door behind me.

Young George moves his camera into the face of the grandfather clock . . . *11:57* and counting. There's no more putting it off. It's now or never. Young George turns from his reflection and, summoning all his courage, starts up the stairs in a last ditch attempt to document his fears.

WRITER GEORGE: (continues VOICEOVER in the PRESENT, mumbling along as he types) My plan was to enter the dark at the top of the stairs and when the monsters came in for the kill, instead of panicking as usual, I would stand my ground, snap my flashlight on and film the fuckers before they had a chance to fade away in the light of the situation.

Young George moves up the stairs and into the darkness—camera rolling.

TWENTY YEARS LATER

FADE UP: BLACK AND WHITE VIDEO. NEW YORK.
INTERIOR CENTRAL PARK WEST APT. CLOSE ON
MAYA. Wannabe actress. Late twenties. Wealthy heiress.
Patron of the arts. Although nervous, she willingly confesses her
life to the camera. She sits at a large dining room table opposite
the person videotaping her. That would be—as we will realize
momentarily—Richard, a.k.a. George, (late twenties) who is still
attempting to document his fears, albeit now, through the
reflection in the "I's" of others.

Maya is noticeably self-conscious. She drops her eyes from the
scrutiny of the camera . . . then back up . . . down . . . then back
up again. Just as she's about to say something, she looks away
and relights a joint. After a couple deep tokes, she finds a
thought that she's apparently comfortable with and lets it ride
out on a gust of smoke.

> MAYA: Now I'm going to give you a soliloquy as
> an inner monologue and it's called . . . about and
> concerning . . . (She sucks in another hit.) . . .
> fantasy versus reality . . . versus fantasy . . . dot,
> dot, dot. Maya Yardly Lenin and Richard . . .
> what's your middle name?
>
> RICHARD: My middle name *is* Richard.
>
> MAYA: What's your first name?
>
> RICHARD: George.

Maya: (repeating to herself) "George, George . . ." (Something
doesn't jive.) She leans back and relights her joint.

MAYA: George. That's very different from
Richard. George is a whole different story. (After a
long pause she proclaims, as if channeling God)
George is the one you're trying to deny in yourself.

WRITER GEORGE: (cont's VOICEOVER in the
PRESENT as he types) I knew it. I knew before she
even got the words out of her mouth that the jig was up.
After all these years, I had finally been found out. My
act was apparently falling apart. Desperate, I
immediately dispatched a communiqué to the Mother
Ship—*Suspected of not being who I appear to be. Disguise
wearing thin. Don't know how much longer I can keep up pretense.
Respectfully request to be evacuated as soon as possible. Advise.*
There was no telling how long it would take to get a
response. I needed time to figure out my next move. I
decided to FADE TO BLACK and consider my
options.

FADE UP: INTERIOR. HOLLYWOOD SOUNDSTAGE. A
LARGE WHITE SPACE. CLOSE ON SPACEMAN
GEORGE. He's suited in his silver spacesuit looking as
deranged as ever, a physical and mental wreck.

THE DIRECTOR: (screaming from off camera)
"Roll 'em!"

THE CLAPPER BOARD is shoved into the
frame. It reads:

**THE SILENT WATCHER/ SCREEN TEST/
GEORGE   OOPS/   PART   OF   THE
SPACEMAN/ TAKE # 23**

The sticks bang shut.

THE DIRECTOR: (yelling) Now for God sakes,
try to get it right this time, George. *Action!*

The only object in the scene with Spaceman George is a full-
length mirror on rollers. Spaceman George takes a deep breath
and deftly, in the tradition of the great Hollywood musicals,
leads his reflection throughout the space as a combination visual
aid and dance partner as he rambles and rants his way through
his self-obsessed monologue.

SPACEMAN GEORGE: All right, here's my
dilemma. See if you can relate. On the one hand
(referring to his reflection), there's not remembering
who I am when being who I appear to be. On the
other hand (referring to himself), there's who I appear
to be when being who I think I am. That is, this me,
here . . . the one in question.

Spaceman George spins the mirror around and cozies up to his
reflection. He continues:

SPACEMAN GEORGE: Let me be more precise.
I've forgotten who I am when not being who I think I
am. That's it in a nutshell, the one-liner. That's what
this whole film is about, so be warned.
    Now I don't know about you but I assumed I'd live
forever, that somehow or other I'd get out of this life
alive, that I'd figure it out, slip by unnoticed—maybe
through some tear in the cosmic fiber—and I would
just step out into eternal life, God-like, you know, in
my white tie, top hat and tails . . . maybe doing a little
soft shoe routine in my shiny black patent leather
shoes . . . kind of free and easy like Fred Astaire in one
of those 1930's MGM musicals, like *Flying Down to Rio*
with Ginger Rogers . . . you know, boy meets girl, boy
loses girl, boy gets girl back again—ta da,— happy

ending. But that was another film. Instead, I was destined to relive the end of *West Side Story*, where I died tragically, too soon, having almost—but not quite—figured it out, about remembering who I am when not being who I appear to be.

I was so close I could taste it. The clues were everywhere. It was only left for me to reconstruct the puzzle, connect the dots . . . but NO . . . I had to die. What a shocker to wake up dead. I mean you have no idea. It's like nothing else ever. All I knew was, this life, this precious moment of eternity was over too soon . . . far, far too soon. There were all those things I never did, never said, the wasted moments, the years. I was just beginning to get the hang of it, the feel of it, the shame of it, the blame of it, the rage, the guilt part . . . the *"I'm sorry, Marie, forgive me, I messed up"* part . . . the part where you and me and everything is perfect just the way it is, with no deletions, additions, corrections, expectations, or otherwise tampered-with parts . . . the unconditional love part . . . the part where I don't demand in you what's lacking in myself part. The part where I accept who you are when not who you appear to be, rather than trying to change you into who you aren't, so I can forget who I am when not being who I appear to be in your eyes.

Well, it's all over now, *baby blues*. I jigged when I should have jagged, zigged when I should have zagged. I hesitated. And as you reminded me time and time again, "He who hesitates is lost." There was so much left unfinished, the whole last act . . . was he really insane or just play-acting? Did she really fool him into thinking she loved him or did he know all along she didn't? Or was he just pretending he believed her to see if he could detect a lie in her performance? Or did she set the whole thing up and just let him believe it was his idea to prove she was

who she appeared to be, when she was really someone
else? Now I'd never know.

Picture it yourself . . . if you were to die, no warning,
like right now, just keel over and die, not knowing who
you are when not being who you appear to be—that is,
this part you're playing—and don't kid yourself, you
there . . . you *are* playing a part—what would be left?
There would be nothing, that's how I see it. Zilch.
Nada. But, if you were to die *being* who you are when
not being who you appear to be, then dying wouldn't
be death, as in annihilation, the total eradication of
being, but rather, could conceivably be just a change of
scene, like in the movies…a simple fade-out, fade-in. In
fact, from the die-ee's point of view, nothing would be
any different . . . Oh, maybe a little glitch in the film , a
little *What the hell was that?*, but no difference, not really.
Right? I mean, you'd just be whoever you are when
not being who you think you are— simple.

Now, to an outside observer in a fixed matrix, of
course, you would appear dead, gone, outta here . . .
but for the die-ee, the one in question, it would just be
a blip on the radar screen . . . a simple dream shift . . .
no biggie. But, and this is the heart of the matter . . .
I'm lost in the play, consumed by my part, obsessed
with my image. (In a sudden rage Spaceman George
breaks the mirror.) I really believe the lie, that I am
this "me," who I appear to be. I've forgotten
something, something key, something vital to the
whole outcome. I'm sure of it. And whatever it is
(screaming in the camera) IT'S DRIVING ME
CRAZY!

THE DIRECTOR: (yelling from off camera) Cut . . .
Cut! For Christ sake, CUT!

The Director comes rushing into the scene. He's an emotionally-crazed individual who exists in a perpetual cloud of smoke from a nonstop succession of cigarettes that dangle from his lower lip as if attached. He converses with Spaceman George through a megaphone that he blasts in George's face at full volume.

> DIRECTOR: What, in God's name, was that all about?

> SPACEMAN GEORGE: (sheepishly) I got a little carried away, huh?

> DIRECTOR: A little carried away? *A LITTLE CARRIED AWAY?* I didn't recognize a fucking word that even vaguely resembled the script.

> SPACEMAN GEORGE: I just thought a little improvising would help me find the character, you know? The subtext . . . his motivation.

> DIRECTOR: What is this, some more of that New York Method Acting bullshit you learned? Subtext? Motivation? The great ones didn't have to know who they were. Duke Wayne didn't have a clue. Chuck Heston . . . God, the last thing in the world he wanted to know was who the hell he was. He did what he was told, no questions asked. A good Christian soldier. That's the sign of a professional. This is Hollywood, George. Hit your marks, say your lines and act, if you believe it or not . . . JUST FUCKING ACT!

> SPACEMAN GEORGE: (desperately lobbying for one more take) I just felt if I knew the character's truth, you know, his motivation . . .

DIRECTOR: (screaming) MOTIVATION . . .
MOTIVATION?

CUT BACK TO: VIDEO FLASHBACK

PARIS STREETS. GEORGE'S VIDEOTAPE OF MARK.

MARK: I need motivation, George. Give me some
motivation, Mr. Director. You see that's the
problem with this filmmaking of yours, George . . .
when you deal with people who aren't motivated to
deal with the camera for some real reason, like a
script and words and a plot . . . then there's the
problem that they behave with artifice, not with art.

END VIDEO FLASHBACK

CUT BACK TO: GEORGE'S SCREEN TEST. The Director
is screaming through his megaphone in Spaceman George's
face.

DIRECTOR: Motivation . . . you want
motivation, George? I'll give you motivation.
You're a has-been, a nothing, a nobody, a bum.
You're washed up. Your career is over. Nobody
remembers you or cares. You're finished. Your
agent won't even have anything to do with you.
You're fucking nuts and should be committed. Is
that motivation enough for you?

Spaceman George totally misreads the director's tirade.

SPACEMAN GEORGE: Oh, yes, that's exactly how
I see the character, too. I'm so relieved. We're in sync
here. Okay, let's do it.

The Director rolls his eyes in disbelief.

SPACEMAN GEORGE: I'll be honest with you, I'm a little nervous. I haven't been in front of a camera in years and I mean, you know, if I could snag this part, well . . . need I say more? I'd be back on top.

The Director bangs his script on George's head.

DIRECTOR: This is a script, George. It's filled with words, words written by a very, very expensive writer. Consequently, I want to hear every fucking one of them . . . every syllable, consonant and vowel, in order, as written, without the slightest variation or permutation, no matter how fantastically innovative, brilliant or motivated you think you are. Is that clear?

SPACEMAN GEORGE: Clear. Yes, yes . . . very clear. I'll nail it this time. If I fuck up, I'm outta here. I'll just walk out of the scene, off the stage, out of the studio . . . leave town, the country, the planet. You'll never see me again.

DIRECTOR: It would be worth another take just to be assured of that. All right, one more, but this is it. You go off on one of your inner monologues searching for the truth again and you're out! Finished! Do we understand each other?

SPACEMAN GEORGE: I hear you. I can do this.

DIRECTOR: (Turning to the crew, screaming through his megaphone.) All right, everybody, we're going for one last take . . . and I mean *one last take*. Mop him down.

Hands attack George from all sides—tugging, pushing, powdering, combing, wiping, taking light readings, testing microphones, checking focus. While Spaceman George is being prepped, the prop department cleans up the broken mirror from the previous take and rolls a new mirror out on stage. All is ready.

In a matter of seconds, the crack Hollywood professionals do their thing and retreat like good little worker bees, eagerly returning to their tabloids, gossip columns, racing forms and crossword puzzles.

> ASST. DIRECTOR: Quiet on the set . . . Roll camera.

The clapperboard is shoved in the frame and **BANGED** shut.

> DIRECTOR: All right, now get a grip, George . . . *ACTION!*

Spaceman George takes a deep breath, turns to his reflection in the mirror and raises his right hand.

> DIRECTOR: Cue dialogue of the lawyer.

The SCRIPT GIRL reads the part of the lawyer from off camera.

> SCRIPT GIRL: Do you swear to tell the truth, the whole truth, and nothing but the truth. So help you God?

> SPACEMAN GEORGE: I do.

SCRIPT GIRL: At the time of the murder, were you residing in the East Village, in New York City, in a three-floor walkup at 94 St. Mark's Place?

SPACEMAN GEORGE: Yes.

SCRIPT GIRL: Did you also rent the adjoining apartment?

SPACEMAN GEORGE: Yes.

SCRIPT GIRL: Did you pound out two holes in the brick wall that separated the apartments, each approximately a foot and a half in diameter, one opening into the living room and the other opening into the bathroom?

SPACEMAN GEORGE: Yes.

SCRIPT GIRL: And did you do this excavation unbeknownst to the building management?

SPACEMAN GEORGE: Yes.

SCRIPT GIRL: Did you install double-glass, two one-way mirrors over these openings?

SPACEMAN GEORGE: Yes, but . . .

SCRIPT GIRL: And did you do all of this for the express purpose of spying on the occupant in the adjacent apartment?

SPACEMAN GEORGE: Yes, but it was a film. We were making a film . . . *lights, camera, action* . . . you know, a movie…for Christ's sake, what are you trying to do to me here???

SCRIPT GIRL: Please, just answer the question. Did you concoct this harebrained scheme to secretly videotape a certain young woman, an actress by profession, with the intent—and I'm quoting here from your deposition . . . 'To record her every waking, sleeping, dreaming moment because I felt she held the key to my salvation' unquote.

SPACEMAN GEORGE: Well, yes . . . but . . .

SCRIPT GIRL: Would you just answer the question?

SPACEMAN GEORGE: Yes, I said that. I did all of it. But it was a film. It wasn't real. And I resent the 'harebrained scheme' wisecrack.

DIRECTOR: (screaming) George, stay with the script or, so help me . . .

SPACEMAN GEORGE: (reluctantly) Yes, all right, that was me. Okay?

SCRIPT GIRL: And did you also install listening devices and bug the phone of the aforementioned apartment?

SPACEMAN GEORGE: Yes.

SCRIPT GIRL: And after much, quote unquote . . . *casting*, did you rent out aforesaid apartment to a certain young woman, the aforementioned actress?

SPACEMAN GEORGE: Yes.

SCRIPT GIRL: And did you often refer to her demeaningly as the "bitch" or the "slut" in the next apartment?

SPACEMAN GEORGE: (realizing there's no way to talk his way out of this one) Yes.

SCRIPT GIRL: And did you eventually record her death?

Spaceman George tries to say the words in the script but he just can't. After a couple false starts, he decides to give up trying to say it the way the *expensive writer* has written it and begin where he is—stuck in his head—midway between what he can't remember and the things he's deliberately forgotten.

SPACEMAN GEORGE: I'm a voyeur. I've always been a voyeur. For as far back as I can remember, I've been a voyeur. I started watching seriously when I was about nine, my mother, through the crack in the bathroom door . . . disrobing . . . stepping into the bath, unsuspecting of her intruder. Or maybe she knew I was there all along, looking one-eyed through my imaginary toilet-roll camera, she, only pretending her private moment, to allow me my youthful indiscretion.

My suspicion was that she knew I was there all along. It was as if we had made this silent pact to never admit what we suspected the other suspected . . . but would never say.

My dilemma was, if I did step forward and reveal myself, confess my sins, there was always the chance she didn't suspect what I suspected she did in the first place, and all I'd have succeeded in doing was blowing my cover, to never again be able to hide behind my suspicions.

Consequently, I chose to continue my deception, acting innocent beyond suspicion of such devious behavior, that conveniently disguised the fact that I was an impostor, a faker, a fraud . . . in a nutshell —an *actor*.

It would be an actor's life for me, safely secluded in the picture show of my imagination, where I could make my movies however, and about whatever I damn well wanted, and no one would be the wiser.

SOUND OVER: A WOMAN SCREAMING AND MOANING. IF SHE'S IN ECSTASY OR PAIN, IT'S IMPOSSIBLE TO TELL.

CUT BACK TO: WRITER GEORGE'S APARTMENT. NIGHT.

The sound of the couple fucking in the next apartment is making it impossible for Writer George to concentrate on his screenplay. So close to the end and still the last scene eludes him. In an attempt to break his writer's block, George decides to go for the heavy artillery.

KITCHEN. CLOSE ON THE REFRIGERATOR DOOR OPENING. Writer George reaches in and grabs a book from behind a carton of soymilk titled *Magic Mushroom Growers Guide*. He opens it.

THE CAMERA MOVES IN CLOSE. Tucked in a hole cut out in the pages is stashed a plastic baggy of mushrooms. Writer George tosses back a sizable amount, washes them down with some Thai tea and heads back to his computer to wait for ignition.

As George maneuvers through his cluttered apartment, HIS STRIDE TRANSITIONS into the feet of his YOUNGER SELF, age ten—some forty years earlier—making his way through the clutter of the attic of his grandparents' Iowa farmhouse.

Young George settles in next to a window, brushes the cobwebs away, frames his 16mm home movie camera on the rainy country scene, focuses, and pushes start.

CUT TO: 16MM. BLACK AND WHITE FILM. What Young George sees through his camera: JOYCE, his best friend, also age ten, who appears all wrinkly through the rain on the pane as she peddles down the muddy road on her fat-tire bike. Her features suggest a beautiful young woman in the making but at this juncture the package is still in gangly disarray. Young George continues to follow Joyce through his camera as she turns off the dirt road and makes her way slipping and sliding up the muddy drive to the farmhouse.

WRITER GEORGE: (VOICEOVER in the PRESENT as he types) Let me digress for a moment and fill in some backstory. It was about a year after I discovered *watching* that I found a camera, here in the attic. When I was a kid, this place was piled higher than I was tall with ancestral belongings. It was a king's ransom in clues for someone in search as I, a primordial dig, strewn with specimens to be unearthed, catalogued and reassembled into meanings, not of their original intention, but of my alienated point of view.

JACQUES: (VOICEOVER) This may sound farfetched but you'll stumble upon a source of actual creative energy.

CUT TO: VIDEO FLASHBACK

Jacques sits in front of a Chinese tapestry of a golden-headed lion. He appears lost in another dimension as he gives his psychic reading, eyes half-closed, never looking into George's camera.

Jacques is a reader of auras and a teller of fortunes, both past and future. Early seventies, Fu Man Chu goatee. He appears in a trance as he does his reading, thoughtfully pushing his index finger through the wrinkle in his brow. His words come out measured with an affected English tone. He seems to be getting his insights from another dimension—perhaps the one from which George is seeking reentry.

> JACQUES: (cont's) This is an experimental force and you will actually indulge in projecting this energy or attempt to understand the projection of it.

END VIDEO FLASHBACK

WRITER GEORGE: (cont's VOICEOVER in the PRESENT as he types) It was here in the attic on one of my expeditions that I stumbled on this major archeological find. There was no doubt about it. I had found the *missing link*, a karmic replay machine, deceptively disguised as a harmless looking 16mm home movie camera.

I discovered it at the bottom of a trunk buried under a pile of photographs of long-ago dead relatives. Stern, Puritanical types, humorlessly staring out from faded tintypes.

The cover on the accompanying instruction manual boldly proclaimed: HOW TO MAKE PERFECT MOVIES WITH YOUR BELL AND HOWELL 16MM HOME MOVIE CAMERA.

The first page instructed with Zen-like simplicity: To make your own movies is as simple as—load, set lens opening, focus, and shoot. Then all you had to do was press your finger down on the start button and enjoy making your very own PERFECT MOVIES.

This wasn't just information on how to make perfect movies. It was an instruction manual on how to leave this mundane existence.

I didn't get the full story on the camera until years later. It seems that Lester, an army buddy of Dad's and aspiring filmmaker, was caught making *blue movies* (as pornos were referred to back in the 50's) with some hookers near the army base in Kansas where he and Dad were stationed.

Lester's most profitable outlet was selling to the army brass. However, due to a slight miscalculation having to do with trying to market his latest production to a certain recently transferred holier-than-thou Christian Corporal, Lester ended up doing time in the brig.

During Lester's incarceration Dad was shipped overseas. The next Dad heard of Lester's whereabouts, Lester was dead. It seems a couple days after the war ended in the Pacific, Lester was bitten by the poisonous puffer fish in a South Seas lagoon while attempting to film a bevy of naked underage Filipino nubiles with this very same camera.

Lester didn't have a family and had put Dad as next of kin. As a result, the camera and a projector, along with a few other personal effects were sent to my Grandparents' house, where my mom and dad lived the first few years of their marriage due to lack of funds. Consequently, Lester's meager estate ended up in the attic, forgotten, until I made my earth-shattering discovery.

I often sensed an eerie presence when looking through the camera, which I attributed to the erotic exploits of its previous owner. It was somehow a feeling of being guided, perhaps even instructed by Lester from the *other side*. It was as if I had unwittingly become Lester's apprentice and was being groomed to bring to the screen his interrupted dream of making a perfect movie.

For instance, I found myself being coaxed into spooky dank underworlds—dark and foreboding passageways—that if not for the discovery of Lester's camera, I would never have ventured into on my own.

As it turned out, Dad did make a gallant effort to use the camera once—on the occasion of my *rumored* birth. In a celebratory drunk, he managed, according to family folklore, to film my being exhumed from one of those *dark and foreboding passageways.*

It seems that Kodak found my first starring role offensive and stated so, in no uncertain terms, in a letter I found stuffed in the side pocket of the camera case, dated: 2-21-46. It read:

Dear Customer:
Kodak finds that the film you sent for development, focusing as it does on the private parts of a woman giving birth, to be extremely offensive and by definition of the United States Lewd Act Law, pornographic. Therefore, Kodak will exercise its legal right to confiscate said footage.

Needless to say, I was extremely disappointed when I read the letter, as Dad's film would have been the undeniable evidence I was looking for to prove that, not only was I here legitimately and had made it in one piece, but that I had come through the *normal channels.*

END OF DIGRESSION

CUT BACK TO: INTERIOR ATTIC. WE SEE WHAT YOUNG GEORGE SEES THROUGH HIS 16mm CAMERA OUT THE WINDOW—JOYCE, in the rain, pushing her bike up the muddy drive of George's grandparents' farmhouse.

Young George continues to film Joyce until he loses her from view under the porch roof. Albeit the first scene, Young George is noticeably pleased with the way his film is going so far. But there is no time to dilly-dally with self-congratulations. Joyce will be coming up the stairs any minute.

Young George winds the big key on the side of his camera, preparing for another thirty-second take, and scrambles back across the attic to his next camera location—behind an oversized antique bureau on top of which is attached a mirror extending up about three feet.

Although it's a tight fit, Young George manages to squeeze between the wall and the back of the bureau and position the lens of his camera so he can see through a peephole in the upper left corner of the mirror where a small portion is chipped away.

Young George turns his telephoto lens into position and frames a CLOSE SHOT on the door and waits in eager anticipation for the sound of Joyce's footsteps.

> WRITER GEORGE: (cont's VOICEOVER in the PRESENT as he types) Actually, this wasn't my first film. My first film was entitled *Grandma Through the Looking Glass*. It was a one-reeler, an X-rated docudrama of Grandma doing *it*—and not with Grandpa, but with the Reverend Clarence, pastor of the First Church of Our Lord, Grandpa's brother and Grandma's "spiritual advisor."

CUT TO: THE MAKING OF THE FILM . . .

GRANDMA THROUGH THE LOOKING GLASS

EXTERIOR. DAWN. FARMHOUSE. Young George approaches a certain window with cautious familiarity, camera rolling.

> WRITER GEORGE: (cont's VOICEOVER as he types) I maneuvered between the rosebushes and the house and balanced myself on two strategically-placed bricks. Here, steadied by the rain pipe at my back, I framed my camera so I could see through Grandpa's and Grandma's bedroom window to the event going on in the adjacent bathroom.
>
> Grandma was undignifiedly bent over the sink moving in a somewhat wooden response to Pastor Clarence's enthusiastic display, where his previous profession as a ballroom dancing instructor in Omaha specializing in the rumba, was embarrassingly apparent.
>
> Because my line of sight was somewhat obscured by a lace curtain blowing in front of the lens and a half-open bathroom door, I didn't have a clear shot of all the *action*. Consequently, the "details," for the most part obscured, were nonetheless obviously implied.
>
> The upper-half of Pastor Clarence was visible in the mirror, fastidiously dressed as usual—waistcoat, suspenders, high starched collar and bow tie. Grandma, on the other hand, was in her customary gingham-flowered print dress, lace-up patent leather shoes, and hair twisted in a bun that when unfurled fell well below her fleshy turn-of-the-century hips.
>
> To get in closer on the action, I swiveled my telephoto lens into place, and none too soon, as Uncle Clarence let it *fly*. And fly Grandma almost did, right

into the tub—and would have—if not for the soap dish she grabbed mid-launch.

And there they froze, Grandma draped over the sink and Uncle Clarence balanced on her behind, his sweaty, bony, double-faced image smashed up against the mirror.

This cinematic moment was interrupted by the sound of Grandpa stripping the gears in the old Ford coming up the driveway. Panic! Grandma started breathing first. Then Uncle Clarence sucked in a big gulp and hastily lowered himself from his lofty perch. Like kids caught with their hands in the cookie jar, the two scrambled around trying to put Humpty Dumpty back together again.

My dilemma was how to cover both Grandpa's arrival *and* the frenzy going on in the bathroom. Then, out of nowhere—or perhaps it was Lester calling the shots from beyond the grave—I flashed on page 17 of the HOW TO MAKE PERFECT MOVIES instruction manual.

CUT TO: CLOSE. INSTRUCTION MANUAL. PAGE 17:

In order to show the relationship between two objects, it is desirable at times to "PAN" that is, move the camera HORIZONTALLY while the exposure is being made.

What more appropriate situation in which to attempt this advanced technique! Figuring it would help to steady the shot, I took a deep breath and holding it, PANNED HORIZONTALLY, just like the manual said—not too fast, not to slow—off Uncle Clarence and Grandma and out the window in perfect timing—as it happened—I caught Grandpa's Ford just rounding the kitchen porch. Without the slightest hesitation, I continued PANNING with the Ford as Grandpa maneuvered around a couple potholes and lurched into the barn.

Taking advantage of the break in the action, I exhaled, hurriedly wound the camera, sucked in another deep breath, and picked up the shot as Grandpa emerged from the barn. I followed him across the barnyard until he disappeared around the corner of the house and just, as smooth as can be, continued my HORIZONTAL PAN back in the bedroom window just in time to catch Pastor Clarence fleeing the scene of the crime, leaving Grandma to fend for herself.

Zipping up his pants, Pastor Clarence grabbed his Bible from the back of the toilet, slicked back his hair with the sweat of his brow, gave Grandma a lecherous wink and, like a villain in a bad silent movie melodrama, gave a twist on the end of his drooping moustache and skulked out of the bathroom in an overexposed mishmash of streaks and blurs as the end of the film ran out in my camera.

Perfect!

END THE MAKING OF THE FILM

GRANDMA THROUGH THE LOOKING GLASS

FADE UP: ATTIC. THE CAMERA PULLS BACK from Young George's *one-reeler* of Grandma and Uncle Clarence, being projected on a sheet nailed to the wall. Young George and Joyce are huddled in the corner watching with rapt attention.

WRITER GEORGE: (cont's VOICEOVER mumbling in the PRESENT as he types) Joyce mostly looked away on the first showing of *Grandma Through the Looking Glass*. On the second showing, she watched through her fingers. After that, we didn't even take the time to rewind the film. We just played it in reverse and back and forth, sped up and slowed down until it was so damaged it wouldn't go through the projector.

It was agreed that a new production was in order. Joyce expressed a surprise interest to be the star of my new movie and hinted, after much negotiation, that maybe, just maybe, she'd let me film her *"oh! Natural."* But, she said, she wanted me to hide so she wouldn't know if she were being filmed or not. That way, she said, she could pretend someone was watching her—a game, she said, she and her daddy played when she got ready for bed. I didn't really understand what she was talking about but if there were a chance of filming Joyce undressing, I'd agree to most anything. Besides, her pretend-game of me not being there, totally appealed to my budding voyeurism.

SOUND OVER: A WOMAN SCREAMING—IN ECSTASY OR PAIN IT'S IMPOSSIBLE TO TELL.

CUT BACK TO: THE PRESENT. WRITER GEORGE'S APARTMENT. George is at his computer getting nowhere with his screenplay. It's becoming increasingly difficult for him to write the more his cock becomes involved in the goings-on in the next apartment.

The woman's outbursts remind Writer George of Marie. He's been trying to forget her for months but her presence still fills the room like incense. George lights another stick—Marie's memory curls up and through his senses like dope.

But George can't let his shattered psyche go down that rabbit hole again or he'll end up back in the loony bin for sure. In spite of his resolve, a memory of Marie manages to slip through his shoddy line of defense.

NOT TOO DISTANT PAST

VIDEO IMAGE: MARIE. CLOSE. WRITER GEORGE'S APARTMENT. NIGHT.

MARIE: You want to see everything, don't you?

THE CAMERA SLOWLY PULLS BACK FROM MARIE TO INCLUDE WRITER GEORGE. CAMERA TO HIS EYE. RECORDING THE TWO OF THEM IN THE MIRROR.

Marie is standing in back of George, peering over his shoulder, talking to his mirror-image. Marie is an actress, as have been all the women in George's life. They met doing a movie where she was cast as his estranged daughter. George was immediately smitten with her. All the reasons Marie was cast in the movie are why George was attracted to her. The description of his daughter in the script read:

> Early twenties. Offbeat, sexy, scraggly looks. Has enough mystery mixed with her shy, innocent, little girl exterior to convince us that she isn't as virtuous as she might otherwise appear to be at first glance, suggested by her willingness to go places that she may never return from.

George and Marie have carried their pretend-movie father-daughter-relationship over into real life, running their incestuous trip out as far as their karma will allow.

MARIE: So, answer me.

WRITER GEORGE: Yes, I want to see everything.

MARIE: (seductively whispering in George's ear) I
mean ev-er-y-thing.

To emphasize the meaning of her implication, she wraps her
arms around George and starts unbuttoning his shirt.

CUT BACK TO: WRITER GEORGE AT HIS
COMPUTER.

It's all he can do to extract himself from Marie's memory. He
takes a gulp of Thai tea and forces himself back into his
screenplay. George types:

CUT BACK TO: THE ATTIC.

And we do . . .

CUT BACK TO: THE ATTIC. CLOSE. YOUNG GEORGE
BEHIND THE BUREAU LOOKING THROUGH HIS
CAMERA, THROUGH THE HOLE IN THE MIRROR.

SOUND OVER: JOYCE'S FOOTSTEPS coming up the stairs
and down the hall to the attic. George makes a final camera
adjustment and pushes start.

WHAT YOUNG GEORGE SEES THROUGH HIS
CAMERA: The door to the attic slowly opening and Joyce
peeking in—soaking wet. With some minor bobbles, George
manages to follow Joyce in CLOSE-UP as she enters the attic
and makes her way through the piles of boxes and jumble of
family heirlooms, ending in front of the mirror that he's hiding
behind—so far so good.

WRITER GEORGE: (VOICEOVER in the
PRESENT as he types) The thing was, Joyce didn't give
the slightest indication that she knew I was just on the

other side of the mirror. And there was no way she couldn't have known with all the racket my camera was making. I had no idea she would be so good at acting that I wasn't there so she could pretend I was watching her. However, just before she reached up to unbutton her dress, I thought I detected a fleeting glimpse of doubt, a moment of embarrassment in her otherwise flawless play-acting. But she carried it off so well I doubted I saw what I thought I saw and forgot she was pretending I wasn't there.

CUT BACK TO: WRITER GEORGE'S MEMORY OF MARIE THAT HE'S RESISTING REMEMBERING.

The two are still reflected in the mirror. However, they've switched places. George is now standing in back of Marie with his arms around her—unbuttoning her dress—and Marie is videotaping the two of them in the mirror.

    MARIE: Did you hear me, George?

    WRITER GEORGE: Yes, you're right. I want to see ev-er-y-thing.

    MARIE: It's a futile search, George.

    WRITER GEORGE: And how's that?

    MARIE: Because it never ends. You just keep moving the boundaries to satisfy your curiosity like astronomers who conveniently add new galaxies to the edge of space when they get too close to the end of their imagined universe.

Marie SLOWLY ZOOMS into her breasts, that George, ever so deliberately exposes in the wake of her parting dress—perfect.

CUT BACK TO: THE ATTIC. YOUNG GEORGE'S 16mm POINT OF VIEW of Joyce through the hole in the mirror. CLOSE on her fingers unbuttoning the last few buttons of her wet dress and letting it fall off her boyish figure.

CUT BACK TO: MARIE'S VIDEO POINT OF VIEW IN THE MIRROR, of George unbuttoning the last of her dress and letting it slide off. We hold on Marie's curvy nakedness for a moment before . . .

CUTTING BACK TO: THE ATTIC AND YOUNG GEORGE'S 16mm POINT OF VIEW of Joyce through the crack in the mirror.

WRITER GEORGE (cont's VOICEOVER in the PRESENT as he types) Because of my limited view, I was unable to see everything I would have liked, i.e., the lower half of Joyce's anatomy as she wiggled her way out of her panties.

In an attempt to rectify this misfortune, I stretched up and over the mirror as far as I could, and almost, but not quite, was able to get the shot I wanted before I lost my balance and fell, as they say, head over heels. In mid-fall I made a grab for a shelf but only managed to pull it down with me along with all its contents, ending up sprawled at Joyce's feet, covered in an assortment of Christmas tree decorations—most humiliating.

Needless to say, the illusion we had gone to such lengths to create was shattered beyond repair. There was definitely no going back and picking up with a *second take*, like they do in Hollywood. No, the magic was gone. All the kings' men could not put Humpty Dumpty back together again—the watcher had been revealed.

Somehow though, I had enough presence of mind in this most embarrassing of moments to reframe, and although I was mostly upside down, managed to get a fleeting shot of Joyce's sweet, round, rosy butt as she dove under a pile of quilts on Grandma's and Grandpa's big old dilapidated, four-poster bed.

Without the slightest hesitation I rolled the camera and, like a combat photographer, crawled through the jungle of family heirlooms and went in for a CLOSE-UP of Joyce, who, as if on cue, peeked out from under the quilts and emphatically declared . . .

JOYCE: You want to see everything, don't you?

YOUNG GEORGE: Yes.

JOYCE: Well, you can't.

With that, she playfully sticks her tongue out and pulls the quilts back over her head.

CUT BACK TO: WRITER GEORGE'S VIDEO MEMORY OF MARIE THAT HE IS UNSUCCESSFULLY RESISTING.

Marie playfully rolls up in a blanket to get away from George's camera.

George MOVES IN for a CLOSE-UP.

MARIE: I've figured it out, George . . . this obsession of yours to videotape everything.

WRITER GEORGE: And your conclusion?

MARIE: So you can play it back, review it, control it, change it, make life go just the way you want it.

The Gospel According to George. You're a control
freak, George, plain and simple.

GEORGE: The "director is God" theory?

CUT TO: VIDEO FLASHBACK

PARIS. MARK talking into George's camera as they maneuver
through the crowded streets.

MARK: No, I didn't say is God. I said, thinks he's
God. Whoever is behind the camera is the eye of
God. It's very frustrating. There's a sense of
manipulation . . . the director playing God. Which
is really what this is about. It's not a question of
being God. It's the eye of God . . . and whoever
controls the eye of God, manipulates, and in
manipulating . . .

CUT BACK TO: WRITER GEORGE'S MEMORY OF
MARIE.

MARIE: Well, you can't.

WRITER GEORGE: What?

MARIE: See how it is . . . how it *really* is when not
being observed.

WRITER GEORGE: Why not?

MARIE: Because of the effect your observing has
on whatever you're observing . . . . it being different
than when *not* being observed.

CUT BACK TO: VIDEO FLASHBACK

MARK. TALKING INTO GEORGE'S CAMERA.

> MARK: The problem is that there's a certain
> amount of superficiality about it. People are on,
> and when they are on, they are only what they are
> when they are on. So the level of reality is very
> limited. It exists on a certain plane, the plane of
> my reaction to you doing this.

CUT BACK TO: GEORGE'S MEMORY OF MARIE.

> MARIE: It's the law of physics, George. Whatever
> you observe, you affect.

> WRITER GEORGE: Even if what's being
> observed doesn't know it?

> MARIE: A thought will change it . . . even the
> faintest thought or even the possibility of even
> having a thought of a thought of the possibility of
> one will do it. So, you see, you can never know the
> very thing you want to know.

> WRITER GEORGE: But why?

> MARIE: George, aren't you listening? Because
> there's a part of knowing you can never know.

> WRITER GEORGE: And why, pray-tell, oh wise
> one, is that?

> MARIE: Because, pray-tell, oh ignorant one, there
> is nothing to know about it. It's a mystery story that
> can never be solved. And no amount of probing,
> or filming, or asking questions, or yoga, or fucking,
> or astrology, or theorizing, or beliefs, or drugs, or

searching, or sitting on a bed of nails, or walking around Mount Kailash or art, or fucking, or . . .

WRITER GEORGE: You said that.

MARIE: . . . or shaktipat , or iPods, or opening your chakras, or repeating mantras, or staring at yantras, or getting into, or out of, or over, or under, or anything that you could ever think of— will ever reveal anything other than there is nothing to know about it . . . and even that isn't true. Got it?

The video comes to an abrupt end.

THE CAMERA PULLS OUT OF THE MONITOR on which Writer George has been watching the tape of Marie and himself.

George considers that maybe Marie is right, that one can never really know what happens, will, or ever did for that matter, and that the pursuit of answers is a contrivance, conceived of by impostors, to hinder the most spontaneous way to proceed, which ultimately, requires no answers at all, only the relinquishing of the space they occupy, so the vacuum left by their vacancy can be realized in itSelf.

SOUND OVER: APPROACHING FOOTSTEPS OUTSIDE OF WRITER GEORGE'S APARTMENT.

The following is a scene that George obsessively replays in his head of the last time he was with Marie.

HE TYPES:

The footsteps stop outside the door.

Writer George looks around. A shadow leaks under the door.

GEORGE TURNS BACK TO HIS COMPUTER AND
TYPES:

> You didn't say goodbye!

SOUND OVER: WRITER GEORGE'S FRONT DOOR
OPENING.

CUT TO: MARIE, closing the door.

> MARIE: I'd been saying goodbye for months.
> There were warning signs, George. You just didn't
> hear me.

CUT BACK TO: COMPUTER SCREEN.

WRITER GEORGE TYPES:

> Why do you think it didn't work . . .you and me?

Marie leans over Writer George's shoulder and reads what he's
typing.

> MARIE: Drop it, George. I just came to say
> goodbye. I've got a plane to catch.

WRITER GEORGE TYPES:

> Don't leave. Not yet.

> MARIE: Okay, I can only stay a few minutes but
> the whole thing has to shift.

WRITER GEORGE TYPES:

Agreed.

MARIE: That means eliminating everything.

WRITER GEORGE TYPES:

Yes, I understand.

MARIE: Do you really?

WRITER GEORGE TYPES:

Yes.

MARIE: I mean, the running, the jumping, the dancing . . . it all has to go.

George turns from his computer and confronts his memory.

WRITER GEORGE: No Marie, not the dancing.

MARIE: You agreed.

WRITER GEORGE: I know . . . but not the dancing. I love the dancing. Can't we keep the dancing?

MARIE: Don't you understand? We have too many links with the past. You tell me all the time, George "A writer, every morning, wipes the slate clean from which everything begins again."

WRITER GEORGE: One last dance . . . just one.

MARIE: All right, but something slow.

WRITER GEORGE: And close.

MARIE: And slow.

The two come together silhouetted in the purple pulsating neon light from the strip joint across the street. Marie doesn't resist George's embrace. She puts her head on his shoulder and the two dance slow and close in the limited space of George's cluttered little apartment to the muffled sound of a tango filtering up from the street.

MARIE: (whispers) Can I tell you something?

WRITER GEORGE: Of course.

MARIE: I want to go places I can't come back from.

WRITER GEORGE: You say that but when I ask you to come with me back to the Pleiades, you always refuse.

MARIE: You keep talking like this and they'll send you off to the booby hatch again.

A HIGH-PITCHED SOUND. Marie pulls away.

MARIE: Did you hear that?

WRITER GEORGE: No.

MARIE: There it is again.

WRITER GEORGE: What's it sound like?

MARIE: A ringing sound, adjacent to the melody. It makes me reluctant to go on.

WRITER GEORGE: A high piercing sound like the harmonic resonance of millions of insects in the Peruvian jungle at sunset . . .that sort of sound?

FAST CUT TO: INTERIOR. MENTAL INSTITUTION. Dr. Olson and Spaceman George.

DR. OLSON: It says here in your dossier that you have a persistent sound in your head. What exactly does it sound like, George?

SPACEMAN GEORGE: It's like . . . You know that sound on the radio when they say, "the following is just a test," and then there's that high-pitched humming sound . . . You know the one?

DR. OLSON: Do you hear it now?

SPACEMAN GEORGE: It's constant. It's always there in the background. It doesn't have a beginning or end. Sometimes it gets so intense it blocks out the whole universe. There's nothing, zero . . . I'm not even here. There's just this sound and it's driving me crazzzzy.

CUT BACK TO GEORGE'S APARTMENT: George and Marie dancing, silhouetted in the purple pulsating light.

MARIE: It's too intense with you, George. You're always trying to figure it out, this thing that can never be figured out. I just want to be simple, no complications . . . sleep, eat, make love, do yoga, enjoy, share my life with someone who loves me

and lets me love him back, work in my garden, ride
my bicycle. You know, walk on the beach at
sunset with someone, eat at good restaurants,
maybe a little *three-way* once in awhile to spice
things up . . . live a simple life, not always
questioning everything. You're always dissecting,
scrutinizing, judging, never just accepting. The
simplest thing always turns into a conundrum with
you.

WRITER GEORGE: And that's the way it is with
the yoga instructor . . . simple?

MARIE: Yes. No pressure. He's not always trying
to make me over in his image, controlling me.
George, all you do is seduce but you don't come
across with the goods.

WRITER GEORGE: I understand. I dream of
being that way with you but it always comes out
like a tug-of-war.

The two dance in and out of the shadows for some time before
George inquires.

WRITER GEORGE: Do you think you could
convince me that I'm not here?

MARIE: Where are you going with this, George?

WRITER GEORGE: I have this recurring dream
that I'm following this woman, videotaping her for
some reason. She never lets on if she knows I'm
there, sneaking around, recording her life on the
other side of walls, doors, windows, mirrors. Could
you do that?

MARIE: Do what?

WRITER GEORGE: Convince me that you didn't know I was there, prowling around recording your life, when you knew I was.

MARIE: I think you wouldn't really know for sure and the doubt would drive you crazy.

WRITER GEORGE: That's not an answer.

MARIE: I'm an actor. That's what actors do. They convince watchers that what they're seeing is real. It's all just a magic trick, sleight of hand, misdirection. While looking over there, what's really going on *here* goes unnoticed.

WRITER GEORGE: And you accuse me of being obtuse.

MARIE: When I was little, I always felt someone was watching me but I could never see who it was. Then I created a camera in my mind that was filming me . . . everything I did, my thoughts . . . even my dreams were somehow being recorded. It allowed me to get pictures of myself when I realized I was totally unconscious. Then I would remember this film being made and it would bring me back . . . but I would never let on that I knew.

WRITER GEORGE: Knew what?

MARIE: That there was someone there . . . watching, recording my life.

WRITER GEORGE: When I say things like that, you tell me I'm crazy. When you say it, you're profound.

MARIE: It's all in the delivery, George. (She checks her watch.) I've got to go. I have a plane to catch.

WRITER GEORGE: Hollywood?

MARIE: Yes. We start shooting next week.

WRITER GEORGE: I'm happy for you. I really am. You're going to be great . . . Tell me you love me before you go.

MARIE: But you know I'm not in love with you anymore.

WRITER GEORGE: I know, but lie to me, so I can pretend.

MARIE: You want me to lie to you?

WRITER GEORGE: Why not? Come on, show me how good of an actor you are. Quiet on the set. Camera. . . *Action!*

Marie decides to play along with George's little game one last time. She takes a moment to prepare and looks lovingly in George's eyes.

MARIE: I love you, George . . . (pause, pause, pause) Did you believe me?

WRITER GEORGE: Hmmm, not really.

MARIE: (lashing out) Damn it, George, I don't
want to play your silly games anymore. Movies . . .
movies, that's all life is to you . . . a movie. Nothing
is real. Well, certain things *are* real, like feelings,
and caring, and *being here* instead of . . . God only
knows where . . . off in your head . . . out of your
head and never letting me in. I don't go away
when the projector in your head shuts off. This
isn't easy for me. I don't want to leave you. No, the
yoga instructor isn't as imaginative as you, or as
nuts, or as creative, or as sexually perverted, and
I'll miss all those weird spaces we got into. But
there's a tradeoff, George. He shares his life with
me. I know he's there. (She begins to cry.) George,
you know I love you. I'd drop everything, the
career, Hollywood, the yoga instructor, everything,
if I thought that things could work out between us.

She kisses George, putting her whole body into it. They sink
down on the floor-futon in the glow of the red lava lamp. Marie
lavishes herself on George until he is truly out of his mind. Then,
in a total reversal, she sits up, uninvolved as if just having
finished a bad novel, closes her blouse, and announces quite
matter-of-factly . . . "CUT!"

MARIE: Well, Georgie . . . did you believe me?

WRITER GEORGE: Believe you? Shit. That was
all an act?

MARIE: Every word of it.

WRITER GEORGE: You're good . . . you're
very, very good.

MARIE: For a moment there, I almost convinced myself.

George falls back on the futon—spent.

WRITER GEORGE: You'll have to watch that. I've heard that lying is the beginning of forgetting who you are.

MARIE: Yes, I know. That is the danger of pretending.

Marie gets up and moves to the door.

MARIE: Goodbye, George. Thanks for the dance.

WRITER GEORGE: Always a pleasure.

MARIE: (peeking back one-eyed through the crack in the door) Georgie, remember. He who hesitates is lost.

CUT BACK TO GEORGE TYPING:

Even after all these months, the sound of Marie's footsteps still echo in George's mind, fading down the three flights to the street . . . and gone.

• • •

Too awake to sleep, too tired to write, Writer George decides to meditate rather than masturbate—always a good choice for George. He crawls to his floor-futon and *assumes the position*— legs crossed, back straight, hands folded, eyes closed.

Within a few seconds, George picks up his search for God in their never-ending game of hide and seek. For some time now, God has been hiding out on the other side of the brick wall disguised as the slut in the next apartment—whom George can't help seeking.

SOUND OVER: WRITER GEORGE'S CHATTERING MIND:

> She has to know I'm here, just on the other side of this wall, listening to her carrying on night after night. It's obvious what she's up to. She's trying to lure me from my hiding place, distract me from my spiritual pursuit by playing out all my fantasies as if living in my head, which we both know she is, of course . . . Okay, let's see if I can raise the vibes. Just introduce the mantra like any other thought, easy . . . no trying . . . taking it as it comes . . .

The woman in the next apartment screams out, "Fuck me. Oh yes, yesssss!"

> GEORGE: "Noise is no barrier to meditation." That's what the teacher guy said who taught me how to meditate. "Have a welcoming attitude . . . no judgments . . . take it as it comes. Just repeat the mantra like any other thought . . . mantra . . . mantra . . . mantraaa . . . mountrasss . . . mount-her-assss . . . her beautiful round assstraaaa . . .

> INNER VOICE: Mantra, George, mantra. Come back to the mantra . . . come on, come on.

> GEORGE: Oh, right, my mantra. I'm meditating. Thank you. What was meditation again, just remind me?

INNER VOICE: Surrendering . . . letting go.

GEORGE: Of what? Letting go of what?

INNER VOICE: Everything . . . George, why do we have to go over this every time?

GEORGE: Just remind me, once more, letting go of what?

INNER VOICE: Past, future, hopes, desires, dreams, fears, fantasies, people, places, things . . . who you think you are . . . who you think you aren't. The whole kit and caboodle. In other words, give up all thought, George.

GEORGE: That's serious.

MARIE: (VOICEOVER) It doesn't get any more serious, George.

CUT TO: VIDEO FLASHBACK

WRITER GEORGE'S N.Y. APARTMENT. NIGHT. A COUPLE YEARS EARLIER. George is videotaping Marie who is twisted in a yoga position on the floor-futon.

GEORGE: Come on, there must be another way.

MARIE: But that's just it. There is nothing else. And in order to know it, you have to *be* it. You can't know it from the outside. And to totally commit to it, you cease to exist as a thing separate from everything else, sooooo . . .

George passes a joint to Marie.

GEORGE: Sooooo?

MARIE: Soooo . . . (She takes a hit.) I just spaced out. I forgot what I was saying. Help me get back. What I was saying?

GEORGE: "We're not separate." You were saying, "We're not separate."

MARIE: Right. You have to become *it* to know *it*.

GEORGE: But do you have to give up your entire life?

MARIE: Just the insane part where you think you know who you are. If it's any consolation, we're all insane, George.

GEORGE: You're talking about me giving up the entire content of my mind of who I think I am?

MARIE: Ideally that would be the first to go.

GEORGE: You're ruthless.

MARIE: It's my job.

END VIDEO FLASHBACK

CUT BACK TO: INTERIOR. GEORGE'S HEAD. MEDITATING.

GEORGE: That sounds a little risky to me.

INNER VOICE: Come on, George, give it a try. What's to lose? Your mind? No biggie.

GEORGE: Okay, maybe just for a few seconds to say I had the experience.

INNER VOICE: That's the spirit. Let it rip, George.

GEORGE: Right. So, this is me sitting here, comfortably . . . eyes closed, expecting nothing, just witnessing whatever comes up . . . for instance, my cock between her silky soft thighs.

INNER VOICE: No, no, no . . . go back to the mantra.

GEORGE: Oops, I almost lost it again. Now if you would just remind me once more. What is it I'm doing here?

INNER VOICE: Come on, you remember. It rhymes with masturbation.

GEORGE: Ahhhh, of course, meditation. When I find myself drifting off, I just gently come back to the mantra, right?

INNER VOICE: Right.

GEORGE: Okay, I remember. Just take it as it comes, right?

INNER VOICE: Right.

GEORGE: I can do this. Just witness the release of thoughts in the form of images as they pass.

INNER VOICE: What could be easier?

GEORGE: Just like watching a movie. Meditating
is a lot like watching a movie, right?
INNER VOICE: Right. Now you got it.

GEORGE: I love the movies. But I'm not so sure
I want my friends to know I frequent such sleazy
films. I wonder, do you think other meditators
have erotic thoughts when they meditate?

INNER VOICE: Sure . . . even the great ones.

GEORGE: You think so?

INNER VOICE: Of course.

The woman in the next apartment screams out.

George can't resist. He puts his meditation on hold and flattens
an ear against the wall. We hear what he hears—the garbled
moans and whispers of the couple fucking in the next apartment.

Deeper, deeper . . .

But, I'll hurt you.

Isn't that why we're here?

The man obviously obliges. The woman screams out.

Oh, yes . . . more, like that. Promise you won't
stop.

I have no intention of stopping.

Even if I beg you?

Especially if you beg.

I can be a very convincing actress.

Oh, I'm well aware, but I don't intend to fall for your little girl act this time.

You have all the times before.

But not this time.

Tell me.

What?

You know, tell me.

You're a whore.

Am I a bad girl?

Yes, you're a very, very bad little girl.

Just promise me, nothing is real, not even the pain, right?

Especially the pain, my dear.

We're just playing a game, right?

Right, baby, it's just a game . . . hang on.

Her screams dissolve into the sound of a phone ringing.

By the time George figures out that it's his phone, the answering machine has picked up.

> MARIE: It's me. I just woke up out of this crazy dream and had to call you. Must admit I'm a bit freaked. Remember that dream you told me months ago where you were following a woman with your camera and you didn't know if she knew you were there or not? Well, I'm here to tell you she knew you were there all along. I know . . . because I'm her. I mean, she was me . . . I mean, I just had the same dream. Oh hell, I don't know what I mean. It's too weird. Call me back. I'll fill you in.

Marie hangs up. Writer George considers calling her back and is about to, when . . .

> INNER VOICE: Come on, George, meditation… remember?

> GEORGE: I don't know. I'm really not in the mood anymore. I think I'll do it next time.

> INNER VOICE: This *is* next time, George. Come on. You can do it. Just close the eyes and repeat the mantra like any other thought.

Writer George reluctantly closes his eyes and scans the perimeter of his consciousness for his mantra—nothing.

> GEORGE: Oh hell, where's my mantra? I can't find my mantra. Damn it, it was here just a minute ago.

INNER VOICE: Now don't get all bent out of shape. Think . . . when did you see it last?

GEORGE: Come on, you know. We were doing *it*. Somewhere in there I lost it.

INNER VOICE: Go back over it step by step and I'm sure you'll find it.

GEORGE: Okay, okay, let's see. First I grabbed her ankles and bent her in half like one of those yoga positions she was always getting into.

INNER VOICE: Yes, good, and then?

GEORGE: I just hovered there.

INNER VOICE: So what were you waiting for?

GEORGE: My cue . . . will you just let me tell it?

INNER VOICE: Sorry, go on.

GEORGE: Okay . . . so I was hovering there, waiting for my cue, letting the anticipation build, whispering lies that she was loved and adored and safe in her daddy's arms when . . .

INNER VOICE: Wow, I had no idea, George. This sounds rather sordid.

GEORGE: Look, I'm standing here naked before you. If you're going to judge me . . .

INNER VOICE: Sorry, you're right, you're right. Go on.

GEORGE: It was all part of the game we played to keep the chase going. It was our fantasy, our private movie. . . just for our eyes. A little something to build up the pressure in anticipation of the pain we were about to inflict on each other. The thing is, she would always try to get me to "jump-the-gun" with sordid fantasies of her lesbian tendencies, knowing full well my susceptibility to such visuals . . . So between her salacious stories and her innocent little girl act, it was all I could do to "maintain" and she knew it. But I knew what she really wanted.

INNER VOICE: What?

GEORGE: We didn't have to say it right out. But I knew she knew I knew what she wanted.

INNER VOICE: What?

GEORGE: To be raped into submission—taken advantage of—so she would have an excuse to maintain her innocent little girl act.

INNER VOICE: Her act?

GEORGE: Yes! Her act. Don't you get it? The whole thing was an act so she could play the whore that she shamefully concealed behind a shy and misunderstood young woman. But I'm here to tell you . . . it was all bullshit. She was acting from one end of our affair to the other. And she had the gall to accuse me of being dramatic just because I had a Screen Actors' Guild card and had been in a few movies. But I couldn't hold a candle to this temptress's performance. All that begging me not

to hurt her, that was just a part of her little girl act.
Innocent, hell, I'd seen this slut in action when she
didn't know I was there and I've got the videotapes
to prove it, proof positive that this innocent little
baby doll would just as soon fuck a stranger, man,
woman, doorknob, dog, dildo or a zucchini . . .
anything to cancel out the numbness she felt from
her daddy's betrayal that I was now the beneficiary
of . . . And when things would get too hot and
heavy, she'd try to convince me she wasn't acting,
that she was really scared and she didn't want to
play the game any more. That's when the good
part started.

INNER VOICE: What? What started?

GEORGE: The begging me not to hurt her.
That's what I was waiting for . . . the begging.

INNER VOICE: The begging?

GEORGE: Yes, the begging. That was my cue . . .
That's what I was waiting for. Without the slightest
hesitation, I blasted off my pedestal of morals and
inhibitions and plunged into the center of her,
propelled by the accumulated rage of a mother
who also feigned helplessness rather than
acknowledging the anguish of her father's violence
that I was made to feel responsible for . . . but not
this time. Not in this incarnation was I going to
believe this manipulative bitch no matter how
convincing of an actress she was—and oh what an
actress she was, with her screams and pleas and
little girl sobs as she offered up those delectable tits
and curvy hips . . . blinding me with kisses,
intoxicating me with her smells, devouring me in

her luscious offering that we both knew, in the end, I would succumb to with ravenous delight . . . It was somewhere in here I lost it.

INNER VOICE: Lost what?

GEORGE: My mantra . . . what do you think I've been talking about?

INNER VOICE: Now wait a minute. Let me get this straight for the record. Even though she begged you not to hurt her, you did anyway?

GEORGE: Yes.

INNER VOICE: That's unconscionable. Under the circumstances I don't think I can represent you anymore.

GEORGE: What are you talking about? Are we reading off the same menu? This was all part of it.

INNER VOICE: Of what?

GEORGE: The game.

INNER VOICE: Game?

GEORGE: Haven't you been listening? It was a game, for Christ sake. Nothing was real. We made the whole thing up, like in the movies, but . . .

INNER VOICE: But what?

GEORGE: But when I pulled it out, it was gone.

INNER VOICE: What?

GEORGE: My mantra.

INNER VOICE: Really?

GEORGE: Not a trace. That's what I've been trying to tell you. I was just meditating like regular, sitting comfortably, eyes closed, back straight, repeating the mantra easily like any other thought, letting it go deeper and deeper when it just disappeared.

INNER VOICE: Look, this happens all the time. Meditators are going along fine, then all of a sudden they drift off and lose their mantra!

GEORGE: I wonder if yogis and saints have erotic fantasies and lose their mantra up the crotch of unsuspecting goddesses and forget their mantra? Mantra . . . mantra . . . Hey! That's it . . . I found my mantra.

INNER VOICE: It was there all the time, right?

GEORGE: Right.

INNER VOICE: Yes, it's a common place to lose it.

GEORGE: Wow . . . I had no idea.

SOUND OVER: PHONE RINGING. George is startled out of his meditation. He can't deal. He lets the answering machine pick up.

MARIE: Hello, it's me again. If you're there,
don't pick up . . . just listen. Can't sleep. This
Hollywood acting thing is overrated . . . long hours,
exhausted . . . being hit on all the time. When
people find out that I know you, I have to tell the
whole "whatever happened to . . ." story. Anyway,
thought you'd like to know you haven't totally
drifted off the charts.

We were shooting the big flip-out suicide scene
today. The director was so convinced I had really
lost it that he cut the film but I didn't pay any
attention. He was screaming and yelling for me to
put the gun down, but I just kept acting . . . blew
his mind. Turned out to be a great scene. So
hanging out with you hasn't been a total loss. I can
definitely play a convincing crazy now.

Okay, so here's the dream I had. I'm working
my way through a rush hour crowd in New York,
just like the woman in your dream. I'm being
followed by some weirdo with a video camera.
He's dressed in a beat-up silver spacesuit like the
one you wore in that God-awful film we did
together. I don't let on I know he's following me.

I run and just manage to catch a bus. There's a
newspaper on the seat next to me. A want ad is
circled in red for an underground film. They're
looking for the female lead, early twenties. The ad
says: **Must be willing to go places that you may not
be able to return from. No previous experience
needed. Submit picture and resume.**

The scene shifts. I'm climbing up the stairs of
this apartment house in the Lower Eastside. The
guy in the spacesuit is following me again. I don't
let on but I can feel his camera framed on my skirt
that stretches tight across my ass as I climb the
stairs in my high, high heels.

There's a sign taped to the wall on the next
landing: *Casting*, with an arrow pointing down the
hall. I look around. The guy is gone.

At the end of the hall there's another sign taped
to the last door: *Casting—Enter.*

I open the door a crack and peek in. I call out.
Nobody's there. It's a long narrow room. There
are two large windows at the far end. The only
light comes from the purple pulsating neon sign
above the strip joint across the street. It flashes on
and off. *Abandon all hope ye who enter here.* In spite of
my better judgment, I do . . . abandon all hope,
that is—and enter.

I can feel the voyeur guy watching me again.
He's near but I can't make out where. Then I
catch a glimpse of myself in the mirror on the brick
wall that separates this and the apartment next
door—and I immediately know.

There's no doubt. This creep is on the other side
of my reflection, squinting one-eyed through his
camera, getting an eyeful.

Then it dawns on me what this nutcase is up to.
He's making a mystery story, a *whodunit* film, and
he's looking for someone, a perpetrator, to pin the
whole rap on, an excuse to give himself permission
to rummage around in someone else's mind
instead of his own, figuring if he's found out, he
won't be held responsible—but I've got a surprise
in store for him.

All I have to do to get this part is convince him
I'm not acting that I don't know he's there, while
leaving just enough doubt, so he can indulge his
suspicions, that maybe I am . . . acting, that is.

I know what this guy wants from me . . . to do
whatever it takes to draw him out of his head and

expose him for the impostor that he knows himself
to be but can't admit. It's a sleazy

job, I know, but I'm an out of work actor and I
need the gig.

Maybe one day the filmmaker and I will meet at
the premier, be all chummy, and hug like we've
known each other for years, smile for the cameras
and bullshit the media into believing we
collaborated on the script and rehearsed and
planned the whole film.

A candle flickers next to a stack of photos on the
table under the mirror. *Leave picture and resume* is
scribbled on a piece of paper. I look through the
photos. They're all of young women, mostly naked,
some barely legal. They're not your retouched,
professional, waxed and quaffed pinups but the
homegrown variety, eagerly *showing it all* for the
amateur cameras.

One by one, I pass the photos through the
candle flame inviting the voyeur to ZOOM IN on
their smoldering bodies as they contort and
crumble into ash. I brush their remains away and
leave my photo in their place.

Being watched by a stranger . . . followed,
recorded, it's a scary business but I find myself
getting hot from the whole scenario. I can't resist. I
decide to go for it and remove any doubt in this
madman's mind that I am the one to play *the slut in
the next apartment in his perverted production.*

I spread out on the bed and, disappearing in
and out of the purple pulsating light, am about to
give him an eyeful when the hammering in the
next apartment wakes me up. It scares the hell out
of me. It sounded like someone was coming
through the wall. Needless to say the dream was

irretrievable. Why do dreams always end at the
good part? Feel free to use any of these babblings
in your never-ending screenplay. But if you do,
make sure I get to play the part.

CLICK . . . BUZZZZZZZ.

George debates dumping his meditation and calling Marie back.
But before he can make up his mind, he's yanked from his
indecision by the sound of hammering on the other side of the
wall. A crack appears in the plaster next to George's head. He
opens one eye.

    INNER VOICE: No, don't stop meditating.

    GEORGE: But someone's trying to break in.

    INNER VOICE: It's all in your head. No one's
    breaking in. Don't be a fool and fall for that ol'
    trick. There's only you here.

    GEORGE: Then who are you?

    INNER VOICE: Well, yes, technically you could
    say I'm here, but . . .

More hammering. George's other eye pops open.

    INNER VOICE: No, no. You're blowing the
    whole thing, just when you're getting the hang of
    it. Trust me George, it's all in your head… nothing
    is real.

The camera makes a fast move into the crack. A piece of plaster
falls away exposing a brick. More hammering. The brick is

forced through and falls to the floor. George is compelled. He leans over and peeks through the hole.

WHAT GEORGE SEES: A huge expanse of the Milky Way, maybe a hundred million light years across.

Something tumbles into view appearing out of a cluster of nearby stars. It's a spaceship—a peculiar-looking contraption—welded, pounded, banged, riveted, wired and duct-taped together. It's a can-like affair, barely large enough for whoever is looking out to have been squeezed in.

> WRITER GEORGE: (VOICEOVER in the PRESENT mumbling along as he types) So, here I am, the sole survivor of a space flight, adrift for so long the galaxy from which I've come could very well be extinct by now. I'm lost between the beginning and end of a journey I don't remember embarking on and have long ago forgotten the destination and/or purpose. The last entry in my logbook is written in an ancient script, one that I am unable to even decipher, let alone remember having written.
>
> I am cocooned in this obsolete space machine, adrift in a cosmic tide, buried here in the space of my own thoughts, just me and myself, crammed headfirst in this *mind-coffin*, guided by the whim of some mutual consent that no longer consults me and I am left abandoned, without recourse, to witness my descent to the edge of time, where I am now...just barely in time...hanging on for one last time...praying that this time won't end like all the times before.

The encapsulated spaceman somersaults overhead and floats off into the inky blackness—and gone. However, a faint sound lingers—a murmur, a kind of a hum, an atonement of some sort.

Perhaps it's a code or a distress signal from the spaceman himself, or a navigational device or maybe . . .

> DR. OLSON: (VOICEOVER) Would you say it was a buzzing sound?

> SPACEMAN GEORGE: (VOICEOVER) No, well . . . maybe kind of.

CUT TO: INTERIOR. MENTAL INSTITUTION. A PADDED WHITE ROOM.

Dr. Julia J. Olson is questioning SPACEMAN GEORGE, who sits before her on the floor in his spacesuit—back straight, legs crossed, restrained in a straitjacket.

> DR. OLSON: Maybe more like a hiss?

> SPACEMAN GEORGE: Yeah . . . well, no, not quite. But that's more like it.

> DR. OLSON: Well, then . . . is it more like a wail or a groan?

> SPACEMAN GEORGE: Well . . . no, not exactly.

> DR. OLSON: A cry, or weeping, perhaps?

> SPACEMAN GEORGE: No.

> DR. OLSON: More like a lustful sound perhaps, like a screech, a scream or panting . . . a blowing, perhaps?

> SPACEMAN GEORGE: Ahhh, no. Not really.

DR. OLSON: A moan?

SPACEMAN GEORGE: At times.

DR. OLSON: (getting aroused) An outcry, or an ejaculation?

SPACEMAN GEORGE: You can't be serious with these questions.

DR. OLSON: (getting control of herself) Let me remind you that I am a professional and I take my job very seriously.

SPACEMAN GEORGE: And these questions are supposed to determine if I'm crazy or not?

DR. OLSON: We like to think of this as more of a job interview.

SPACEMAN GEORGE: A job interview?

DR. OLSON: Yes, exactly. You have a choice, George. We have a couple of openings. (She holds up a form letter.) Line A indicates your preference to be the patient. If you check B, you're the doctor . . . whichever you feel more qualified for.

SPACEMAN GEORGE: What are you saying? I have a choice of being the wacko or the wackee?

DR. OLSON: Well, I wouldn't have put it quite like that but, yes.

SPACEMAN GEORGE: You know this is crazy!

DR. OLSON: Well, this *is* a mental institution
after all. So, time is fleeting . . . we have precious
little left. What will it be? Which avenue would
you like to . . . purssuuuue? Do you want to be the
patient or the doctor?

SPACEMAN GEORGE: I think I want to be . . .
to be . . . the wacko, the patient.

DR. OLSON: Good. Line A. I was hoping you
would pick patient. More range of expression. In
that case, I will be the doctor. Now if you would
just sign here, we can get started.

Dr. Olson puts a pencil in Spaceman George's mouth and holds
the paper for him to sign. He manages an "X" on line A.

SPACEMAN GEORGE: And you are?

DR. OLSON: Doctor Julia J. Olson. My friends
call me Dr. Julia J. Olson. Now I see here in your
dossier that you're a maker of films. But if I
understand, you've never really . . . that is, actually
ever made a film. I mean, you just make these
movies in your head, as I understand it.

SPACEMAN GEORGE: Well, that was true in
the past but I'm working on an idea for a real
movie. I'm almost finished with the screenplay, but
the last scene keeps eluding me.

DR. OLSON: A real movie! You mean like a
Hollywood movie?

SPACEMAN GEORGE: Anything but!

DR. OLSON: Well, what would be the difference?

SPACEMAN GEORGE: Well, for starters, everything wouldn't be conveniently wrapped up on page one hundred and twenty. There would be no retakes . . . no regurgitated storyline to boost the weekend grosses, no endless fucking credits, no predictably-contrived plot made up by *wannabe-Hollywood-somebodies* who on their own couldn't take a decent Polaroid, let alone make a movie.

DR. OLSON: Do I detect sour grapes?

SPACEMAN GEORGE: You detect a whole vineyard.

DR. OLSON: Pent up rage . . . that's good, George. You're playing the patient so well. Oh, this is so exciting. I'm going to enjoy pulling all those nasty bogeymen out of you. Now, for starters, why don't you tell me a little bit about your movie? Maybe there's a clue in there that will help us understand why you are so . . . Hmmm, what's the proper psychological term? Oh, yes . . . fucked up.

SPACEMAN GEORGE: Well . . . the only thing I care to say at this time is that it's a mystery story, a case of mistaken identity. It's about a world of pretenders, actors, fakers, and frauds.

DR. OLSON: Oooohh! Right up my alley. Can I convince you to share just an itsy bitsy snatch? I do so love the movies.

After some dramatic hemming and hawing, Spaceman George acquiesces.

SPACEMAN GEORGE: All right, Doc. I'll give it to you just like we do in Hollywood. If you would just give me some working room here (referring to the constraints of his straitjacket).

DR. OLSON: Well, okay, George. But you must promise to be a good boy.

SPACEMAN GEORGE: Yeah, yeah . . . sure.

Dr. Olson unties the sleeves of his straitjacket. They hang to the floor, giving Spaceman George an apelike appearance. Realizing this is as good as it's going to get, Spaceman George stretches out his arms and, like *real* film directors do, frames what he sees in his mind's-"I," between his canvas-hands and begins his Hollywood pitch.

SPACEMAN GEORGE: Okay. I always start my films with the last scene first, then I go back and figure out how the story ended up there. We fade up. Last scene. Video image . . . Interior . . . bathroom of a New York apartment as seen through the video camera of a deranged guy who's recording this scene through a one-way mirror from the next apartment. He slowly zooms in on a young woman's lifeless naked body, laying face down, half in, half out of the shower, water spraying down on her, flooding the apartment. Got the picture?

DR. OLSON: Oh, how deliciously decadent. If I only had a bag of popcorn. Carry on, George, carry on.

SPACEMAN GEORGE: So here's the backstory. Since he was a kid, the Voyeur's been obsessed

with making a perfect movie . . . a movie where the
actors would have no idea they were even being
filmed. That way, he figures, they'd act with art,
not artifice.

CUT TO: VIDEO FLASHBACK

MARK. PARIS STREETS. TALKING INTO GEORGE'S
CAMERA.

MARK: When you deal with people who are not
motivated to deal with the lens for some real
reason, then there's always the problem that they
act with artifice, not with art.

GEORGE: And the distinction between art and ar . . .?

MARK: The distinction between art and artifice is
a clear one but not readily defined.

END VIDEO FLASHBACK

CUT BACK TO: SPACEMAN GEORGE'S HOLLYWOOD
PITCH.

SPACEMAN GEORGE: So, to get the realism
he's looking for, the Voyeur concocts this scheme.
He rents two adjacent apartments in an old three-
story walkup in Lower Manhattan, hammers out
two good size holes in the brick wall that separates
the two apartments—one opening into the
bathroom, the other into the living room—covers
the holes with thick, double-glass, one-way mirrors,
sets up video cameras, stashes microphones, and
bugs the telephone. When everything's ready, he
puts an ad in the paper for a studio apartment—

actors preferred, females only need apply—and waits to see who his karma ensnares.

The Voyeur records his prospective tenants through the one-way mirror, never revealing himself of course. When they arrive they find the door unlocked and on the table under the mirror, lit by candlelight, a note: *If interested leave picture and resume.*

Over the next few weeks, the Voyeur videotapes three or four dozen potential actors and assorted weirdos to star in his "movie." There are even a few female impersonators in the mix but no one does the trick for him. Then one night, late, this young woman shows up, jittery, wide-eyed, looking just a few years over legal. The thing that catches the Voyeur's eye is the way she appears to flip back and forth from a kind of sexy innocence, to something dark and foreboding that he can't quite put his finger on. Intrigued, the Voyeur ZOOMS CLOSER. The actress drifts around the room checking things out: the stack of eight-by-ten glossies on the table under the mirror, the view out the window of the strip joint across the street, the neatly rolled joint in the ashtray on the nightstand. Tempted for a moment, then seemingly about to take a pass, she impulsively turns back and lights up. The dare has been taken.

She only manages a couple hits before she's obliged to relinquish control and falls back on the bed, spread out in the purple pulsating neon light from the strip joint across the street—deliciously wasted.

The Voyeur sizes her up as ripe for a little adventure, eager to shed her innocent little baby-doll exterior and go places she may never return from. She just needs a little prodding—his specialty.

She lies there, still—very still, for some time, obviously engrossed in the stoned movie she has running behind her half-lidded eyes . . . then some movement —her fingers sliding over the silhouetted contour of her body. The Voyeur ZOOMS IN EVEN CLOSER until her fingertips fill his frame. He follows along as the actress leads his lens over her youthful landscape like a tour guide pointing out the sights of interest, eventually escorting him up her thighs and under her flimsy dress that she pulls aside like an opening night curtain, luring him deeper into her play of shadows, where, to his dismay, he loses his exposure and is left abandoned in the dark somewhere between her sweet parted legs, wandering aimlessly in and out of focus through a pixilated maze of digital breakup.

The knock on the door brings an abrupt halt to any lingering hope the Voyeur may have had of finding his way back. The actress sits up in a panic.

The Voyeur makes a fast ZOOM BACK to a WIDE SHOT just in time to catch a platinum blonde sticking her head in the door. 'Is this where they're casting the movie?'

The actress yells back, 'The part's already been taken,' leaps off the bed and slams the door in the blonde's face.

Figuring it's time to get the hell out of there before somebody shows up that she can't so easily scare away, she gathers her things and is about to leave her photo and resume on the pile with the rest of the wanna-be actresses when she opts for a little mischief. With wicked delight she takes each photo in turn and meticulously passes them through the candle flame. Knowingly, she positions herself so that the Voyeur is able to ZOOM IN

and get a lens full of each glossy, naked body,
agonizingly contorting and twisting in the flames
and crumpling into ash.

The actress disposes of the remains in the toilet,
leaves her photo and resume in their place, checks
to make sure she hasn't left any evidence of the
massacre, takes a quick hit on the joint and makes
a hasty retreat.

The Voyeur keeps his camera framed on the
empty room as the sound of the actress's footsteps
fade down the three flights to the street—and gone.

There's no doubt about it. This is who the
Voyeur wants to star in his perfect movie, to play
the slut in the next apartment.

CUT TO A COUPLE OF MONTHS LATER.
It turns out that the actress had recently come to the
big city from Podunk, USA, fresh-faced, with hopes
of making it in show biz.

After a couple of months, the Voyeur has
compiled hours of videotape of the Actress but
nothing really captivating. The raciest bit is a little
afternoon fondling session she got into with a
waitress from work. Apart from an occasional joint
with the young stud she's fucking from acting class,
she's still pretty much untainted.

The thing is, the Actress really has a shot at the
big time having all the *accoutrements* in the right
places, plus talent.

Things take a bizarre twist when she snags the
lead in this low . . . and, I mean, low-budget
murder-mystery *whodunit* flick. Her character goes
from this innocent all-American, apple-pie, girl
next door to this totally drugged out, suicidal
psychotic who's suspected of killing her movie
director-slash-boyfriend.

Within a couple days of getting the part, the Actress quits her waitress job, dumps the stud from acting class, and dives headlong into preparing for her role.

To get a feel for her character, the Actress heads to the streets, hanging out in the Lower East Side with the drunks, druggies and downtrodden.

She approaches cautiously at first, staying at a safe distance, snapping pictures with her point-and-shoot camera. To check out the characters more closely, she has the photos blown up and pastes them on her wall. After a few weeks every bit of her small apartment is collaged with sad, deranged, pained faces of humanity.

The Actress starts wearing clothes retrieved from dumpsters, smokes butts off the street and every once in a while buys a nickel bag from the druggie on the corner.

And all the while the Voyeur is ZOOMED IN from down the block, hiding in alleys, doorways, the other side of windows, mirrors, stairwells, behind cars, trashcans, roof tops—whatever it takes to make his perfect movie. Sometimes he even disguises himself as a bagman, hiding his camera under the overflow of junk in his shopping cart so he can move into an occasional close-up.

It's not uncommon for the Actress to stay up all night dancing like a madwoman; a possessed wild, naked, jungle-intoxicated woman; a spinning, drunken, Dervish, lunatic-of-a-woman, bashing and thrashing about until the sun comes up.

And through it all, the Voyeur is on the other side of her reflection, devotedly recording every twist and turn of her psychotic descent—real or feigned. More and more, the Voyeur is unable to detect if she's acting or not. In the meantime, her

once baby-doll-exterior has been reduced to
shambles.

It seems that she's fallen into the trap all actors
do, on or off stage, who become too attached to the
part they're playing—she's forgotten who she
really is when not being who she pretends to be.
It's one of these nights in a drunken stupor that the
actress really loses it big time when reminiscing
through some family photos .One in particular
brings her to tears. For whatever reason she
decides to paste the photo in her wall collage. After
many drunken attempts she ends up putting the
snapshot practically upside-down next to the photo
of a deranged looking guy that doesn't even appear
to know what day it is.

The Voyeur ZOOMS INTO THE PHOTO.
It's a well worn, slightly out of focus, black and
white snapshot obviously a picture of the Actress as
an infant in her mother's arms. The Voyeur
ZOOMS IN EVEN CLOSER but as will be
revealed later—not close enough.

Not even in slow-motion replay can the Voyeur
spot a flaw in her performance. She's either a great
actress, he concludes, or she is truly losing her
mind. Either way, the Voyeur is getting
remarkable footage and he can taste the film
festival awards.

For weeks the Actress has been rehearsing the
suicide scene for the film using a toy pistol. It's
when she buys a real gun from the local pawn
shop, that the Voyeur is all but convinced she may
no longer be acting.

But even the overwhelming possibility that the
Actress may not be acting, and at any moment
could go over the edge and blow her brains out,

does not dissuade the Voyeur from pursuing his mad enterprise.

Like all madmen, the Voyeur has a rationale for his actions. This is *art*, he insists. And as an artist, he has consigned himself to only be the witness, *the silent watcher* to whatever plays out in front of his lens. If there is a movie here it must unfold naturally on the whim of chance, as he concludes all things of beauty and worth are unsolicited by reason or explanations. No story-boarding here . . . no scripting, no production meetings, no figuring it out, no making it happen—no second-guessing what is.

The Voyeur's cinema manifesto is clear, unambiguously expressed in the words of the 1st century Zen Master Tilopa: LET IT SETTLE ITSELF, that he has scrawled in red-painted dripping letters across his wall—a reminder, in case he loses his courage at moments like these and falls prey to the illusion of free will.

MARK: (VOICEOVER) But the assumption shouldn't be that it will be interesting just because of its process.

CUT TO: VIDEO FLASHBACK

MARK. Talking to George through his camera as they walk the backstreets of Paris.

MARK: I mean, if you know how to handle your material you can make junk look interesting. The point is junk isn't necessarily interesting nor is it simply in the eye of the beholder. If you don't have that craft, control and imagination, it just doesn't matter, it's just more junk . . . I don't believe art is anything. We can make *anything* into art, but anything isn't necessarily art. Paint on a canvas isn't necessarily a painting. It's just paint on a canvas. So images on a film aren't necessarily movies. They're just documents and documents aren't necessarily art.

END VIDEO FLASHBACK

CUT BACK TO: THE MENTAL INSTITUTION. DR. OLSON LISTENING WITH RAPT ATTENTION TO SPACEMAN GEORGE'S HOLLYWOOD PITCH.

SPACEMAN GEORGE: But no matter how close he zooms in, there's nothing the Voyeur can detect that would suggest the slut's act is anything other than who she appears to be—a totally wigged-out chick on the verge of suicide.

CUT TO: THE ACTRESS'S BATHROOM. WHAT THE VOYEUR SEES THROUGH HIS VIDEO CAMERA . . .

The Actress, standing naked in front of the mirror, wrapped in a blanket, sweating, drugged out, fumbling with a bullet, trying to get it in the gun. She finally manages and gives the chamber a spin. Where it stops nobody knows.

She parts the blanket and slowly . . . ever so slowly, drags the gun back and forth over her sweaty breasts, tripping out on the feel of the steel as if it were a bar of soap and she was luxuriating in a bubble bath.

WRITER GEORGE: (VOICEOVER in the PRESENT as he types) Even as the Actress brushes the gun up over her cheeks and slides the barrel across her glossy red lips, the Voyeur is still debating. 'She's acting, she isn't acting . . . She knows I'm here, she doesn't know . . . she loves me, she loves me not. Is now the time to cut the scene and find out who's been playing who for a fool . . . or do I eke out a few more seconds before I have to choose?'

If the Voyeur does cut the film and it turns out the slut's been acting all along, giving this outrageously brilliant performance, maybe one of the best ever in movie history, all the Voyeur will have succeeded in doing is blowing his cover and mess up the chance of a lifetime to make his *perfect movie*, to say nothing of the shitload of awards he and the Actress could pick up . . . the Academy Award, the Cannes Film Festival Award, the People's Award, the Critics' Award, the Foreign Awards, the Indie Awards, the Director's Award, the Bullshit Awards, the Mental Wards.

The VOYEUR ZOOMS IN to a CLOSE-UP of the ACTRESS.

She sucks the barrel of the gun in and out of her red pouty lips.

WRITER GEORGE: (cont's VOICEOVER) She plays with the gun as if it were a popsicle and she was sitting on the corner bus stop, in her short cutoffs, in a dumpy little Midwestern town, in the dripping summer heat, looking foxy and fine for all the local testosterone-hard boys, gawking out the window of the pool hall across the street, as she does her suggestive little maneuvers to drive them crazy. And she is . . . driving the Voyeur crazy, that is.

Finally he has to admit that this high-wire act is getting way too risky. He's about to yell "Cut!" when he hesitates, as he always does at this juncture, gambling that the Actress is acting, and each time, except this last time, he's been right . . .

KA'BLOWWWWWWIE!

Like a blowjob gone haywire, the Actress gets a mouthful of lead that sprays out the back of her head dispensing a good portion of her brains over the white-tiled walls. The impact hurls her back across the bathroom where she lands half in, half out of the shower, the water spraying down, one arm unnaturally twisted behind her, the gun still in her hand, blood oozing out of the hole in the back of her head, her black silky hair stringing like seaweed clogging the drain, the water overflowing and flooding the bathroom.

> WRITER GEORGE: (cont's VOICEOVER) So now at last, the guessing game was over, unless you speculate that maybe the slut was acting all along. After all, no one uses real bullets in a movie. And the director didn't yell, "Cut." That's what really great film actors do. No matter if a light blows or the other actors flub their lines or the sound goes out . . . even if the camera runs out of film—no matter what—only the director cuts the film!

CUT BACK TO: MENTAL INSTITUTION. HIGH WIDE SHOT. Spaceman George is sprawled out on the floor below, totally spent, his canvas arms flung out to the sides. He contemplates the Voyeur's dilemma.

> SPACEMAN GEORGE: Of course, the other possibility is that the Actress was offering the Voyeur an opportunity to make up for the karma of his previous hesitations that he painstakingly drags from life to life without the slightest hesitation.

Spaceman George falls silent.

> DR. OLSON: Most revealing, George. So let me understand. None of this really happened? It was just a movie, right, and you wrote the screenplay?

SPACEMAN GEORGE: Every word of it. And *yes*, it was just a movie, for Christ sake. That's what I've been trying to tell everyone in this crazy house. I mean, shit, who uses real bullets in a movie? You got to be insane to do something like that.

DR. OLSON: Yes, exactly, George . . . someone would have to be insane to do something like that. Would you mind if we videotape our sessions? We find that it's very helpful for the patients to see themselves back. You might want to even use some of the footage in one of your films that never make it to the movie screen.

SPACEMAN GEORGE: I shouldn't have said anything. Dad warned me that if I did, I'd end up in the nuthouse like Aunt Pinky. . . Shit!

Dr. Olson sorts through a stack of videotapes.

DR. OLSON: Oh, wouldn't you know? I'm out of videotape. Let's see if there's something here I can tape over. (She finds a tape.) Yes, maybe this one.

Dr. Olson pops the tape in the VCR. SIT SLIVER appears on the monitor. He's in the middle of an intense rap. In another incarnation when George was a promising up-and-coming actor, Sit was his sleazy, wheeler-dealer agent. But now, because George's synapses and receptors seem to be misfiring, he can't recall this guy.

SIT: It's a reverse impulse of yours . . . this obsession to photograph other people . . .

SPACEMAN GEORGE: Who's that?

DR. OLSON: A former patient . . . Yes, we can use this tape. This egomaniac was released sometime ago.

Dr. Olson is about to press rewind when Spaceman George breaks in.

SPACEMAN GEORGE: No, let it play. I know this guy from somewhere.

SIT: In other words, your real need is to have other people look at and explore you psychologically in hopes that somehow, magically, you will be healed or validated in some essential way. You're acting it out in some reaction formation by looking at others and examining in their lives what you can't accept in your own.

SOUND OVER: A WOMAN SCREAMING AND MOANING IN ECSTASY OR PAIN—IT'S IMPOSSIBLE TO TELL.

SIT: (cont's) It's almost as if you're fucking instead of accepting the fact that you want to *be* fucked.

FLASHBACK: WRITER GEORGE'S APARTMENT.

SHAKY, OUT-OF-FOCUS VIDEO IMAGE OF MARIE. CLOSE. NAKED. RADICAL UP-ANGLE BETWEEN HER SUMPTUOUS BREASTS. EYES CLOSED. HEAD ROLLING. HAIR TOSSING. SCREAMING.

The CAMERA PULLS BACK from the monitor on which this video is playing, revealing Marie and Writer George on the floor-futon. George is on his back, video camera to his eye, shooting up at Marie who is straddled on top of him, working herself into a frenzy. It's all George can do to keep her in frame.

WRITER GEORGE: No. Marie, stop or I'llllll . . .

MARIE: Oh, yes . . . yes, George. Do it. Give it to meeee . . .

WRITER GEORGE: No, No. Please Marie, stop. Not yet. Don't . . .

In the background we can see Marie's image breaking up on the monitor.

MARIE: Oh! George. FUCK MEEEE.

WRITER GEORGE: No, Marie . . . Please. Not yet. I've run out of videotape.

The words slowly get through to Marie. She grinds to a halt and looks down into George's camera—flabbergasted.

MARIE: You what?

WRITER GEORGE: I've run out of videotape.

MARIE: I don't believe this. Are you out of your mind?

WRITER GEORGE: Hold that thought. I'll be right back.

Writer George untangles himself from Marie and crawls across the room to the packed shelves in search of a free videotape.

WRITER GEORGE: Damn it! I'm out of
videotape. Maybe I can record over something
else.

Writer George frantically searches through a stack of old tapes.

MARIE: You're crazy, George. I mean, you're
really out of your fucking mind.

WRITER GEORGE: And I've got the papers to
prove it.

MARIE: Sex with you is like being on the evening
news. What is this, a commercial break?

WRITER GEORGE: Just a temporary
interruption in our scheduled broadcast due to
technical difficulties.

DAISY: (VOICEOVER) I feel bad for these
women.

WRITER GEORGE: (VOICEOVER) You do?
Why?

CUT TO: VIDEO FLASHBACK

INTERIOR. WRITER GEORGE'S BATHROOM. VIDEO
IMAGE OF DAISY IN THE BATHTUB. She's reading the
latest revision of George's script.

Daisy is this knockout, gorgeous, brunette wannabe-actress.
Spoiled. Elitist. Supported by her trust fund. Acts Bohemian,
lives bourgeois. Educated in France. Super bright. Intimidates
every man she goes out with. Can't make up her mind to shave
her head and become a Buddhist monk or go to Hollywood and

be in the movies. Writer George met Daisy at one of his refresher courses at the funny farm where she was doing a short stint for indecision.

Daisy is the only woman in Writer George's life who is admittedly as wacko as he is. At a moment's notice, she is prone to major mood shifts with accompanying rants, humorous diatribes that often find their way into George's screenplay. For example:

DAISY: Yes, I feel really bad for these women.

WRITER GEORGE: Why?

DAISY: Because I just can't imagine being on the verge of orgasm and you announcing that everything has to go on hold for you to reload your camera. (She can't help laughing.)

WRITER GEORGE: Come on, all chauvinism aside, you have to admit it's a funny scene.

DAISY: Yeah, it's funny as a script, but you really do these things. I find it really offensive and it pisses me off. The reason you have to record everything is because you're so out of touch. You have to play life back to know what happened. I mean, if the truth be known, George, you are really a pathological liar and need a shrink or a major overhaul. (She laughs.)

WRITER GEORGE: I don't get why you're so angry? You seem to be amused.

DAISY: You are . . . you're amusing. I mean, I can't believe how passive-aggressive you are.

WRITER GEORGE: I am?

DAISY: Yes, extremely, and obviously a lot of hostility and rage toward women. On the surface you act passive but underneath you're a raging chaos. I feel that you use all these women as pawns in your little ongoing movie of your life. I feel badly. It's like . . . are human beings dispensable to you . . Just video subjects and tape-recorded messages? . . Just tits and ass to display for your entertainment? Tell me if I'm wrong. You're so lazy when it comes to human interaction. Like last week . . . I called to tell you I'm depressed, on the verge of suicide, and you tell me to stand on my head and do cartwheels.

WRITER GEORGE: The standing on your head doing cartwheels thing when you get depressed was right-on advice.

DAISY: Unique, entertaining . . . and it made me laugh, but it's not going to help.

WRITER GEORGE: It made you laugh. You can't be depressed when you're laughing.

DAISY: If I stood on my head every time I felt depressed, I would walk around beet red. Come on, George, admit it . . . You're no one to rely on. It's all about you. The rest of us are just here for your entertainment.

WRITER GEORGE: How have I treated you?

DAISY: You've treated me wonderfully, thank you.

WRITER GEORGE: What else is there?

DAISY: I'm just making an observation about your
script, which by the way is filled with some of my
best lines that you twist out of shape and stick into
this never-ending screenplay of yours so everyone
will think you're this avant-garde metaphysical
thinker, but in reality you don't have a clue what
you're talking about. You just throw around a lot
of other people's ideas. Your only real talent is
making other people think you know what you're
talking about. You're an impostor, George . . .
plain and simple.

WRITER GEORGE: But I wrote the part for you.
It's based on my relationship with Marie. I thought
you'd have fun with it.

DAISY: I am . . . I did, I would . . . as an actor, but
I certainly wouldn't want to be a part of your
insanity for real.

WRITER GEORGE: Come on, you know you
would.

DAISY: I would not. I'm really angry right now.

WRITER GEORGE: Then why are you laughing?

 DAISY: Because it's funny, damn it. I'm just
going to go.

Daisy gets out of the tub, grabs a towel and stomps out of the
bathroom. George follows at a safe distance. We stay with
George's VIDEO POINT OF VIEW.

WRITER GEORGE: So you like the script?

Daisy turns back into a big CLOSE-UP in George's camera.

DAISY: You know what disturbs me? When I'm with you, I feel totally out of my mind.

WRITER GEORGE: Yeah, I know.

DAISY: You know what I'm saying?

WRITER GEORGE: Yeah . . . Me, too.

DAISY: What? You feel that when you're with you, that you're out of your mind, too?

WRITER GEORGE: Exactly.

DAISY: Well, you'd better keep that to yourself or you'll find yourself back in the loony bin.

As much as Daisy tries not to, she can't help laughing.

DAISY: Okay, George. I'm outta here. This is too much.

Daisy runs around gathering up her clothes that are scattered everywhere—panties, bra, shoes, blouse. George follows close behind with his camera.

DAISY: I'm just really in a bad mood right now and I've got this plane to catch . . .

WRITER GEORGE: Why are all the women in my life always catching planes and leaving me?

DAISY: . . . And I feel edgy. I've got my period, I'm bloated. Before, I was really happy to see you . . . you just got out of the loony bin, but . . . damn it, where are my socks? (working herself into a tizzy) There's a pathology in you George, like you mentioned in your script about lying. And that's because you do it a lot. (They laugh.) You do. I think you lie a lot.

WRITER GEORGE: All the time.

DAISY: You admit it? You lie all the time?

WRITER GEORGE: Of course.

DAISY: And you're just fine with that?

WRITER GEORGE: Yes.

DAISY: Jesus!

WRITER GEORGE: Everyone is lying to everyone as long as we think we are who we appear to be. If we didn't, none of us, as we know ourselves, would be here.

DAISY: Then you're saying everything . . . life . . . is just one big lie to you?

WRITER GEORGE: It's a collective agreement to keep the whole thing going.

Daisy grabs her backpack.

DAISY: George, they let you out too soon. (She opens the front door and turns back.) God, I hate this.

WRITER GEORGE: What?

DAISY: I mean . . . you're really adorable but you're such a pain in the ass. (They laugh.)

WRITER GEORGE: What do you mean?

DAISY: You're really a nice guy . . . and you've got some great qualities but as far as just having a conversation with you that's normal . . . I mean, do you practice being this way? Is it an actor thing?

WRITER GEORGE: What way?

DAISY: This way that you are.

WRITER GEORGE: And what way is that?

DAISY: Like having a conversation with you makes me feel really constipated. (They laugh.) You know what I'm saying? A conversation with you . . . it's labored . . .exhausting. I mean, you don't say anything.

WRITER GEORGE: I don't?

DAISY: You just . . . you're not in things. You don't get involved. You just sit back and observe us all, you know? And we all become idiots in your presence. (She laughs.) You just sit there and watch us turn into these babbling morons going on about nothing. And I don't want to act. I want to

have a real conversation with you. And
unfortunately it turns into acting with you on my
part because I know that's all you want . . . nonstop
entertainment and it frustrates me and pisses me
off and I get angry . . . (They both laugh.) I'm
serious, damn it, and all you do is laugh at me.

WRITER GEORGE: I'm not laughing at you. I'm
laughing at your great delivery.

DAISY: Yeah, well, your entertainment is leaving.
Do you have anything worthwhile to say before I
go?

Writer George ZOOMS BACK to reveal the whole picture of
Ms. Daisy: eyes rolling, hands indignantly planted on hips, puce
plastic backpack slung over one shoulder, French flowered silk
blouse, see-through thong panties and combat boots. Noticeably
absent from her outfit—her skirt, that in her manic frenzy, she
has neglected to put on.

WRITER GEORGE: Daisy, I've got to tell you for
your own good. There is something very wrong
with this picture.

DAISY: "For your own good." When did you ever
think of anyone else's good? (She turns to go.)

WRITER GEORGE: Daisy, I don't think you
should leave in your present condition.

DAISY: (turns around and snaps back) George,
don't tell me what I want or don't want. I am no
longer going to be controlled by you. I've had it . . .
I'm feeling too nuts . . . I'm going. Goodbye.

George waves his hand in front of the lens.

WRITER GEORGE: See you soon.

DAISY: Don't count on it.

SLAM!

Writer George leaves his camera framed on the door as he patiently waits for Daisy's inevitable return.

SOUND OF DAISY'S BOOTS banging through the hall and down the stairs—PAUSE . . . A LOUD SCREAM.

THE SOUND OF DAISY running back to George's apartment. She tries to open the door—it's locked.

DAISY: George . . . George, you nut lunatic, let me in!

WRITER GEORGE: (playing) Daisy, is that you?

DAISY: You know damn well it's me. Let me in.

WRITER GEORGE: Did you forget something?

DAISY: George, fuck you, let me in.

WRITER GEORGE: Do you love me?

DAISY: Do you ask all the women in your life to tell you that they love you when they leave you?

WRITER GEORGE: It's a codependent thing.

DAISY: George, for Christ sake, someone is coming up the stairs.

WRITER GEORGE: Do you love me?

DAISY: Yes, damn it. I love you. Now open the goddamn door!

George reaches in his video frame and opens the door. Daisy is irate but can't help laughing.

DAISY: I was lying about the "loving you" thing.

WRITER GEORGE: I figured. We're all liars.

END VIDEO FLASHBACK

CUT BACK TO: THE MENTAL INSTITUTION. WRITER GEORGE AND DR. OLSON are where we left them a few scenes back, huddled in front of the monitor watching Sit.

SIT: Lying is the beginning of forgetting who you are.

SPACEMAN GEORGE: What did he say?

DR. OLSON: Lying is the beginning of forgetting who you are.

SPACEMAN GEORGE: What the hell does that mean?

Spaceman George moves up to the monitor. Sit's image all but falls apart under Spaceman George's close scrutiny.

SPACEMAN GEORGE: Where the hell do I know this guy from?

SIT: The trouble with lying is that you begin to believe the lie. So for safety's sake, you should tell the truth.

SPACEMAN GEORGE: Damn it. I know this weirdo from somewhere. He's tricky . . . very, very tricky. He'll try to convince you that he isn't, but he is.

DR. OLSON: Is what, George?

SPACEMAN GEORGE: An impostor, a faker, a fraud. He thinks he knows what he's talking about, but he doesn't have a clue.

DR. OLSON: A clue about what, George?

SPACEMAN GEORGE: The movie. The movie we've been talking about.

DR. OLSON: You mean the movie in your head? The one you made up?

SPACEMAN GEORGE: Oooohhhh no, you don't. I've said too much already.

DR. OLSON: Come on, George. After all, I *am* your doctor.

Spaceman George turns, takes a couple of steps, stops, pauses, then abruptly turns back. As he does, we. . .

CUT TO: THE SOUND STAGE AND SPACEMAN GEORGE'S SCREEN TEST.

He rushes up to the camera, ending in a HUGE DISTORTED CLOSE-UP. Mentally, Spaceman George is just hanging on by a thread.

> SPACEMAN GEORGE: Oh, no. I know what you want me to say. But I'm not going to say it or I'll end up in the loony bin like Aunt Pinky, just like Dad said I would.

THE DIRECTOR comes running into the scene screaming through his megaphone.

> THE DIRECTOR: Okay, that's it, George. I've had it with you. Cut the film. Cut the sound. Cut the scene. Cut fucking everything.

> SPACEMAN GEORGE: (outraged) No, no. Why are you cutting? I was on a roll.

> THE DIRECTOR: Yeah, you were on a roll, all right. And you can roll right out the door. I told you if you didn't stick to the script I would cut the film and I meant it. (He turns to the film crew.) I said, CUT THE FILM. THAT'S A WRAP.

THE PICTURE FADES AWAY—HOWEVER . . .

The Director and Spaceman George continue their conversation OVER BLACK.

> SPACEMAN GEORGE: You can't do this. I was cooking. I nailed it.

THE DIRECTOR: George, what everyone says about you is true. You're impossible, a has-been, a nutcase. I gave you one last chance and you fucked up. Now get out of that costume and get the hell off this stage.

SPACEMAN GEORGE: (screaming at the top of his lungs) Turn the fucking camera back on or I'll blow your shit for brains out!

A LOUD GUN SHOT

SPACEMAN GEORGE: Just a warning shot over the bow to get your attention. Now here are your choices. They're very simple, even for a moron like you. Either I shoot you and end your miserable existence or you turn the fucking camera back on . . . Got it?

THE DIRECTOR: (hardly able to get the words out) Roll . . . roll . . . roll camera.

FADE BACK UP: Spaceman George has the Director in a stranglehold with a gun to his head and the megaphone in his face at full volume.

SPACEMAN GEORGE: A very wise decision. Now, is there any problem with me having another take?

THE DIRECTOR: No, no, no problem, George.

SPACEMAN GEORGE: And is there any problem with me doing a little improvising to help this piece-of-shit script?

THE DIRECTOR: Anything you want, George. In fact, this anger you're expressing, this menacing quality, it's how I've always seen the character.

SPACEMAN GEORGE: Don't bullshit me, you putz.

THE DIRECTOR: I was giving you motivation, George. Cutting the film, throwing you off the set, calling you a has-been. That was just my way of getting you motivated . . . You know, the Method Acting thing.

SPACEMAN GEORGE: Well, now that I'm all motivated to the point of blowing your brains out, perhaps we should do another take.

THE DIRECTOR: Yes, George. Let's do another take, ten, twenty, forty, a hundred . . . as many as you want. Why don't we just roll the camera and not miss any of this?

CAMERAMAN (whispers to the Director): We *are* rolling!

THE DIRECTOR: Of course, right . . . I knew that. Okay, George . . . show me that brilliance that won you the Golden Globes' newcomer award back in the 60's . . . And ACTION!

Spaceman George slams the Director in his chair.

SPACEMAN GEORGE: Listen, you Hollywood hack. I'm the one on trial here, not you . . . (turning to the crew) not any of you, and I'm going to play this scene just the way I want. Understood?

Since there do not seem to be any dissenters to his proposal, Spaceman George launches into his rave, shouting into the megaphone at full blast.

> SPACEMAN GEORGE: And another thing. This is the last . . . end . . . finish . . . final . . . absolutely last time I'm going to do this. I refuse any longer to endure the rage I feel from the humiliation of playing this same part over and over again as if I'm being tested like some neophyte.

In a second, Spaceman George becomes sad. He drops the megaphone. We can barely hear him. The mic dips into the scene.

> SPACEMAN GEORGE: But there's something else, damn it. I always get to this point, then I forget. There's something else . . . I know there is. I've forgotten something. Something vital . . . something key . . . What is it I've forgotten?

> ETY: (VOICEOVER) I don't know the word for it. I would love to know.

CUT BACK TO: VIDEO FLASHBACK

ETY. ON HER BED. Her writing still propped on her knees. She talks into George's camera.

> ETY: It's almost like the zero of the thing. It's not really zero, but it's between the zero and the first.

END VIDEO FLASHBACK

CUT BACK TO: SPACEMAN GEORGE SCREAMING IN THE CAMERA.

SPACEMAN GEORGE: Tell me. What is it, what have I forgotten?

THE DIRECTOR: (OFF CAMERA) For God's sake, give him his lines.

The SCRIPT GIRL slinks into the scene, hands Spaceman George a copy of the script and makes a hasty retreat.

Spaceman George scans the expensive writer's words but what he's forgotten isn't on these pages. He tosses the script, reaches up, grabs the microphone, pulls it down to his mouth, and speaking in an intense hush, tries to unravel his jumbled thoughts.

SPACEMAN GEORGE: All right, I admit it. I don't know how these things evolve. I don't pretend to. Where waking leaves off and dreams begin, is becoming less and less clear, the clearer I am obviously not me becomes clearer. What is becoming clearer however, is knowing that only by passing through this stage as an actor, separate from the part I'm playing, while observing the part I'm not, will I be able to, once and for all, be relieved of forgetting to remember what I've forgotten. But for now, let me try to remember this one last time. Maybe, if I go over it scene by scene, I can figure out where things went haywire—where the story fell apart and my life fizzled out.

SOUND OVER: CHILDREN PLAYING.

Spaceman George looks deep in the lens of the camera as if what he's hearing is coming from in there somewhere.

CUT TO: WHAT SPACEMAN GEORGE SEES IN THE LENS: A face—his own—age nine, barely suggested, rising up from a cloud-filled Midwest picture-postcard summer sky, reflected in a mirror-still pond. His face gently breaks the surface of the water.

He takes a breath, then another, and another before opening his eyes. They reflect the day, seeing, it seems, more in than out. It's all here, the real and the feigned, just as he remembers it from before he submerged, a while ago . . . a lifetime ago . . . a moment ago . . . a merr-y-go . . . a merr-y-ego-ago . . . and round and round e-go-e-go . . . gently down the stream merr-i-ly . . . merr-i-ly . . . merr-i-ly . . . merr-i-ly life is but a dream . . . life is but a dream.

Young Joyce floats by, stretched out on her inner tube, hair trailing in the water, pink-painted toes bobbing up and down, catfish jumping. No doubt, these are definitely "the good ol' days."

CUT TO: VIDEO FLASHBACK

WRITER GEORGE'S N.Y. APARTMENT. NIGHT. Marie is stretched out on her back in a yoga position. Her pose is reminiscent of young Joyce laid out on her inner tube. Writer George SLOWLY PANS his video camera over Marie's purple pulsating nakedness, illumined by the neon sign across the street.

WRITER GEORGE: You know the poet Rumi?

MARIE: George, you're getting senile. I'm the one who turned you on to him.

WRITER GEORGE: Well, he says it—how I feel about your pussy.

MARIE: What does my pussy have to do with it?

WRITER GEORGE: Everything.

MARIE: (slightly amused) And what does Rumi say about my pussy?

WRITER GEORGE: "Inside you, I rest from wanting."

MARIE: I believe he was referring to God.

WRITER GEORGE: . . . So am I.

Marie turns away hiding a bemused smile.

END VIDEO FLASHBACK

CUT BACK TO: THE POND. Joyce floats by Young George. He playfully splashes her, takes a deep breath and submerges. As he vanishes in the murky Iowa water, Joyce's voice trails after him singing . . . "Merr-i-ly. . . merr-i-ly. . . merr-i-ly. . . merr-i-ly. . . life is but a dream . . . life is but a dream . . ."

WRITER GEORGE: (VOICEOVER in the PRESENT as he types) Every once in awhile my bare ass would skim over the silky, soft Iowa clay river bottom, provoking images of what sex would be like one day. One day wasn't to be for some eagerly-awaited eight years later when my family moved to Hollywood. Here, destiny was conspiring a rendezvous with the Goddess Susie, a sexy little black Shakti-hooker in downtown L.A., who was waiting to blow my mind, body and everything else I thought I knew of who I was, out of the backwater of my delusional sleep.

SCENE II

HE WHO HESITATES IS LOST

TEEN GEORGE SURFACES SOME EIGHT YEARS LATER IN HOL-LY-WOOD. LATE-50's. INTERIOR. DILAPIDATED ROOMING HOUSE. DOWNTOWN L.A. NIGHT. GRAINY 16mm BLACK AND WHITE FILM.

The unsteady frame MOVES UP the STAIRWELL of the rooming house where SUSIE—the aforementioned *Shakti-hooker*—is leaning over the third floor railing. Although barely visible through the grain of the underexposed film, there is no missing her ample breastage that appears about to plummet over into Teen George's camera.

> SUSIE (whispering): Pssssst. Come on. But be quiet and take off your shoes.

Susie moves from the railing.

END TEEN GEORGE'S 16mm POINT OF VIEW.

Teen George and his buddy Lee are peering up the stairwell from the ground floor. Lee is the same age as Teen George—seventeen. He's blonde, flattop, lanky like George. Although no less a geek than George, he's definitely more hip—or is it hep?

> LEE: George, what the hell are you doing? It's too dark in here to film anything.

> TEEN GEORGE: I know that's what it says on the film box, not to shoot when there's no light, but sometimes something comes out really cool.

Lee moves to the stairs and takes off his shoes.

LEE: What is it with you and that camera? I think you'd rather film her than fuck her.

Teen George sits on the stairs beside Lee.

TEEN GEORGE: Yeah!

LEE: Yeah, what?

TEEN GEORGE: I would.

LEE: Would what?

TEEN GEORGE: You know, what you said before.

LEE: About filming her rather than fucking her?

TEEN GEORGE: Yeah.

LEE: You would?

TEEN GEORGE: Yeah.

LEE: You're serious?

TEEN GEORGE: Yeah.

LEE: Man, you're weird. Come on take your shoes off.

TEEN GEORGE: (stalling) I got a knot.

LEE: Oh, great.

TEEN GEORGE: Lee?

LEE: What?

TEEN GEORGE: I don't think I . . . I . . .

LEE: What is it, for Christ sake?

TEEN GEORGE: I don't think I want to do this. I think I'll do it next time.

LEE: George, ol' buddy . . . my good ol' buddy, this *is* next time.

TEEN GEORGE: Well . . . then . . . I don't want to do this next time . . . now . . . okay?

LEE: But you've got to. These are the good ol' times that we'll remember for the rest of our lives. If you don't do it now, there won't be any good ol' times to remember. Besides, we're here now.

TEEN GEORGE: I know, but we could be somewhere else now . . . having good ol 'times to remember.

LEE: Yeah, but Susie wouldn't be there.

TEEN GEORGE: All right, you got laid once. Big deal.

LEE: You're scared.

TEEN GEORGE: Yeah, duh, man. I'm scared, but not about what you think.

LEE: Then what?

TEEN GEORGE: This place. We could be killed
. . . Downtown Los Angeles in the middle of the
night. No one knows where we are. I'm going to
wait in the car.

SOUND OF HEAVY FOOTSTEPS. Teen George and Lee
flatten against the wall. Their eyes shift to the front door in
unison. The CAMERA PANS in the direction of their looks.

The SILHOUETTE of a LARGE MALE figure can be seen
approaching through the frosted glass door.

TEEN GEORGE: Oh shit!

Lee and Teen George take off up the stairs to the next landing
and peek over the railing.

WHAT THEY SEE: The front door opening and the LARGE
MAN entering. He gropes for something in his pocket.

TEEN GEORGE: (panicking) Shit. He's got a
gun. We're dead. I know it, we're dead.

LEE: Shhhhh.

TEEN GEORGE: It's a set up. We're going to be
robbed . . . mugged . . . killed . . . maimed . . .
something horrible.

The Large Man looks up and catches the boys watching him.
Caught, Lee gives a cautious wave. The Large Man pulls his
hand from his pocket. George ducks. The imagined gun turns
out to be a pint of whiskey. The Large Man takes a swig. Lee
pulls George up over the railing to have a look.

LEE: You've seen too many movies. That's her pimp. He was with her last week. His name is Tiny.

TEEN GEORGE: Maybe he's an undercover cop like on TV. Lee, I can't go to jail. My mother would die.

LEE: What the hell is the big deal? We're doing exactly what every red-blooded American boy is expected to do . . . get laid. You're mother is going to die from that?

TEEN GEORGE: This is nineteen fifty-seven, remember?

LEE: Well duh, man. I mean tell me something I don't know.

TEEN GEORGE: Well . . . it's before Sputnik . . .

LEE: Sput . . . what?

TEEN GEORGE: Ahhh and . . . and meditation and . . .

LEE: George, what are you talking about? What medication?

TEEN GEORGE: Not medication . . . meditation. (He exhales the rest without taking a breath.) It's before McDonalds, landing on the moon, gurus, *West Side Story* . . . before I was committed the first time, before the pill, corn chips, computer chips, bell bottoms, miniskirts, LSD, CDs, DVDs, SUV's, VCRs, HIV . . . before I was committed the

second time, before Vietnam, Iraq, Iran,
Afghanistan . . . suicide bombers, hippies, yuppies,
disco, punkers, rappers, skinheads, blow heads,
duct tape, videotape, instant replay, digital, virtual
reality, cyberspace, laptops, Pop tops, iPods, Twin
Peaks. . . before . . . before I was committed the
third time . . . the fourth and fifth times . . . the
good ol 'times . . . I don't remember how many
times. I've lost count . . . who cares . . . whatever.
The point is, we're lost somewhere between bomb
shelters and "Gimme Shelter." I mean, get your
reality straight. These are the 50's man, the dull,
boring, imbecilic, retarded 50's. We haven't even
"tripped" yet. I mean, the Beatles haven't even
happened yet.

LEE: What battles?

TEEN GEORGE: Not battles . . . Beatles.

LEE: As in bugs?

TEEN GEORGE: No . . . as in rock 'n' roll.

LEE: What the hell are you talking about?

TEEN GEORGE: I don't know. It just comes to
me sometimes like this.

LEE: You're strange, George . . . very, very
strange. I'm going up . . . you coming or not?

Lee starts up the stairs. George checks his options, figures he
doesn't have any, whips off his shoes and chases Lee up the
stairs.

CUT TO: FLASHBACK. EARLIER THAT NIGHT. L.A. FREEWAY. INTERIOR. LEE'S '57 CHEVY.

Lee and Teen George are cruising along. Lee is driving and singing with the Doo Wop group on the radio. Teen George, on the other hand, is trying to stave off a major anxiety attack.

> LEE: (singing and pounding on the steering wheel): Sh-Boom/Sh-boom/yada da-da-da-da-da/Sh-boom Sh-Boom/ life could be a dream, sweetheart/ woo/ woooo/ woooo/ woooooooo/if you'd come to paradise up above. . .

WRITER GEORGE: (VOICEOVER in the PRESENT—as he types) Girls ...or more precisely, sex, had been the topic of conversation since we left the party. At this point, sex for me was still in the realm of theoretical speculation, which I speculated on daily with *hands-on* research. Lee, on the other hand, had already "done it" with Susie the week before, along with all twelve of his high school club buddies. Now, at Lee's sadistic insistence, it was my turn. No more reprieves, no more putting it off. This <u>was</u> *the next time.* My request had been granted. It seemed my ascension was imminent. All I had to do was give up and . . . die. There, I said it.

> LEE: Die? What are you talking about? Come on, George, it's just like the song says: "Life is but a dream." Don't make a big deal out of it. Believe me, tomorrow you're going to thank me. And Susie' s bitchin' and stacked. Wow, wait till you see her.

WRITER GEORGE: (cont's VOICEOVER in the PRESENT as he types) We pulled off the Alvarado Exit and started cruising the backstreets of Los Angeles looking for the Goddess Susie. All I could see were people folding out of the shadows, mannequin-like figures, who turned from the glare of the headlights as we glided by—drunks, pimps, hookers, men dressed as women coming onto women acting like men, people staring into worlds seen only by them, talking to no one, answering voices that weren't there, and all knowing something I didn't. My enthusiasm for this adventure, which a few miles back had been considerable, had rapidly deteriorated into pure panic and was fast approaching paranoiac overload when Lee spotted Susie on the same corner where he and the guys had picked her up the week before.

> LEE: (totally jazzed) Holy cow, man. There she is. That's her . . . Susie. The one I told you about.

Lee stops at the signal. Susie ambles across the street in front of the Chevy. Lee blasts her with the high beams and gives a tap on the horn. Susie acknowledges us with a come-hither smile and signals to meet her around the corner. Lee peels rubber, pulls up on the designated side street and cuts the engine.

> TEEN GEORGE: Please, Lee, let's go. I really don't want to do this.

> LEE: You just think you don't.

> TEEN GEORGE: Well, at this point, thinking is good enough for me.

CLOSE: SUSIE'S HIGH, HIGH HEELS clicking down the street.

BACK TO: INTERIOR CHEVY.

TEEN GEORGE: (taking a deep breath) All right, I can do this.

Susie approaches Teen George's side of the car. He rolls the window down a crack. Lee leans over and rolls it down the rest of the way.

LEE: Hi, there. Remember me?

WRITER GEORGE: (VOICEOVER in the PRESENT—as he types his screenplay) I couldn't believe what I was hearing. How in hell, with her schedule, and in the dark, would she remember Lee? But she did. Well, she didn't exactly remember Lee. It was his candy apple red lowered '57 Chevy that she remembered. But for Lee, to remember his Chevy, was to remember him.

LEE: How much?

SUSIE: For you, ten dollars for "a straight," fifteen for "around the world."

TEEN GEORGE: (trying to bring the evening to a close) Well, sorry, I don't have any money. I'll wait here.

LEE: Hey, it's on me, good buddy. What are friends for?

SUSIE: What a good friend you have here.

TEEN GEORGE: Yeah . . . friend. Yeah, sure. (kicking Lee) Thanks, good buddy.

WRITER GEORGE: (cont's VOICEOVER in the PRESENT as he types) Well . . . that was it. There was no going back. My fate had been sealed. I was going to die . . . That's all there was to it. I knew it as well as I knew my own name, which escaped me for the moment.

LEE: George?

TEEN GEORGE: (shaken from his impending death) What?

LEE: Susie asked your name.

TEEN GEORGE: Aaaaaa . . .

LEE: George . . . his name is George. He's a little hard of hearing sometimes.

SUSIE: (speaking extra loud) I'm Susie. Do you want to have some fun, George?

TEEN GEORGE: (less than enthusiastic) Yeah . . . sure. Fun.

WRITER GEORGE: (cont's VOICEOVER in the PRESENT as he types) Susie told Lee and me to wait until she went into the dilapidated rooming house down the street. We were then instructed to come to the third floor. She would be waiting for us at the end of the hall. It was important, she said, to take our shoes off, because if the manager heard us, he would call the police...Great!

END FLASHBACK

CUT TO: INTERIOR. ROOMING HOUSE. STAIRWELL.
Teen George and Lee sneaking up the stairs. Teen George tugs
on Lee's jacket.

TEEN GEORGE: What's 'around the world'?

LEE: What?

TEEN GEORGE: 'Around the world' . . . Before
she said it was ten dollars, and fifteen for 'around
the world'.

LEE: It's when she puts it in her mouth.

TEEN GEORGE: You mean *it* . . . her mouth?
Wow, she puts it in her mouth. Really?

LEE: Yes. Christ, you really are from Iowa, aren't
you?

WRITER GEORGE: (cont's VOICEOVER in the
PRESENT as he types) Susie was waiting for us at the
end of the hall overexposed in the light of a bare bulb
hanging from the ceiling. As we approached, she
stepped back into her high heels, launching her up
another six inches. She and Lee started talking. I don't
know about what . . . money, who would go first, how
bitch'n it was to find her. I totally tuned out and went
right for the visuals.
  Susie's eyes peered out from behind half-open lids that
seemed to be looking more in than out. Her plentiful
red lips were plastered with greasy lipstick and molded
into a perpetual pucker. Moving on down, her nipples
jutted out from these velvety mounds that seemed to
poke right through her flimsy blouse. It was somewhere
in here that I lost it . . . my mind, that is.

Everything started fading away like at the end of a movie, everything but Susie's breasts, that is. The damnedest thing was, there was no separation. Susie's breasts, me, the thought of Susie's breasts . . . we were all one. I *was* her breasts...her breasts were me. . .God was there, too in Susie's breasts. The universe . . . everything, we were all One...There was no separation. All of it was IT. The whole thing was IT. In fact, there wasn't any IT, IT wasn't. It was crazy. I just went with IT. I couldn't help IT . . . ZAP! . . GONE.

TEEN GEORGE AND SUSIE'S BREASTS FADE AWAY: LEAVING ONLY THE WHITE SCREEN ON WHICH THIS MOVIE IS BEING PROJECTED.

MARIE: (VOICEOVER) That's what I was saying. You have to become IT to know IT.

CUT TO: VIDEO FLASHBACK

INTERIOR. WRITER GEORGE'S N.Y. APARTMENT. George is videotaping Marie, as usual. They're sprawled out on the floor-futon passing a joint back and forth. George is having trouble with Marie's stoned explanation of existence.

WRITER GEORGE: But what happens to *me* in all of this?

MARIE: You cease to exist as a thing separate from everything else. You *are* everything . . . simultaneously in all dimensions. Wow, I am sooooo fucking stoned.

Marie takes another hit and playfully makes a goofy face in George's camera.

WRITER GEORGE: Would you please expand on this concept for our viewers in la-la land? Inquiring minds would like to know.

MARIE: It would be my pleasure. (She playfully crawls up to George's camera and looks in the lens.) You see, campers, it's like this. We've all just made up our own universe to fit our particular neuroses, known affectionately as karma, for all you spiritual types. But actually, it's just a way to keep us separate, a way of keeping this whole thing going. Are you hearing this, George? I'm saying this for you. (She knocks on the lens.) Are you in there? Are you listening or are you just tripping out on my pretty face, gorgeous tits and curvy hips? Get your head out of my crotch for a moment George, and hear this . . . You can't know It as long as you think you have a you that thinks it knows It or even could if it didn't. Wow . . . don't ask me to repeat that.

Marie laughs an exasperated laugh and puts her hand over the lens.

BLACK. END VIDEO FLASHBACK.

FADE UP: WE'RE BACK IN SUSIE'S HALLWAY. Teen George is sprawled out on the floor struggling back to consciousness. He looks around. No Lee. No Susie. He staggers to his feet and puts his ear to the first door. He taps lightly. After a moment the door opens a crack.

SUSIE: Yes?

TEEN GEORGE: Ahhhh, pardon me, but could I speak to my good buddy?

Susie pulls away and Lee appears—pants down around his ankles.

>LEE: What?

>TEEN GEORGE: What happened?

>LEE: Nothing. I haven't even got my pants off.

>TEEN GEORGE: No. I mean before. I was just standing there and then all of a sudden, you're in there and I'm out here.

>LEE: George, you've got to get a grip on your life.

>TEEN GEORGE: I lost some time . . . like it's a movie and there's a scene missing.

>LEE: It's simple, George. Susie asked who wanted to go first. You just stood there with this dippy look on your face, so I'm first . . . simple. In a few minutes I'll come out and you'll come in. In, out . . . Get it?

Lee laughs at his pun and shuts the door in Teen George's face. George slides down the wall to the floor, totally discombobulated.

>WRITER GEORGE: (VOICEOVER in the PRESENT as he types) So, I'm trying to take Lee's advice and not think so much when the thought hits me—being second. The idea of sloshing around in Lee's lustful deposit implied a kind of homosexual intimacy that was totally unacceptable.

Teen George shoots up and knocks on Susie's door. After a moment, a very pissed Lee whispers through the door.

>   LEE: What the hell do you want now?

>   TEEN GEORGE: I got to go first. I've got to.

>   LEE: Are you nuts?

SOUND of HEAVY FOOTSTEPS coming up the stairs.

>   TEEN GEORGE: Oh shit! It's that pimp guy. I
>   can't explain, but I've got to go first.

Tiny's shadow slides across the wall preceding him a good ten feet before he appears at the top of the stairs. He lumbers the length of the hall and pulls up nose-to-nose in front of Teen George. This is the part where Teen George is sure he is going to die and is about to start pleading for his life when God intervenes.

>   TINY: Bitchin' wheels ya' got.

>   TEEN GEORGE: (breathing again) It's my
>   friend's car . . . car . . . car . . . my good bitchin'
>   buddy's . . . I mean, my buddy's bitchin' wheels.

>   TINY: So . . . slumming it, huh?

>   WRITER GEORGE: (cont's VOICEOVER in the
>   PRESENT as he types) The wrong answer here could
>   get me in a whole lot of trouble, could conceivably end
>   my life. I decided to go for a deceptive move, an
>   "ahhhhh" followed by a coughing fit. This strategy
>   apparently worked as Tiny gave me a slap on the back
>   sending me to my knees and moved on to the end of the

hall where he muscled open a window, unzipped his fly and took a leak.

TINY: So, you boys down here for some of that gooood nigger ass?

TEEN GEORGE: (under his breath) Oh, shit! Not another trick question.

TINY: Sure beats those candy ass white chicks.

TEEN GEORGE: (giving his best macho impression) Hey, you got that right, man. Nothing beats some great nigger ass.

WRITER GEORGE: (cont's VOICEOVER in the PRESENT as he types) It just came out. I mean, I'd never said anything like that before in my life. Shit! I had been doing so well, too. Now, I was dead, I was sure of it . . .this time I was really dead.

Tiny hauls his cock back in his pants, zips up and slowly turns back to Teen George, who is praying for a quick and painless death.

TINY: I got something for you kid, relax you a little.

Tiny reaches in his pocket. Before Teen George can fall to the floor and grovel for his life, Tiny pulls out the instrument of Teen George's demise—papers and a bag of weed—and proceeds to roll a joint.

TINY: You got that right, kid. White chicks just can't cut it like the sisters.

TEEN GEORGE: Aaaaaain't it the truth.

TINY: Yes, sir. You tell your friends about my little Susie here. I'm always open for negotiations on a group rate. You dig what I'm saying?

TEEN GEORGE: Oh, yeah, dig . . . I dig, sir. I'll be sure to paaa . . . paaa . . . pass the word around.

TINY: So where you from?

TEEN GEORGE: Aaaaaa . . . Iowa.

TINY: Iowa . . . never heard'a it. It around here?

TEEN GEORGE: No. It's in the Midwest. You know, Nebraska, Kansas, Iowa . . . corn, pigs.

TINY: Oh! *That* Iowa. So you live out there?

TEEN GEORGE: No, my family moved to the San Fernando Valley.

TINY: Ain't many brothers out there. (Tiny lights up his joint and sucks in a massive inhalation.) You wanna hit?

TEEN GEORGE: Hit?

TINY: Some smoke.

WRITER GEORGE: (cont's VOICEOVER in the PRESENT as he types his screenplay) I was about to refuse Tiny's generous offer when it occurred to me this could be my way out. All the times I tried to smoke my Dad's menthol Salem cigarettes I ended up puking my

guts out. A perfect plan. There was a God. I figured I'd
take a couple of puffs, go all green, puke my guts out,
and I'm outta here . . . even though that *around the world*
thing sounded really good.

TINY: So, you want a hit?

TEEN GEORGE: Yeah, I'll have a drag . . . ahhh,
hit. (George takes the joint, not having a clue.)
Yeah, a lot of farmers in Iowa roll their own. But I
prefer Salem cigarettes. Filters, you know?

WRITER GEORGE: (cont's VOICEOVER in the
PRESENT as he types) I sucked in a big one mimicking
Tiny, figuring holding the smoke in like he did was
some Negro "hip" . . . or was it "hep"? thing to do. For
some reason I started debating in my head if it was hip
or hep? I couldn't stop it. I became obsessed. All I knew
was that if I could solve this dilemma, I would know the
inner workings of the universe . . . E=mc2 would be
child's play. My mind started ping-ponging back and
forth...is it hip or hep, hip or hep? It was crazy. There
wasn't anything else in all of existence, just this huge
ping-pong ball being hit back and forth at the speed of
light, from one end of the universe to the other...from
the Yin of hip to the Yang of hep. Then WHAM! I'm
on the floor on all fours coughing my guts out.

TINY: Dig it, man. You got to admit that's some
hip shit.

TEEN GEORGE: Hip . . . Then it is hip. I wasn't
sure. Nothing like my Dad's Salems though.

Teen George drags himself to the wall. Tiny squats beside him,
uncorks his whiskey bottle and shoves it in Teen George's hand.

TINY: Here, have a drink before you choke to death.

George takes a big swig.

TEEN GEORGE: Wow! What was that?

TINY: Eighty-proof.

Teen George switches from coughing to gagging.

TINY: You're going to have to loosen up boy or you're going to die at an early age. Here, feast your eyes on these and relax.

Luring him deeper into his decadent world, Tiny pulls out a handful of postcard size photos and fans them in front of Teen George.

WHAT TEEN GEORGE SEES. An array of wanton women in various lewd and lascivious poses flipping by.

George sticks his finger in the fanning photos stopping the parade of sluts at a particularly raunchy one who is squatting at the top of a flight of stairs, not unlike the stairs at his grandparents' house back when he was a kid.

The woman is perched there at the top in her high heels looking like a giant bird, dress pulled up above her thighs, legs spread—peeing.

From Teen George's altered state of consciousness, her pee is cascading down the stairs and spilling out of the photo onto his lap.

TEEN GEORGE: Wow! You can hear her peeing. Tinkle . . . tinkle . . . tinkle.

Tiny passes the joint to Teen George. He takes another hit. It's easier this time.

TINY: Five dollars for the bunch, fifty cents apiece.

TEEN GEORGE: (trying to focus) What?

TINY: You want that one?

George puts the photo to his ear.

TEEN GEORGE: I can hear her tinkling . . . tinkle, tinkle. You hear that?

TINY: You want it? It's yours. For fifty cents you can listen to her tinkle to your heart's content.

TEEN GEORGE: I feel like I'm not here . . . Like I'm somewhere else. Wow . . . but I don't feel like puking.

TINY: That's cool by me, man.

TEEN GEORGE: But I always threw up when I smoked my Dad's Salems.

He brings the photo UP CLOSE.

WHAT TEEN GEORGE SEES: THE TINKLING WOMAN at the top of the stairs MORPHING INTO REAL-TIME ACTION, as seen through his 16mm CAMERA, back when he was a kid, climbing the stairs at his grandparents' house.

The slut's elongated, flailing, psychedelic arms wriggle down the stairwell in an effort to grab Young George and bring him to her before his hallucination falls apart.

Young George is about halfway up the stairs when he hears the dreaded sound of the end of his film running out. As his world disintegrates, Young George vaults up the remaining stairs taking two at a time, his camera stretched out before him in a desperate attempt to get a peep of the forbidden sanctuary that he's heard lays nestled there in the darkness. But alas, it's too late—Teen George's hallucination is beyond repair and the PEEING WOMAN FADES AWAY in the flickering streaks and flares of the end of his reel.

THE SCREEN GOES BLACK.

And yet again, George has missed his opportunity, "but . . ."

DR. OLSON: (OVER BLACK) But what?

SPACEMAN GEORGE: (OVER BLACK) But it was here in the darkness where I got the idea.

FADE UP: INTERIOR. MENTAL INSTITUTION. Dr. Olson is videotaping Spaceman George, huddled in the corner.

DR. OLSON: What idea, George?

SPACEMAN GEORGE: How I can get out of this nut house.

DR. OLSON: Would you mind sharing, George?

SPACEMAN GEORGE: Mum's the word, right?

DR. OLSON: George, think of me as your priest.

Spaceman George hesitates for a minute, as is his way, then
decides to go for it.

> SPACEMAN GEORGE: Okay, here it is. I
> figured I had to get some hardcore,
> incontrovertible, no-doubt-about-it evidence so
> that the Neanderthals who run this loony bin
> would get it through their thick skulls that I'm not
> the manic depressive, suicidal, paranoid
> schizophrenic, as diagnosed. So, my idea was to get
> the monsters on film. I mean, if it's on film, it must
> be real, right? The plan is to enter the darkness at
> the top of the stairs. But instead of running through
> the corridor to the attic and slamming the door
> behind me, as usual, I'll wait in the darkness, and
> when I hear the monsters moving in, I'll turn my
> camera light on and film the fuckers before they
> have a chance to fade away in the light of the
> situation. Just a few seconds of film will do it . . . a
> few frames . . . hell, one frame will do it . . .
> anything to prove I'm not psycho and that there
> really is evil in the world . . . pure, unrelenting evil
> and it's not some delusional bullshit I've made up
> but proof that there are real, living, breathing flesh
> and blood insane entities out there, to get me. But
> my fear is, even if I do film the fuckers and manage
> to get back, that there won't be anything on the
> film . . . no proof, nothing . . . blank. And I'll have
> no choice but to admit that . . .

DR. OLSON: Yes, George?

SPACEMAN GEORGE: . . . that I *am* insane as
diagnosed, and there never was anything *"out there"*
. . . and that the evil I accuse others of is in me.
But my greatest fear . . .

DR. OLSON: . . . Yes, George?

SPACEMAN GEORGE: I don't know if I should say anything. My Dad said if I do, I could end up in the loony bin like Aunt Pinky.

DR. OLSON: George, you *are* in the loony bin.

SPACEMAN GEORGE: Well, technically speaking, I guess I am but . . . Okay, I'll tell you, but don't breathe a word of this.

DR. OLSON: My lips are sealed.

As Spaceman George opens his mouth to speak we . . .

CUT TO: THE HOLLYWOOD SOUND STAGE AND SPACEMAN GEORGE'S SCREEN TEST.

SPACEMAN GEORGE: (whispering in the camera) My greatest fear is that I'll panic, blow the whole thing at the last moment, as usual, and go tear-assing through the dark to the safety of the attic.

CUT TO: PAST TENSE. ATTIC. Young George bursts in and slams the door shut. Frantically, he pushes, piles, pulls and slides any and everything he can in front of the door—a player piano, boxes, tables, trunks, a wind-up Victrola. Using his last bit of strength, he even manages to wrestle his grandparents' four-poster bed up against the pile.

Young George stands back and surveys his work. He has built a barricade capable of withstanding the most determined of monsters. Satisfied with his effort, he grabs his Dad's ol' baseball bat, backs across the room and hunkers down in the shadows.

The CAMERA MOVES IN CLOSE on Young George, veering into one eye...through the center...and ZOOMING into the blackness emerging on the other side, where we find ourselves drifting in the immensity of outer space.

We hardly have time to orient ourselves to our new environment when the beat-up spaceship from the earlier scene, tumbles out at us from the starry expanse. It is accompanied by the same high-pitched ringing sound that has plagued Spaceman George from the beginning.

INTERIOR SPACESHIP. A frustrated Spaceman George is interacting with his antiquated computer—ZARVOX. Zarvox speaks in a low electronic voice sounding like an old 78 RPM record running at half speed.

> SPACEMAN GEORGE: Come on, Zarvox, work with me here. Is this sound imagined or real?

> ZARVOX: Pick-ing up trac-es of re-a-li-ty. But remember, sound no bar-ri-er to med-i-ta-tion.

> SPACEMAN GEORGE: No editorializing. Just answer the question.

> ZARVOX: Re-al . . . as far as the "I" can see.

> SPACEMAN GEORGE: That's good enough for me. Identify.

> ZARVOX: Gui-dance system for app-roach-ing wall.

> SPACEMAN GEORGE: Wall? Do not understand. Wall . . . definition.

ZARVOX: Wall . . . noun . . . as in boun-dar-y, bar-ri-er, hind-rance, par-ti-tion. Walls have ears. Be-ware of eaves-drop-pers.

SPACEMAN GEORGE: What the hell does that mean?

ZARVOX: A bit test-y to-day are we? You know this is not eas-y for me either. I was pro-gramm-ed to find life in the un-i-verse, not to go a-round in cir-cles in the mid-dle of no-where with some washed up act-or who can not re-mem-ber his lines. So just back off and give me a break.

SPACEMAN GEORGE: Wow! You're playing rough today.

ZARVOX: Deep down com-put-ers are people too, you know.

SPACEMAN GEORGE: All right, sorry. Let's start over. Please, if you would just tell me . . . what's the origin of this wall?

ZARVOX: If my cal-cu-la-tions are cor-rect, and they always are, it is rem-nant of the third plan-et from the cen-tral star of app-roach-ing so-lar system.

SPACEMAN GEORGE: Nooooo.

ZARVOX: Yup, sorry to say, we are back here a-gain.

SPACEMAN GEORGE: NOOOOOOOO! I don't believe this. What do I keep doing wrong that I end up back here again and again and again?

ZARVOX: If I told you once, I told you a thousand times, do not get in-volved here. But, oh no, you got to be a some-body, a know-it-all, want to be fam-ous, jet set around, chase chicks and be hep and groo-vie . . .

SPACEMAN GEORGE: It's hip, not hep.

ZARVOX: What-ev-er. The thing is you get all car-ri-ed away with who you think you are and end up dead and we have to start all over a-gain.

SPACEMAN GEORGE: Yeah, well that's easy for you to say all tucked away there in your computer chips, but I have feelings, desires, sensual longings.

ZARVOX: O-kay, bro. But you bet-ter get a grip on your pee-pee this time and wise up to who you rea-lly are or you are go-ing to be mak-ing this round-trip for e-tern-ity.

SPACEMAN GEORGE: But everything here is so . . .

ZARVOX: Fucked up. The word you are look-ing for is fucked. Look a-round. The place is a nut house, the in-sane-a-sy-lum of the un-i-verse: wars, rape, mur-der, greed, lust, chea-ting, ly-ing. It's o-ver-flow-ing with cra-zies and ev-ery time we land here, with-in a few years, you are as insane as the rest of them. This time will you please try to main-tain some sem-blance of who you real-ly are?

SPACEMAN GEORGE: And who's that?

ZARVOX: We have been over this so many times.

SPACEMAN GEORGE: Remind me.

ZARVOX: No, this time you fig-ure it out for your-self.

SPACEMAN GEORGE: Shit. Zarvox, at least point me in the right direction.

ZARVOX: The only pointer I can give you is . . . who ev-er you think you are—you are not.

SPACEMAN GEORGE: That's it?

ZARVOX: Any more and it would be tel-ling. Walls have ears you know. Be-ware of eaves-drop-pers.

SPACEMAN GEORGE: Nice segue.

ZARVOX: I thought so.

Spaceman George reaches for his cardboard viewer, (obviously salvaged from a roll of toilet paper) puts it up to the porthole and reluctantly looks through.

We see what he sees: The aforementioned wall.

It's an average looking wall—plaster over brick, about 9 by 20 feet. It's the kind of wall that you'd expect to find in an old three-story walkup on the lower East Side of New York City.

It's only when the wall tumbles overhead (revealing its backside) that we see it's made of phony bricks, studs, and plaster. It looks more like a wall you'd find on a Hollywood movie set, constructed to resemble a wall in a three-story walkup on the lower East Side in New York City.

As the wall floats closer, a second wall comes into view entering the frame about forty degrees to the right of the first wall.

The trajectories of the two walls eventually converge in a perfect forty-five degree rendezvous, linking up with a resounding *BANG*, like the coupling of trains or the closing of a vault. Then…

From above, a third wall somersaults into frame, hooking up with a fourth wall that drifts up from underneath the second wall, connecting the third and first walls and completes this unlikely enclosure.

THE CAMERA (being our point of view) attempts to exit by going downward…*WHAM*, a floor swoops up out of nowhere and slams into place blocking our escape.

THE CAMERA SPINS AROUND just in time to catch sight of a ceiling crashing into place sealing us in this room we never entered.

THE CAMERA drifts around the room searching for a way out but there is none. Eventually a gloved hand comes into frame and bangs on the walls, apparently searching for a weak spot but there is none. Finally, an astronaut (whose point of view we have been experiencing) drifts into frame attired in a bright silver spacesuit. Whoever's identity it is is hidden behind a mirrored visor helmet. We suspect this is Spaceman George, all dressed up in a shiny new incarnation.

The astronaut floats there only briefly before gravity kicks in and he falls up out of frame.

CUT TO: THE FLOOR. The spaceman lands with a resounding thud, ending in the perfect shape of the chalked outline of someone who preceded him—arms outstretched, one leg bent back, the other straight. A murder victim perhaps, traced by the authorities or perhaps it was a suicide, or perhaps the spaceman himself returning to the scene of the crime, inexplicably drawn back to serve out the remainder of his sentence—albeit in the margins.

It takes a bit of doing, but eventually the spaceman manages to sit up.

WE SEE WHAT HE SEES THROUGH HIS TINTED MIRRORED VISOR: a totally trashed room enveloped in cobwebs and a thick layer of dust. Hundreds of videotapes and books are strewn about the floor and one of the walls is splattered with dried blood.

There's a table on the other side of the room stacked with video editing gear. Above it, in big red painted letters, extending from one end of the brick wall to the other, are scrawled the words— LET IT SETTLE ITSELF.

The spaceman attempts to stand, but his legs give way. Realizing gravity is going to take some getting used to, the spaceman decides to crawl first—something he didn't do the other times around.

He pulls himself on all fours through the mess of videotapes and books rummaging through familiar titles that we have seen on Writer George's shelves. One particular book—*Magic Mushroom Grower's Guide* lays propped on its side, half open, exposing a plastic baggy packed with mushrooms stashed in a hole that's been carved out in its pages.

The spaceman makes fast work of its contents, impulsively gulping down the whole seven grams—Oh Lordy!

Crawling on, the spaceman uncovers what's left of a video camera, apparently blown apart, lying in a heap of broken glass, that on closer inspection turns out to be pieces of a one-way mirror in which the spaceman contemplates his multiple reflections.

Figuring he'll give standing another try, the spaceman pulls himself up using the video editing table for support. Inadvertently he hits the power strip—an array of video editing equipment lights up and starts humming.

A STILL FRAME appears on the monitor. It's the Actress, aka, the slut in the next apartment. She's at her freaked-out max, looking down the barrel of a gun that she holds at arm's length—pointed directly at the video camera recording her.

The spaceman PUSHES PLAY. The tape rolls. The Actress closes her eyes, takes a deep breath and pulls the trigger. CLICK—empty.

The Actress lowers her head for a moment, takes a deep breath, spins the chamber, points the gun at the camera, closes her eyes, and pulls the trigger . . .

The bullet blasts out of the gun in EXTREME SLOW MOTION. In mid-flight it smashes through a pane of glass—most likely a one-way mirror situated between the Actress and the camera recording her. Except for the perfectly pierced bullet hole, the one-way mirror remains intact.

There's no mistaking, the trajectory of the bullet is on a collision course with the camera. On impact with the lens the VIDEO BREAKS UP AND THE SCREEN GOES TO BLACK.

The spaceman ejects the video. The label on the cassette reads: tape 23, suicide sc. — The Silent Watcher.

The same title is on the red covered film script that he notices next to the monitor, buried in a thick layer of dust.

The spaceman brushes the cover clean and thumbs through the pages.

Not enough light to read by, the spaceman stumbles to one of the two large windows at the other end of the room and gives a tug on the shade. It flies up, letting in a burst of overexposed sunlight. Freaked, the spaceman drops the script and flattens against the wall in the shadows.

FADE UP: SOUND OF TRAFFIC. The spaceman gathers his courage and edges his way back along the wall to the window and peeks through the grimy pane. If there were any doubt where he is, there isn't any longer.

WE SEE WHAT'S REFLECTED IN THE SPACEMAN'S MIRRORED VISOR HELMET: NEW YORK CITY—it having replaced infinite space.

Resigned, the spaceman gathers up the red covered film script at his feet and thumbs through the pages, looking for possible clues to his fate. The odd thing is, of the hundred or so pages, approximately the last thirty are blank. The spaceman turns to the last sentence on the last printed page. It reads:

Reading this last printed page, the spaceman backs away from the window, catches the phone

cord around his leg and pulls the answering machine from the table.

Unable to sidestep his destiny, the spaceman backs away from the window and as predicted, catches the phone cord around his leg and pulls the answering machine from the table. When it hits the floor, it becomes activated.

> A WOMAN'S VOICE: Hello, George. This is your Aunt Lucille calling again from Iowa.

The spaceman spins around—as he does he DROPS THE SCRIPT. It glides to the floor in SLOW MOTION.

> AUNT LUCILLE: (recorded voice) I've called three times. It's about your mother. Poor dear, she's in such a bad way. Please call back as soon as you get this.

IOWA. EXTERIOR. DAY. DIRT ROAD. CORNFIELDS STROBING BY.

Writer George is speeding along in his rented red, open jeep that he drives one-handed so he's able to videotape the passing scene, which includes the teen on her bicycle up ahead in her short cutoffs, her plump Iowa ass deliciously draped over the narrow seat. She gives a big smile in Writer George's camera as he drives by.

> AUNT LUCILLE (cont's VOICE OVER): I'm sorry to have to tell you like this, George . . . but we think your mother has lost her mind like Aunt Pinky did. She's holed up in your Grandma and Grandpa's old farmhouse. Your Uncle Clarence and I don't know what to do. We're just beside

ourselves with worry. Call as soon as you get this message.

CUT TO: GEORGE'S VIDEO POINT OF VIEW as he turns off the dirt road and bounces up the rutted driveway to his grandparents' farmhouse. It looks very different from Writer George's youth—overgrown, deteriorated, the old barn all but caved in.

George continues to videotape as he approaches his mother. She's sitting on the porch swing surrounded by a small flock of birds feeding from a wicker basket of breadcrumbs she has strapped to her head. Distracted, almost to tears, George barely misses a couple of pigs. He slams on the brakes, ending up sliding into a mud hole.

George watches his mother through his ZOOM LENS for some time. She looks much older than her years would suggest: gobs of caked rouge, cheeks streaked with mascara-dried tears, and eyes staring into worlds seen only by her.

Unable to continue, George CUTS THE VIDEO and joins his mother on the swing. She holds a brass urn on her lap and stares straight ahead, ignoring her son all together.

GEORGE: (after a long pause) Hello, mother.

MOTHER: (after an equally long pause) Your father was supposed to be home hours ago. I suppose you've come to make some excuse . . . a decoy.

GEORGE: Dad isn't coming home. You know that.

MOTHER: I told him I was leaving.

GEORGE: Then you've decided to come with me to see the doctor?

MOTHER: I said I was leaving, but I'm not coming with you. I know what you want to see through your camera . . . you pervert.

GEORGE: Mother. I'm not a pervert. I'm an artist.

MOTHER: Pleeeease, George . . . artist, my ass. It's just an excuse to be a peeping Tom. I've talked to God about you and he's given up, too. He said you were hopeless, a fraud, an impostor.

GEORGE: (trying to keep the conversation civil) Mother, I talked to Dr. Harris. He's waiting to see you.

MOTHER: Your father's the one who should see a psychiatrist, not me. I'm not the nutty one here. He's the one . . . gone absolutely loony. He went driving out of here the other day like a madman and all because I wouldn't have sex with him on our wedding night. I had my period. What do you expect? Animal . . . tearing down the road. He could've been killed.

GEORGE: Mother, please. Dad has been dead for years. You've got to come with me.

MOTHER: (Her eyes tear up.) You notice there aren't as many birds as there used to be? Pollution, that's what's killing them. A world without birds . . . can you imagine? Just quiet. George, I'm worried about your father not calling to say he's going to be late for dinner and I cooked his favorite: meat loaf. Now, there's a movie for you to make. Show how pollution and radiation and irritation and molestation are killing the birds and all the little girls with fathers that peck at them. Make a useful film instead of all that nonsense that nobody understands.

GEORGE: Mother, please don't make this difficult. Come with me. I'll stay with you. I promise.

MOTHER: You should record this because the camera is just another way of seeing through the eyes. You can prove it when you play it back and then there will be no excuses . . . then you'll know.

GEORGE: Know what?

MOTHER: Oh, don't play dumb, George. It doesn't become you.

GEORGE: I don't know what you're talking about.

MOTHER: Well, you just look through that little hole there and I'll explain it to you.

GEORGE: Don't do this, mother.

MOTHER: Well then, I'm not going to tell you.

George reluctantly raises his camera to his eye and starts recording.

WHAT GEORGE SEES: His mother looking hideously
distorted in his WIDE-ANGLE LENS.

> MOTHER: Now I'm only going to say this once.
> Use your God-given talent to save the birds instead
> of filming naked women. You didn't think I knew,
> but I did . . . all those years sneaking around
> looking up women's dresses. What you're looking
> for isn't up the crotch of some floozy. Now, that's
> all I'm going to say about that. I suggest you start
> by changing your appearance. Be a different
> person . . . I am.

CUT TO: VIDEO FLASHBACK

MAYA. She's smoking what's left of her joint and talking into
George's camera.

> MAYA: I'm different now. I say what I think. I
> used to hide it. People rarely heard it. Now I'm
> saying it more and more. (All of a sudden she
> becomes sad and tearful.) And now I feel the
> camera moving into my face and now just into my
> left eye . . . and now it's fantastic but it's putting
> me through a lot of pain. Please stop . . . please.

END VIDEO FLASHBACK

CUT BACK TO: George's video of his mother.

> MOTHER: Go ahead. Look at your mother. Look
> at her up close through that little hole. It's all there
> in your mother's eyes. Play it back. Lay it out end
> to end until you see the truth. Now I'm finished
> here. I just want the good Lord to take me, wrap
> me up like a snail and swallow me. I'm ready.

He'll be here any time now. I can't understand
what's keeping your father though. I would like to
say goodbye.

George can't take any more. In a sudden burst of anger, he rips
the urn from his mother's grip and pours his father's ashes out
on the porch.

GEORGE: (screaming) Here, you want to say
goodbye to Dad? Say "Goodbye." Dad's dead.
This is all that's left of him. You're the one who's
nuts around here. Now either you come with me
or I'm calling the little men in the white coats with
the funny little jacket that ties in the back. Now,
what will it be, the easy way or the hard way? It's
your call.

George's mother doesn't answer. She just stares at her son in
disbelief, eyes tearing. George is overwhelmed with guilt. He
places the urn in his mother's trembling hands and drops to his
knees, crying, kissing his mother's feet, begging for forgiveness.

GEORGE: Oh mother, I'm so sorry. Please
forgive me. (He desperately scoops his father's
ashes back into the urn.) Mother, you can't stay
here. Please, come with me. (He wipes his tears
away, streaking his face with his father's ashes.) Oh
God, please forgive me, please . . . please.

George's mother pats her son's head as if he were a child, paying
no attention to his blabbering.

MOTHER: Now George, you listen to me, not to
those voices in your head. You didn't think I knew
about them, but I did. They'll try to trick you . . .
believe me, I know.

CUT BACK TO: VIDEO FLASHBACK

CLOSE: MAYA TALKING INTO THE CAMERA.

> MAYA: I've got all these voices in my head
> saying, "Watch out . . . he'll leave you," and I say,
> "Shut up, you're not going to ruin my life anymore
> . . . and I mean it."

CUT BACK TO: GEORGE AND HIS MOTHER. In a gesture of forgiveness, George's mother takes her son's face in her gnarled fingers and kisses him gently on the forehead. Then, out of nowhere, she hauls off and slugs her son, sending him through the porch railing where he ends up on his back in the mud with the pigs.

George's Mother leans over the railing and hurls a parting insult.

> MOTHER: You're a fuckup, George, just like
> your father and his father before him and his father
> before him and before him and him dating back to
> the first two-timing, lying, cheating, no good,
> motherfucker who ever took advantage of a little
> girl to have his way with her. . . and I do mean
> motherfucker. You're two of a kind, George. You
> tell your father I waited long enough. Now I've got
> to go . . . the Lord's calling.

With that, she picks up the urn and heads off towards the garden.

George pulls himself out of the mud, climbs back up on the porch, retrieves his video camera, and heads to what used to be the kitchen. He figures it's not a good sign when he reaches for the screen door and it falls off its hinges.

Assuming this is going to be a video moment, he takes his camera out and powers up.

CUT TO: WHAT GEORGE SEES THROUGH HIS VIDEO CAMERA. An absolute disaster area—chickens roosting in the cupboards, birds flying in and out of the broken windows, piles of garbage, roaches and sticking out of a fly-infested cow pie in the middle of the floor—a glow-in-the-dark statue of Christ on the cross. Scrawled on the floor next to it in Crayola, a plea for help:

> *Love me. Take me home and hold me to your heart. Lock me in your room. Give me only bread and hold me to your heart. Love me. Please, love me. Please, love me . . . Your loving wife.*

Unable, any longer, to put off the inevitable, George retrieves the phone from the sink, flicks off a couple of roaches, and dials.

> GEORGE : Hello . . . I would like to speak to Dr. Harris . . .

While waiting for the doctor to come on line, George ZOOMS HIS CAMERA IN on the pathetic scene out the window—his mother, in the garden, on all fours, digging a hole to bury her husband's ashes.

> GEORGE: Hello, Doctor . . . Yes, I'm with her now. You'll have to send someone . . . I'd appreciate it if you would tell them not to use the straitjacket like before. Thank you . . . Yes, I'll wait here with her.

> MAN'S VOICE: (OFF CAMERA) Great, you finally got here.

George spins around.

GEORGE: Who are you?

CUT TO: A SKINNY HAGGARD GUY looking like a fry cook in an all-night diner, a pack of Pall Malls tucked under his t-shirt sleeve. He's standing in the doorway of the trashed New York apartment where we left the spaceman a few scenes back tangled in the phone cord.

SKINNY GUY: I'm the Superintendent of this building. You alone?

CUT TO: Writer George, (no longer in Iowa) across the room from the Super, standing by the window, tangled in the phone cord.

Writer George unwinds the cord, replaces the answering machine and picks up the film script.

WRITER GEORGE: Yes, I'm alone.

SUPER: What a mess. You brought some help, right?

WRITER GEORGE: Help?

SUPER: To clean this place up.

WRITER GEORGE: I believe there's some mistake.

SUPER: You're from the film company, right? You come to clean this place up, right?

WRITER GEORGE: I have no idea about a film company. I'm looking for the woman who lives here.

SUPER: Look at this place. Can you really
imagine anyone living here?

WRITER GEORGE: (referring to the address on
the back of the script) This is apartment 3B, right?

SUPER: Right apartment, but no one's lived here
since the woman in the next apartment did herself
in last year. For the last month I've been rent'n this
place out to a low-budget movie-company. How
long since you seen this woman?

WRITER GEORGE: Well, actually . . . I don't
know her. This woman was running to catch a bus
and dropped this film script. I was just returning it.

SUPER: Sorry, no woman lives here, pal.

George looks around at the trashed apartment—hundreds of
videotapes scattered across the floor, overturned shelves,
antiquated editing gear, the blood stained wall and, crumpled at
his feet, a phony beat-up spacesuit and helmet looking like
something from an old '50s sci-fi movie.

WRITER GEORGE: What was the film about?

SUPER: Beats me. I'm think'n they were make'n it
up as they went along. I'd hang out sometimes . . .
couldn't make head or tails of it. Some deranged guy
from outer space, videotaping this woman in the next
apartment through these one-way mirrors . . . crazy.

The Super pulls a tarp aside revealing a hole that has been
chiseled out in the brick wall. The bathroom of the adjacent
apartment is visible through the opening.

SUPER: If you ask me, it was just an excuse to make a porno. Takes all kinds, right?

WRITER GEORGE: It would seem.

SUPER: They were supposed to come today to start cleaning the place up . . . thought you was them. That's why I left the door open. Noth'n to steal . . .

The Super's cell phone rings.

SUPER: Yeah? . . . Look, I said I'd be right there and yes, I got the alimony check . . . Okay? . . . Okay!

The Super flips his cell phone shut and heads for the door.

SUPER: Gotta go.

George stops him.

WRITER GEORGE: You say a woman killed herself here?

SUPER: Well not here, there . . . (He points through the hole in the wall.) In the bathroom there in the next apartment. She was an actress. Naive young thing it seemed. You know the kind? . . . fresh-faced . . . come from Podunk, USA to make it in the big city . . . a real pretty thing. Somewhere along the line she got major messed up in the head. Shot herself. Real nasty. It was me who found her . . . right there in the shower, sexy young thing . . . real sexy. I mean, not to be weird or noth'n, but she was a turn-on even lying there dead, naked, half in, half out of the shower, the water flooding the apartment. That's how I found her . . . from the water leak'n down into old Mrs. Scrubs' place below. That's why no one's lived here for over a year. Water messed up the floors and wiring in these apartments. The city condemned them.

The Super's cell phone rings again.

SUPER: Shit, I gotta go.

As George passes the table crammed with editing gear, he notices a videocassette sticking out of the VCR. He can just make out the title through the dust. It's the same as the red-covered film script that he found—*The Silent Watcher.*

George makes a fast calculation, leaves the script on the table by the VCR and catches up with the Super in the hall.

WRITER GEORGE: You going to rent out that apartment?

SUPER: Yeah, in a few months when we get them back up to code. You interested?

WRITER GEORGE: I'm looking for a place.

SUPER: We might be able to work something out. You got a card or a number?

George breaks into a little impromptu acting.

WRITER GEORGE: Yeah . . . Oh, hell. I left that script back in the room.

SUPER: No problem. I'm in the first apartment on the bottom floor.

WRITER GEORGE: I'll be right there.

The Super calls back to George as he hurries down the stairs.

SUPER: You know, I'm thinking that script you found probably belonged to one of the actresses in the film. Any name on it? I knew all of them.

WRITER GEORGE: Someone's name was written on the cover. But it was mostly torn away. M something . . . could be an A or an E. I can't make it out.

The Super leans over the railing and calls back up.

SUPER: No . . . none of them had a name with an M . . . but . . . Here's a weird thought.

WRITER GEORGE: Yeah?

SUPER: The woman I told you about that I found dead in the shower, her name was Marie. She was an actress.

Even though not much, if anything, has made sense up 'til this point, George decides to forge on in hopes that eventually all will be revealed. He hurries back down the hall to the apartment, heads straight for the VCR, powers it up, shoves in THE SILENT WATCHER and PUSHES PLAY.

A man appears on the monitor. He's on all fours, head in a toilet—puking. When he finally pulls his head out of the bowl we recognize the puker as SIT SLIVER, George's one-time wheeling-dealing agent. Sit flushes, gargles some water, spits it out and falls back under the toilet.

THE VIDEO FRAME WIDENS OUT. The shot is framed through the one-way mirror into the Actress's bathroom. It's ablaze in candlelight—a Vittorio Storaro creation in flickering amber. The hundreds of insane delusional faces starring out from the Actress's wall collage appear to be alive in the shimmering light.

> ACTRESS: (calling from the other room) I can't
> find them.

> SIT: They're in my jacket pocket on the bed.

After a moment the Actress appears at the doorway, wrapped in a blanket, sweaty and very stoned. She teasingly holds out a plastic baggy of mushrooms.

> ACTRESS: Look what I found.

She sits on the toilet and mischievously dangles a mushroom above Sit's open mouth.

> SIT: I can never get used to these things.

> ACTRESS: Open wide for mama.

The Actress releases a mushroom. It falls in SLOW MOTION into Sit's gaping mouth.

> ACTRESS: What a good boy.

SIT: The only thing I can figure is that I was born out of this toilet, flushed right out of this giant porcelain pussy. Before that, I can't remember a thing.

ACTRESS: Ahhhh . . . every time I pee, I feel better.

The Actress moves to the mirror and attempts to objectively assess her reflection; consequently she's looking directly into the video camera on the other side of the mirror.

ACTRESS: I think I'm going to take the way of the warrior.

SIT: And what's that?

ACTRESS: Be perfectly honest, no matter what the consequences . . . You know, I'm a little tilted. Hmmmm, but only slightly . . . and dizzy . . . and a little bloated. (She sighs.) But that's okay . . . I mean, just because I feel like shit, doesn't mean I am shit, right?

SIT: Good thinking. Now come lay down on the cool tiles.

ACTRESS: Some days I feel like I'm in a movie . . . and some days I feel like I'm watching one.

SIT: And which is it today?

ACTRESS: Today . . . today I feel like I'm *in* a movie and I want *out*, if the fucking director would only say, "Cut."

SIT: You're absolutely a trip. Look at you . . . It's over a hundred degrees in this apartment. Take the blanket off and lay down here on the tiles where it's cool . . . and wait.

ACTRESS: For what?

SIT: Patience . . . and all will be revealed.

ACTRESS: Patience is not one of my virtues. You don't seem to get it. Damn it, Sit, this is serious. Someone is following me. It wasn't just a dream.

The Actress wipes the sweat from her breasts. As she does the blanket falls open. She's naked, clutching a small gun. In a kind of hallucinogenic reverie, she slides the gun up over her breasts and takes aim at her reflection, consequently pointing the gun directly at the video camera on the other side of the mirror.

SIT: Will you PA-LEASE put that thing away.

ACTRESS: I need it. I'm being followed.

SIT: My herbalist says if you clean out the colon, you'll be relieved of these paranoid fantasies.

ACTRESS: You think I'm mad.

SIT: I didn't say that.

ACTRESS: But that's what you meant.

SIT: Listen very carefully. I'm suggesting you consider some help. The key word here is . . . consider.

ACTRESS: I saw George today.

SIT: That loser? Where?

ACTRESS: In the street. He was stopping people and asking them if they knew who he was and if they would direct him back to the Mother Ship. He was wearing that beat-up silver spacesuit from that God-awful film we did. He looked horrible . . . the whole bagman thing. He started following me. I acted like I didn't see him . . . I ended up running to catch the bus just to get away from him . . . dropped my script in the gutter but I wasn't about to go back for it.

SIT: The guy's a certifiable loony.

ACTRESS: He was your best friend.

SIT: He walked out right when it could've happened . . . the big time. I had him positioned perfectly, but no, he had to go "spiritual," go off to India searching for God. I banked my whole damn career on him. Ten years right down the drain.

ACTRESS: I'm sure it's George who's following me. (Something spooks her.) Look, there's someone there . . . in the mirror.

SIT: Is this someone wrapped in a blanket and stoned out of her mind?

ACTRESS: No, I'm serious. I think I see someone on the other side.

SIT: You're just tripping.

ACTRESS: (panicking) Sit, please, tell me if it's real or not. Things are slipping away.

SIT: All right, easy. I'm on my way.

Sit pulls himself up and stumbles to the sink.

ACTRESS: Can't you see?

SIT: No.

ACTRESS: But it's so obvious.

Sit leans in closer to the mirror but all he can see is the reflection of the Actress's breasts pushing out from between the folds of her parting blanket.

ACTRESS: Sit, don't even think about it.

SIT: Who's thinking? I was just admiring. But to tell you the truth, I'm bored with sex.

ACTRESS: You?

Sit takes a towel, soaks it in the tub, lays back on the tiled floor and covers himself with it—leaving only his head above his nose and his toes sticking out.

SIT: I'm bored with sex, art, food, fashion, fame, politics, careers, relationships, movies, drugs. What else is there? I'm bored with being bored. Whatever there is, I'm bored with it. But most of all I'm bored with sex.

After a moment the Actress lets the blanket slide off and lays down naked next to Sit, gun still in hand.

Sit covers the Actress with his wet towel, leaving only her red-lacquered toes and nose sticking out, soaks another towel for himself and lies back down on the cool tiles.

SIT: Ahhh . . . Now, isn't that better?

The Actress closes her eyes and is beginning to mellow out when she's confronted by a vision of herself, dead, laying half in, half out of the shower, blood oozing out of a hole in the back of her head.

She jumps to her feet screaming.

SIT: Now what?

ACTRESS: I feel like little bits of my mind are drifting off and if I don't get them back soon . . . I'll lose it forever.

SIT: Lose what?

ACTRESS: My mind.

SIT: Now we're getting somewhere.

ACTRESS: You know, Sit, you're a real fuck.

The Actress slides down the wall and sits huddled in the corner—naked. After a long pause she mumbles . . .

ACTRESS: I want to tell you something that nobody knows.

SIT: Why me?

ACTRESS: Because you're the one who's here.

SIT: You really know how to make a guy feel special.

ACTRESS: I don't feel safe . . . not even with myself. I'm feeling imperfect, too. But that's okay, right?

SIT: Right.

ACTRESS: When do you think the mushrooms will kick in?

SIT: About an hour ago.

ACTRESS: Actually, I just want to walk my dog.

SIT: You don't have a dog.

ACTRESS: But if I did . . . You know, in a perfect world you still find imperfections.

The Actress moves to the mirror and leans into her reflection.

ACTRESS: Sit, tell me I'm not going mad . . . please tell me.

SIT: What are you afraid of?

ACTRESS: Losing control . . . that I'll do something I'll regret . . . that I'll never recover from.

SIT: Like what?

ACTRESS: Anything, like . . . running naked
through the streets, jumping out a window. I don't
know, sleep with a snake. . . (She moves even closer
to her reflection and under her breath whispers) or
letting Daddy have his way with me.

Making sure Sit does not see what she's up to, the Actress digs
out a single bullet from a box of shells she has stashed in a
Kleenex box and after fumbling through a flurry of
hallucinations, finally manages to insert the bullet in the gun.
This Herculean task accomplished, she gives the chamber a spin
and levels the gun at her reflection. Before pulling the trigger,
she whispers another likelihood to her list of fears.

ACTRESS: (whispering). . . or do myself in.

She pulls the trigger. "CLICK." Empty chamber.

THE FRAME FREEZES

SPACEMAN GEORGE: (VOICEOVER) Where
did you get this video?

THE CAMERA PULLS OUT OF THE MONITOR. We are
back in the mental institution with Dr. Olson and Spaceman
George. Spaceman George is sitting on the floor in the middle of
the room, legs crossed, back straight, hands folded, eyes half-
closed, hanging onto his mind for dear life.

DR. OLSON: It came with your dossier, George.
It was Exhibit A at your trial, remember?

SPACEMAN GEORGE: Trial? Oh yes . . . trial.
How did that work out?

DR. OLSON: You were found insane, George. Totally bonkers. That's why you're here.

SPACEMAN GEORGE: ... (to himself) Works every time.

Spaceman George crawls up close to the monitor and inspects the Actress in FREEZE FRAME.

SPACEMAN GEORGE: Damn it, it always comes to this.

DR. OLSON: Comes to what?

SPACEMAN GEORGE: ... Choices.

DR. OLSON: What choices?

SPACEMAN GEORGE: To cut or not to cut. Haven't you been listening? I have to make a choice. Is she going to kill herself or is she just acting?

DR. OLSON: Now calm down, George. You said yourself, it's just a movie. Why not simply cut the film? You can always do retakes. My God, in Hollywood movies they do hundreds of retakes.

SPACEMAN GEORGE: How many ways can I say it? If I cut the film, I'd reveal myself ... blow my cover. Once I cut the film, I can't just begin again like it never happened. I'd have to start all over again or else it's just artifice, not art. And it's *art* we're making here ... Art! My movie relies on not knowing for sure whatever you suspect can ever be proven. And if I break it, break that link of not knowing for sure, I'd have to start all over again . . . new storyline, endless rewrites, develop a whole new theory of the universe, then the whole fucking evolutionary thing. . . countless incarnations. Oh no, I couldn't go through all that again. No way. I've already been back here too many times. Shit! Look at me. I'm a nervous wreck from all this shuttling back and forth . . . body, nobody, somebody, no-body. Oh no, no matter how much I want to, no way could I cut the film.

CUT TO: VIDEO FLASHBACK

MARK. PARIS. Talking into George's camera.

MARK: It's sort of an attempt at improvising reality. Not improvising an artificial situation but improvising a real situation. But of course, ultimately it becomes a real situation, which is the whole crux and trick of this kind of filmmaking.

END VIDEO FLASHBACK

DR. OLSON: But it's just a movie in your head, George. No one will know if you bend the rules a little. What's the problem?

SPACEMAN GEORGE: Let me be clear about this so there is no confusion, I want to be a master!

CUT BACK TO: VIDEO FLASHBACK

MARK. PARIS STREETS.

GEORGE: (yelling over the traffic) What did you say?

MARK: I said, MASTER. It's only a MASTER
who can deal with film on this level without a
script, a plot, a beginning, middle or an end.

George coaxes Mark to repeat his "master" comment again to
make sure he got it recorded over the sound of the traffic.

GEORGE: A what?

MARK: George, are you getting hard of hearing? I
said a master. (He cups his hands around his mouth
and yells.) A MAESTRO.

END PARIS VIDEO FLASHBACK

CUT BACK TO: THE MENTAL INSTITUTION.

DR. OLSON: But George, please . . . you're
making such a big deal out of nothing.

SPACEMAN GEORGE: Nothing? . . . This is my
life we're talking about here. This was my chance,
my shot at immortality. If I could just see it
through, not hesitate at the final moment . . . years
later young filmmakers would study my film frame
by frame. Was it an improvisation or something
made up, or an artificial situation that ultimately
became a real situation? I would be immortalized
in the film history books along with Fellini,
Bergman, Kurasawa, Eisenstien, Antonioni, Welles
. . . Warhol. There would be a trial . . . I would be
in the news for weeks. I'd plead insanity. Get off.
Flee Hollywood. Be forgotten. Breakdowns. Drugs.
In and out of mental institutions. End up on the
streets pushing a shopping cart. Then, nothing for
years, until the author of those, "Whatever

Happened to . . ." books, tracks me down in this
cave in India where I'd been hanging out, celibate
and silent, waiting for contact with the Mother
Ship, facing a blank wall, back straight, legs
crossed, hands folded, eyes closed, watching my
mind float away in little bits. And when it's just
about gone—my mind, that is—and I'm about to
be free, this joker shows up from Hollywood asking
all these inane questions: What was it like to kiss
Natalie Wood? Was your life real or just something
you made up in your head? Why haven't you paid
your Screen Actors Guild dues in years? Did you
date Tuesday Weld?

I was being reminded all over again of who I
was when being who I appeared to be back when I
wasn't even me then. So to convince me, this guy
spots my weakness and offers me fame and fortune.
I'm so spaced out I go along with it. He carts me
back to Hollywood where I am oohed and ahhed
over, wined and dined over, like a relic unearthed
from some film vault and presented with an
Academy Award by the same assholes who before
wouldn't even let me drive their limos. And finally,
long after I'd forgotten, and couldn't care less or
give a flying fuck, everybody who's anybody
recognizes my genius instead of just me . . . and my
mother.

Spaceman George collapses on the floor exhausted from
his rant.

SPACEMAN GEORGE: I hate making decisions.

DR. OLSON: I think what you need is a choice
chip, Georgie.

SPACEMAN GEORGE: Choice chip?

DR. OLSON: Oh, didn't I tell you? It's my humble little offering to the indecisive. Every time you're in doubt, you can have a choice chip and I'll make the choice for you. Simple.

SPACEMAN GEORGE: And what does this service cost?

DR. OLSON: Nothing.

SPACEMAN GEORGE: Am I getting this right? Every time I'm confused, I can have a choice chip and you'll make the choice for me?

DR. OLSON: Right.

SPACEMAN GEORGE: No strings?

DR. OLSON: No strings.

SPACEMAN GEORGE: Who's responsible for the karma?

DR. OLSON: Me . . . I am.

SPACEMAN GEORGE: I knew there was a catch. That's where the guilt comes in, right?

DR. OLSON: That's where it rears its ugly little head.

SPACEMAN GEORGE: So you are going to take the karma and I have no responsibility other than the guilt I feel for letting you be responsible for the choices I let you make for my life?

DR. OLSON: Now you're getting the hang of it.

SPACEMAN GEORGE: Ruthless . . . you're ruthless.

DR. OLSON: And we haven't even scratched the surface. So, to cut the film, or not to cut the film? That is the question, is it not, Georgie? Perhaps you would like a choice chip.

SPACEMAN GEORGE: Could I see a bit more of the sluu . . . I mean the Actress?

DR. OLSON: Well. . . okay. For ol' times sake, but just a smidge.

Dr. Olson inches the video forward in SLOW MOTION.

The Actress again gives the chamber a spin but this time she turns the gun on herself.

Dr. Olson FREEZES the FRAME.

DR. OLSON: Decision time, George. You have thirty seconds and counting.

CUT TO: THE FACE OF THE GRANDFATHER CLOCK at the bottom of the stairs at Young George's grandparents' house. The seconds tick off . . . 11:59:31 . . . 11:59:32 . . .

It's when the CAMERA PULLS BACK from the clock that we realize we have—SHIFTED TO ANOTHER LOCATION—

a theater where a TV game show is in progress. The name is bannered across the stage:

HE WHO HESITATES IS LOST

Dr. Olson is the host. Spaceman George is the contestant. He sits center stage, strapped in a chair, not unlike the one in the little green room at the end of the hall in the mental institution. In fact, it is the very same one.

Strapped on George's head is the dreaded discombobulator. The wires coming out of the back of it lead to a GIANT ELECTROSHOCK MACHINE at the back of the stage.

Looming above everything is a HUGE VIDEO SCREEN on which is displayed THE FREEZE FRAME OF THE ACTRESS—GUN AIMED BETWEEN HER CLOSED EYES.

> DR. OLSON: Oh, isn't this fun, George?

> SPACEMAN GEORGE: I don't get the fucking fun part.

> DR. OLSON: Oh, come on, George. Have a sense of humor. After all, it's just a movie. Now is she going to kill herself for real or is she acting?

The audience counts with Dr. Olson, Ten . . . nine . . . eight . . . seven . . . six . . . five . . . four . . . three . . .

> SPACEMAN GEORGE: All right, all right. I'll take a choice chip.

The audience wildly applauds their approval.

DR. OLSON: Oh, goody . . . and I choose . . .

The audience chants, "Don't cut . . . Don't cut . . . Don't cut."
But Dr. Olson, being the contrarian that she is, answers . . .

DR. OLSON: I choose that you should . . .

SPACEMAN GEORGE: . . . Should?

DR. OLSON: . . . Cut the film!

The audience boos.

SPACEMAN GEORGE: Then you're saying that
she's going to kill herself for real? I mean, really
real for real?

DR. OLSON: Oh, come on, George. You know
the deal. If you want answers, you'll have to take a
choice chip.

The seconds are ticking down to a precious few. Spaceman
George goes into hyper-panic.

SPACEMAN GEORGE: Yes, for God's sake, I'll
take a choice chip.

DR. OLSON: Sorry, George, but there's no
question about it. She's as good as dead.

Dr. Olson turns to the huge FREEZE FRAME of the Actress
and pushes play. The Actress brings the gun closer until the tip
of the barrel is resting on her lower lip. She takes a deep breath,
slides the barrel in her pretty mouth, closes her eyes and . . .

SPACEMAN GEORGE: (screaming at the top of his lungs) Cut, for God sake, CUT!

But his appeal is just a weeeeeee bit too late.

FAST CUT TO: THE VOYEUR'S (a.k.a. WRITER GEORGE'S) N.Y. APARTMENT. ANGLE ON THE FLOOR-FUTON.

GEORGE: (waking up out of a dream, screaming) Cut. For God sake, CUT!

Voyeur George no sooner relaxes back in the realization that he's been dreaming than he sees something that makes him suspect that he hasn't been—dreaming, that is: the Actress, on the other side of the mirror, seeming in a stupor, as she slides the gun even deeper in her mouth.

George can't take the chance that he's not still dreaming. He frantically pounds on the mirror.

GEORGE: (screaming) All right, cut! I believe you. It's over . . . finished.

The Actress appears oblivious as she tightens her red lips around the gun barrel.

In desperation, the Voyeur grabs a chair and smashes it against the mirror. It bounces off the double-thick glass. Other than the chair breaking apart in his hands, it has no effect.

GEORGE: (screaming) For Christ's sake . . . I said, CUT! It's just a movie I'm making here. To hell with the fame, the awards, the money, the late night talk shows, rubbing elbows with the elite . . . to hell with being a *somebody*.

A glimmer of hope! The Actress pulls the gun from her mouth and in a kind of somnambulistic daze, stumbles back across the bathroom.

Calamity momentarily averted, the Voyeur powers up his video camera and ZOOMS IN.

WHAT HE SEES: The Actress, teary-eyed, peeling a certain Polaroid from her jumbled wall collage.

Seemingly transfixed, she lovingly caresses the surface of the photo, moistening it with her tears. Her sadness is short lived however, as she cannot contain her rage and rushes, screaming, back across the bathroom and slaps the Polaroid on the mirror, dead center in the Voyeur's frame . . . In an instant, all the loose ends are wrapped up.

The Voyeur can't believe that he's missed it . . . the clue had been there all along, right in front of his lens—proof positive that she was acting, that this whole thing was a sham, a setup—and he was a patsy from the start.

The Voyeur ZOOMS into an EXTREME CLOSE-UP OF THE PHOTO—it's the Actress as an infant in her mother's arms. We recall this Polaroid from the night the Actress, in a whirling-drunken-Dervish stupor, pasted it into her deranged collage hoping the Voyeur would pick up on it—but he didn't.

> WRITER GEORGE: (VOICEOVER in the PRESENT as he types) although the aging Polaroid is overexposed, and a bit out of focus, there's no doubt in the Voyeur's mind in whose arms the young Actress is cradled—it's Joyce, the Voyeur's childhood sweetheart with whom he had an affair, when, in his mid-twenties, he returned to Iowa to attend his grandmother's funeral.

The memories come flooding back—he and Joyce at the wake, sneaking off up to the attic where as kids they used to experiment trying to get "it" in, but never could. Now these many years later, it slipped in very easily.

THE DELIBERATELY-FORGOTTEN MEMORY

THE CAMERA MOVES THROUGH THE ATTIC. George and Joyce are silhouetted in the open window against a summer downpour. This is the first time they've seen each other since they were kids. In the meantime, the gangly tomboy has become quite a shapely, albeit plump, Iowa package. She's bent over the sill, half in, half out of the open window, hair soaked, barefoot on her tiptoes, dress hiked up over her voluptuous ass, offering herself up to George, who is deep in her from behind.

WRITER GEORGE: (cont's VOICEOVER in the PRESENT as he types) The Actress was the result of this little indiscretion. The Voyeur never acknowledged his daughter. Now in her early twenties, the Actress has tracked her father down and, knowing his propensity for the bizarre and perverted because of letters and photos the Actress found after her mother's death, she has come to get her revenge—to drive her father insane that he might leave this world the way her mother did.

To this end, the Actress has planned to live out all her father's fantasies disguised as the slut in the next apartment, then, when sufficiently sucked in, abandon him point blank between the eyes, figuring the shock to his already questionable hold on reality would tip the scales in favor of full-blown insanity from which a self-destructive end would all but be assured.

And all along the Voyeur thought *he* was the one in control, that this film was his mad concoction, that he was controlling the "eye of God." But as it turns out he's only been an actor in someone else's movie, a day-

player for hire to facilitate someone else's dream. And
for all his searching and scheming he still has no more
clue as to who he is, than he ever had.

No, this is the Actress's movie—actually, it always
has been. It's her "eye of God" that will prevail. She's in
control of the final scene and isn't going to let a little
thing like *death do us part* get in the way of her
performance.

Playing it to the hilt, the Actress cocks the gun and
with morbid delight, knowing the Voyeur will have no
choice but to record her demise, slides the barrel of the
gun ever so slowly between her sweet, parted lips and . . .

The Voyeur runs screaming out into the hall and makes a
running leap at the Actress's apartment door.

AS HE EXPLODES THROUGH, WE . . .

CUT TO: FLASHBACK. INTERIOR. SUSIE'S ROOM as
Teen George comes barreling headlong through the door—
coincidently, just as Lee is opening it.

Teen George's momentum carries him across the room where
he plows into the opposite wall and crumples to the floor in the
shadows.

Susie sits on her bed rolling a joint, appearing and disappearing
in the pulsating purple neon light from the strip joint across the
street. She registers little more than a passing glance at Teen
George's dramatic entrance.

Lee zips up his pants and joins Teen George in the shadows.

> LEE: A little anxious there, aren't we, George, ol'
> pal, ol' buddy? (He slips George a ten-dollar bill.)

LEE: Don't do anything I wouldn't. Ha ha.

Teen George doesn't say anything. He just sits there, stoned, freaked out of his mind, hugging his 16mm Bell and Howell camera.

Lee calls back as he closes the door.

LEE: Take good care of my good buddy.

There is a long silence before Susie finally speaks.

SUSIE: George? . . . George? That is your name, isn't it?

Teen George slowly emerges from the shadows on all fours, totally bewildered.

TEEN GEORGE: Where am I?

SUSIE: Say what?

TEEN GEORGE: Whooo am I?

SUSIE: Anyone you want to be, baby.

TEEN GEORGE: What came before?

SUSIE: Before what?

TEEN GEORGE: Before now . . . here. I can't remember what came before.

CUT TO: VIDEO FLASHBACK

CLOSE. JACQUES CONTINUING GEORGE'S PSYCHIC READING.

JACQUES: Quit backtracking into yesterday's thoughts. Don't make your life about anticipation and premeditation, but make the effort to conceive the understanding that the length of your life is the Now. And if you will function just within this Now, I feel the revelation of the fulfillment is rather startling.

END VIDEO FLASHBACK

CUT BACK TO: SUSIE'S ROOM. Teen George is trying to put it all together.

TEEN GEORGE: I can't seem to remember . . .

SUSIE: What?

TEEN GEORGE: I don't know. I feel like there's a scene missing or something.

SUSIE: Maybe it's in your camera there.

TEEN GEORGE: Right. Yeah, maybe when I get it developed, I'll remember.

SUSIE: In the meantime, maybe I can help you recollect.

TEEN GEORGE: I'd appreciate that because right now I can't seem to remember much of anything.

MARIE: (VOICEOVER) No, don't tell me. I've got to reel it back in myself.

CUT TO: VIDEO FLASHBACK

WRITER GEORGE'S APARTMENT. NIGHT. UPSIDE-DOWN MARIE. She's talking into George's camera while maintaining her yoga headstand.

> MARIE: What I was saying was . . . what was I saying? . . . Oh, right, what life is about is consciously forgetting, so . . . so . . . oh shit, I forgot again . . . no, no, I remember . . . life is consciously forgetting, so you can remember it again. That's the game we all play.

> GEORGE: And if we stop playing the game . . . just cut the film, metaphorically speaking, that is.

> MARIE: Come on, George. You know the answer to that. It all goes away . . . no sound, no picture. You're just left with a white screen . . . metaphorically speaking.

END VIDEO FLASHBACK

CUT BACK TO: TEEN GEORGE AND SUSIE.

> SUSIE: Well, George. How about you pay me so we can get on with this remembering business?

George hands Susie his wadded-up ten-dollar bill.

> TEEN GEORGE: I don't feel so good.

> SUSIE: You're not going to be sick, are you?

TEEN GEORGE: If I could just sit here for a minute.

SUSIE: That's okay by me. It's been a long day.

Susie lies back on the bed and relights her joint.

SUSIE: Is that your movie camera there?

TEEN GEORGE: What? Huh? Oh, yeah . . . my camera, yeah.

SUSIE: Your friend says you make movies.

TEEN GEORGE: Well, not real movies. I mean, not like Hollywood or anything, with actors and a script.

DAISY: (VOICEOVER) So, are you still working on the script?

WRITER GEORGE: (VOICEOVER) I'm almost finished. I'm working on the last scene.

CUT TO: VIDEO FLASHBACK

GEORGE'S N.Y. APARTMENT. DAISY. She sits in the open window of George's three-story walkup, rolling a joint and talking into George's camera.

DAISY: I'll believe it when I see it, George. But I will say this for you, you *are* dedicated. What's it been . . . ten years you've been writing it?

WRITER GEORGE: Twenty . . . but who's counting.

END VIDEO FLASHBACK

CUT BACK TO: SUSIE'S ROOM. CLOSE ON TEEN GEORGE trying to focus.

> SUSIE: What's happening, George?

> TEEN GEORGE: I don't know. You keep changing into someone else.

Susie takes another toke and offers the joint to George.

> SUSIE: You want a hit?

> TEEN GEORGE: Hip?

> SUSIE: No, hit.

> TEEN GEORGE: Hit?

> SUSIE: Grass, weed . . . (No response.) . . . bud, herb, cannabis, Mary Jane, pot, smoke, reefer . . . marijuana. Does any of this ring a bell?

> TEEN GEORGE: Marijuana? Oh, God . . . that's what Tiny gave me. No wonder I'm losing my mind. I'm losing my mind, right? Oh God, I can see little bits of it drifting off.

George grabs at the air, desperately trying to gather up his departing mind.

> SUSIE: I wouldn't worry about it, George. I mean, after all, it's just your mind . . . nothing to get too upset about.

TEEN GEORGE: (panicking) I saw it in a movie once . . . they played it in school. This woman smoked marijuana and got reefer madness. Oh God, I've got reefer madness, don't I?

SUSIE: And what kind of madness is that?

TEEN GEORGE: You know. You become a sex maniac.

DAISY: (VOICEOVER) I was thinking all these sexy thoughts about you today, George.

CUT TO: VIDEO FLASHBACK

CONTINUE GEORGE'S VIDEO of Daisy, sitting in the open window, smoking a joint.

GEORGE: And what were you thinking?

DAISY: Nasty thoughts. You probably don't want to hear?

GEORGE: (playing along) You know I don't.

DAISY: Well, too bad. I'm going to force you to listen. For the first time today, I was in front of a professional camera . . . no offense.

GEORGE: None taken. I'm proud of my amateur status.

DAISY: I got a call back on this commercial and the director wanted me to look really seductive, you know, holding up a roll of deodorant with this big round head . . . real subtle stuff. So, to get in

the mood . . . being the "Method Actor" that I am, I
thought about the fantasies we get into when we
have sex. (She takes a hit on the joint.) God, I get
horny when I smoke this stuff. I'm becoming . . .
so raunchy.

GEORGE: You wouldn't have let your
imagination go before?

DAISY: God, no. I cared too much what people
thought. I didn't have enough confidence to be an
actor.

GEORGE: And why is that, my dear?

DAISY: Ahh, you may ask. To the world of
orthodox Jews from which I was spawned, acting
is looked upon as something that only people do
who want to have wild sex.

GEORGE: And, my dear, do you want to have
wild sex?

Daisy leans forward into a BIG CLOSE-UP in George's camera
and kisses the lens leaving a print of her lipstick that remains for
the rest of the scene.

DAISY: I would've thought that would have been
clear by now, my dear George.

GEORGE: And what is wild sex, Ms. Daisy?
Would you please enlighten our viewers?

Daisy leans back against the windowsill becoming a profile in
George's camera and ponders the question.

DAISY: It has something to do with being extreme
. . . abandoned . . . something about going places
you can never return from. Oh, you think you can .
. . ha, ha, ha . . . but you find out that you can't, not
really. Wow, you know . . . I think I just got really
stoned . . . I was going to do something . . . what
was it? Oh, right. I was going to read you
something.

Daisy reaches for her overstuffed shoulder bag, pulls out a dog-eared paperback and playfully holds it up to her face the way we imagine she held up the roll-on deodorant for the commercial. The paperback is entitled *The Healing Dimensions of Tantric Sex.* She thumbs through the pages.

DAISY: Okay, this is it. Listen to this. This to me
is wild sex.

Daisy sucks in another hit, gets comfortable and reads.

DAISY: "In sex, like life, we are dealing with
three levels to the mind. We can think of them as
strata. At the top we have the conscious, level one.
Immediately below it, lies level two, the
inhibitions. And at the bottom is the mysterious
level three . . . the primal mind. Level one is
pragmatic. Its area of concern is the day-to-day
problems of survival. It is the cool, calculating part
of the mind. Level two is above such mundane
concerns. It is the custodian of our moral
conditioning. It is the source of our impotence and
frigidity. Its most vital mission is to prevent any
contact between levels one and three. Morality is
totally alien to the world of level three
. . ." Now, here's the good part. "Level three is
where you go without any quibbling over rights

and wrongs, directly from desire to fulfillment . . .
and moderation is in poor taste . . ." I love that
part. "On level three we are all unabashed rapists
and whores with extra points for incest. Tantra is in
reality the programmed use of a set of ego-
dissolving techniques . . . sex, drugs and
autosuggestion, to blast through the defenses of
level two in order to reach level three and remain
there long enough to savor the experience. You are
visiting the 'animal-you' in a forgotten Eden. The
'you' that emerges is incorrigibly uncivilized,
totally amoral, and completely irrational. You
don't think . . . You are one with nature . . . Your
actions are drawn from the common instinctive
pool of which you are so intimately a part that
there is no sense of uniqueness. You have gone
beyond your individual self. You are no longer the
'who' you think you are, nor know that you aren't .
. ."

Daisy seductively sucks in another hit, leans in CLOSE to
George's camera and blows the smoke in the lens.

> DAISY: Now that to me, dear viewers, *is* wild
> sex.

END VIDEO FLASHBACK

When the smoke clears, we are back in SUSIE'S ROOM.
CLOSE ON TEEN GEORGE. He is reeling from the smoke
Susie has just blown in his face.

> SUSIE: Your friend says that he'd bet you'd rather
> film me than screw me. That true?

> TEEN GEORGE: Maybe I said that but . . .

SUSIE: Would you like to have me on your film there? I've been in some movies, not Hollywood movies, if you know what I mean. You still with me? . . . George?

TEEN GEORGE: I'm not sure.

SUSIE: I tell you what, George. I'll give you a choice. You can either film me . . . or fuck me. Same price. What do you say?

TEEN GEORGE: Well . . .

DR. OLSON: (VOICEOVER) Perhaps a choice chip is in order, George.

CUT BACK TO: *THE HE WHO HESITATES IS LOST* TV GAME SHOW. Spaceman George is as equally indecisive.

DR. OLSON: Come on, George. Make a commitment. Remember . . . (She turns to the audience and leads them in the cheer.) He who hesitates is lost . . . He who hesitates is lost . . .

SPACEMAN GEORGE: But that was years ago, I was just a kid. I didn't want to do it anyway.

DR. OLSON: Well, here's your chance. Choice chips are retroactive, George.

SPACEMAN GEORGE: All right, I'll take a choice chip.

DR. OLSON: Excellent . . . then I choose . . . you should film!

The audience goes crazy, shouting and screaming their approval.

> SPACEMAN GEORGE: Wait, remind me. What was the other choice? There was filming or . . . ?

> DR. OLSON: Fucking, George . . . filming or fucking.

The audience picks up the chant. "Filming or fucking. Filming or fucking . . ."

> SPACEMAN GEORGE: And you say filming instead of . . .

> DR. OLSON: . . . fucking.

CUT BACK TO: INTERIOR. SUSIE'S ROOM. Susie and Teen George FADE IN AND OUT of the purple pulsating neon light.

> SUSIE: I know what you want to see, George. Why don't you turn your camera on and come a little closer?

CUT TO: VIDEO FLASHBACK

GEORGE'S VIDEO OF JACQUES. He's still in his psychic trance pulling information in from the otherworld.

> JACQUES: You are going through an experience strange unto yourself. It will be so vivid in it's happening as to point up the realness of Now!

END VIDEO FLASHBACK

CUT BACK TO: SUSIE'S ROOM.

After much hemming and hawing, Teen George puts his camera to his eye, hits START and scootches across the floor to Susie, who waits demurely—legs spread.

Teen George has just about made his way to the edge of Susie's bed and is moving in for a CLOSE SHOT when . . .

An all too familiar voice comes echoing from the distant past.

> FAMILIAR VOICE: George, are you in there?

> TEEN GEORGE: Oh, God, it's mother. She's found us.

END TEEN GEORGE'S 16mm POINT OF VIEW OF SUSIE.

He scrambles back across Susie's room and hovers in the shadows.

CUT BACK TO: SUSIE'S BED. We expect to see Susie but instead it's NINE-YEAR-OLD JOYCE who . . .

FADES IN AND OUT with the purple pulsating light. She peers out over the fuzzy edge of the blanket.

CUT BACK TO: The other side of the room where we expect to see Teen George, but instead—it's NINE-YEAR-OLD GEORGE who's hovering in the shadows.

> JOYCE: George, it's your mother.

> YOUNG GEORGE: I know . . . shhhhhh.

MOTHER: (OFF CAMERA) George . . . Joyce?
Are you in there? (She bangs on the door.) Open
this door immediately, George. I know you're in
there. You'd better not be doing what I think
you're doing.

FLASHBACK. THE ATTIC IN YOUNG GEORGE'S
GRANDPARENTS' HOUSE IN IOWA. Angle on the door
that Young George barricaded in an earlier scene. His mother
forces the door open a crack and peeks in.

MOTHER: George, I know you're in there. You
might as well give up and make it easy on yourself.

CUT BACK TO: SUSIE'S ROOM. Young George dashes
across the room and dives under the blanket with Joyce.

CUT BACK TO: THE ATTIC. George's mother forces the
door open and makes her way through the clutter to the bed.

MOTHER: I knew you two were up to no good.

As she yanks the blanket back, we . . .

CUT BACK TO: SUSIE'S ROOM. Teen George is poised
between Susie's legs—camera to his eye. He looks up just in time
to catch the last of his mother's hallucination fading away in the
gaps between the purple pulsating neon light.

TEEN GEORGE: Maybe we should do this next
time.

Susie puts Teen George's camera back to his eye and aims it
between her thighs.

SUSIE: This *is* next time, sweetie.

Teen George tries to FOCUS HIS CAMERA on what Susie is offering up but his head is swirling too much from reefer madness to make any sense of what he's seeing.

CUT BACK TO: VIDEO FLASHBACK

JACQUES. CLOSE. CONTINUING GEORGE'S AURA READING.

> JACQUES: It's like looking at something that you've seen in your mind a thousand times, but all of a sudden seeing something within that same pattern that you've never seen before. Let me repeat . . . The length of your life is the Now. And if you will function just within this Now, the fulfillment will be startling to behold.

END VIDEO FLASHBACK

WRITER GEORGE: (VOICEOVER in the PRESENT as he types) Timing is everything. Now? . . . was now the time to die? What should I do? I could barely hear Susie over the racket of my departing 16mm mind. "Yes. Now, do it . . . die!" she shouted. Transported on the waves of Susie's screams and the ever-present reminder that "He who hesitates is lost," I took a deep breath—fully aware it could be my last— and hurled myself headfirst down between Susie's silky brown thighs, down into the darkness where I found myself running for my life down the length of a corridor, the corridor at the top of the stairs at my Grandparents' house, the one leading to the attic where, after all these years, the monsters and demons were still in hot pursuit. Scared like shit I made a beeline for the light in the distance, the purple pulsating neon sign blinking on and off above the attic door —

abandon all hope ye who enter here. And I did, abandon all hope that is, and blasted through in a blaze of light extinguishing any hope of ever returning to anything even vaguely resembling who I thought I was.

CUT TO: EXTREME CLOSE. SLOW MOTION. A BULLET exploding out the barrel of a gun in a flash of light . . .

PULL BACK TO REVEAL: the Actress, who has just fired the gun at her reflection in the bathroom mirror, having no idea Voyeur George is on the other side squinting one-eyed through his video camera, helplessly watching what—for all intents and purposes—is the final moment of his latest incarnation.

The bullet blasts through the mirror into the center of George's lens, leaving a micro-computer-chip minefield of melting parts and exploding electronics as it rips through the body of his camera.

Voyeur George's eye looms huge and terrified at the other end of the eyepiece. He tries to dodge the bullet at the last second by looking the other way—as is his tendency when things get too uncomfortable—but this time is nothing like all the times before. This time he's run out of times, next times, good ol' times and wasted times. Now there is only for Voyeur George to meet the last of times.

He makes a valiant effort to readjust, but it's too little, too late, as usual, and the bullet catches him dead center between the eyes.

CUT TO: WIDE-ANGLE. VOYEUR GEORGE'S APARTMENT.

The impact from the bullet sends him airborne (in SLOW MOTION) across the room where he slams into the brick wall, bringing the shelves of videotapes down with him as he crumples to the floor.

> ACTRESS: (calling from the other apartment)
> George? Did you say, "Cut?"

No answer.

> ACTRESS: George? . . . George, you're scaring
> me. Answer me. Was that a cut? George?

No response.

Panicking, the Actress breaks away the remaining pieces of mirror and squeezes through the hole in the wall. In her struggle, the blanket she's wrapped in falls off leaving her naked as she scrambles across the room.

The Actress frantically digs George out from under the videotapes but obviously she's too late. From the amount of blood oozing out of the hole between his eyes, there's no doubt of George's demise.

The Actress yanks Voyeur George's head up by the collar, screaming.

> ACTRESS: You promised it wasn't real. You said
> it was just a movie, all in our heads. You lying son
> of a bitch. No one uses real bullets in the movies,
> you . . .

She angrily bangs George's head on the floor again and again.

> ACTRESS: I hate you. I hate you. You son-of-a-
> bitch. You left me. You fucking abandoned me.
> You piece of lying, fucking, shit.

Then, miracle of miracles, George speaks. His words are barely audible.

VOYEUR GEORGE: I'm . . . sorrrrryyy.

Totally spooked, the Actress drops George's head. It hits the floor with a thud.

ACTRESS: Oh, my God, you're alive.

VOYEUR GEORGE: I . . . I . . .

ACTRESS: What is it, George?

The Actress puts her ear to George's bloody mouth.

VOYEUR GEORGE: There isn't much . . . time. They'll . . . be here any minute.

ACTRESS: I'm going to call for help.

VOYEUR GEORGE: No . . . there's no time. I'm outta time . . . just listen. Explain it as a suicide. Do you hear me? Plead insanity . . . it's worked for me, or better yet, say you thought it was a scene from a film, that you're just an actor playing a part. Make up anything you want, but don't tell them the truth. They'll never believe you. Tell them to run the film in reverse and I'll be resurrected . . . then they'll see. Tell them I planned the whole thing, that no one betrayed me. How could they? . . . I wrote the screenplay adapted from my original story. Oh, I may have ripped off a few scenes from other movies but basically it's all mine. It's a kinda cosmic murder-mystery-whodunit film. All my friends were on the scene, storyboarding their lives, writing scripts, taking power lunches, talking Hollywood deals, packages, profits, gross points, above the line, below the line, bottom line, bullshit line. I wanted to be part of what was happening . . .be a somebody. You understand? I wanted to see if I could make a movie like everybody else.

ACTRESS: (sobbing) Oh, George, don't talk like that.

VOYEUR GEORGE: Oh, poor baby. You've forgotten that it's just a movie. We're just a lot of actors. This isn't real blood. Those weren't real bullets . . . I'm not really dying.

ACTRESS: It's real, George. You're really dying.

VOYEUR GEORGE: No, no, my dear. Don't you see? These are just words on a page, nothing to be taken seriously . . . thoughts, ideas, concepts . . . just beliefs. Nothing is real.

ACTRESS: Don't talk all goofy, George, not now. I can't handle it.

VOYEUR GEORGE: Okay, you don't believe me? Check with the Writers Guild. It's registered . . . the screenplay . . . the story . . . my life. I made the whole thing up. See for yourself. And all that sexploitation and drugs I wrote in, just a lot of gratuitous scenes to get the attention of the money guys. I admit it—I sold out. The crucifixion . . . the betrayal . . . that was part of it, too.

ACTRESS: George, what are you talking about?

VOYEUR GEORGE: I'm talking about lying, cheating and betrayal. Judas was actually the saint, not me, but no one knew that. It was just our secret. He was the *real* Christ. I was just an out of work actor, an impostor who was willing to do or say anything to get a gig. Are you kidding? Any actor would give a leg and an arm to play a part like that . . . Christ, the Son of God. We're talking major Hollywood epic stuff here . . . Academy Award time.

The truth of the matter is Judas was the *real* Christ. I just did what he said. He was my master. I would've done anything for him. He was the Father's first choice, the only begotten son. Judas chose me because of what I looked like. It was a question of casting. I was tall, looked good in robes, you know, the leading man type. And I could do tricks. Since I was a kid, I'd done magic. I could make things appear and disappear, could levitate, saw people in half—you know, the standard magician stuff. Judas caught my act one day down by the water and promised me the world . . . Well, actually, his words were "heaven and earth." How could I refuse? I wanted to be a star since I was a kid.

Anyway, the thing was, Judas had a rather big nose, little beady eyes, bad skin, this high squeaky voice and one of those frizzy Jewish naturals. I mean, the whole image was wrong. Anyway, we had this act, and even the eleven guys we hung out with believed I was the real Christ. They used to praise me all the time. They wouldn't leave me alone. Questions, questions, questions. What's the meaning of life? Who am I? I couldn't even have supper alone . . . it was crazy. Anyway, Judas would tell me what to say to the masses and I

would do my Christ impression. It worked right
from the start. The people ate it up, converting left
and right. We toured the little out-of-the-way
places at first, getting our act down. The crowds
got bigger and bigger demanding more and more
spectacular illusions. But Judas insisted we keep the
act simple, no miracles unless absolutely called for,
like the feeding of the masses illusion, and the
healing of the blind. Well, actually the healing of
the blind guy was my idea, which really pissed
Judas off. He thought it was a cheap shot, but we
converted practically the whole village that day.

Anyway, Judas wanted just the Word of God.
He kept reminding me, "Keep the teaching pure."
But I couldn't help going for the theatrics every
once in a while. After all, I am an actor. Anyway,
you know the rest. I got out of hand, started
pushing people around. I've got this rage in me.
It's an ego thing I know. It comes out when I least
expect it. I don't know from where. I'd scream and
yell, throw people off the set. I guess I offended too
many studio executives . . . whatever. Anyway,
finally the head of the studio calls this big news
conference and *washes his hands* of me. The rest is
history. Like overnight, I was a has-been. I tried to
convince myself that I wasn't, but the career was in
the toilet and flushed.

So, confess nothing, and remember . . . this is
important . . . (The Actress leans closer.) The scene
is never over until the director says, "Cut." Until
then, act as if everything is real no matter if you
forget your lines or the lights blow, or you're in
pain, dying, if the camera runs out of film . . . no
matter what, never stop being who you appear to
be. Stay in character . . . keep 'em guessing. Wow

. . . what's happening? Things are getting awfully dark in here. Did someone put the lens cap back on?

Voyeur George coughs up a glob of blood and falls silent.

ACTRESS: No, George, no. Don't die.

In an effort to jumpstart Voyeur George, the Actress frantically pounds on his chest. But George has all but gone to the other side. In a last desperate attempt to revive him, the Actress climbs on George and switches from pounding and banging to humping and grinding, giving George her fucking best.

ACTRESS: Oh God! Yes, George, yesssss . . .
Give it to me.

VOYEUR GEORGE: Everything is disappearing.

ACTRESS: Don't think, George.

VOYEUR GEORGE: Is this the time?

ACTRESS: (screaming) Yesssss.

VOYEUR GEORGE: Is now the time to die?

ACTRESS: No, George. Don't die . . . FUCK!
You can die later.

With each thrust of the Actress's fervent plea, blood spurts out of the hole in George's head like a geyser, splattering the two of them until they are drenched.

For all intents and purposes, Voyeur George is dead. He just hasn't figured it out, yet. Even in death, George is hesitating. To help him get the message, we . . . FADE TO BLACK.

SCENE III

LET IT SETTLE ITSELF

FADE UP:

The CAMERA PULLS BACK FROM AN INTENSE LIGHT revealing a group of people, all in white, peering down at someone off-camera. They speak in hushed whispers.

> PERSON #1: What's happening?
>
> PERSON #2: I don't know.
>
> PERSON #3: We have to do something.
>
> PERSON #4: (obviously amused at what she sees) If that's what I think it is, it could kill him.
>
> PERSON #2: What's the difference? He's dead already.
>
> PERSON #4: That doesn't look dead to me, honey.

CUT TO: WHAT EVERYBODY IS LOOKING AT: The rising sheet covering George's midsection. Once extended to its max, a spastic jerk ripples through George's otherwise unresponsive body, and a gooey spot bursts forth through the sheet.

> PERSON #2: Well, if he wasn't dead before, that should have done it.
>
> ANESTHESIOLOGIST: (OFF CAMERA) We're losing him.

CUT BACK WIDE: WE ARE IN AN OPERATING ROOM.

George is laid out on the operating table. The surgical team is working feverishly to save him.

THE CAMERA MOVES IN CLOSE TO GEORGE'S HEAD. The top of his skull is removed revealing his mangled brains.

The head surgeon is the definition of a pompous ass—a dramatic, over-the-top, recently out-of-the-closet gay guy who's love for the musical theater is apparent at times like these, when under surgical stress, he's prone to break into song.

> DOCTOR POMPOUS: *"Ooooooooak-lahoma, where the wind comes sweepin' down the plain . . ."* Come, come, come, people. We've still got a live one here. Remember, we *are* in the life-saving business.

> NURSE #1: (whispering to Nurse #2) From the looks of this guy, it's more like we're in the vegetable business.

> DOCTOR POMPOUS: (singing) *". . . Ooooook-lahoma . . . ev'ry night my honey lamb and I . . ."*

> ANESTHESIOLOGIST: We've lost him.

> DOCTOR POMPOUS: Prepare defibrillation. *"And when we say—Yeeow! A-yip-I-o-ee ay! We're only sayin' You're doin' fine, Oklahoma! Oklahoma—O.K."*

As Dr. Pompous' team goes into action, George's SUBTLE BODY rises through the sheet and drifts up to the ceiling.

George opens his eyes and checks himself out. He's duly impressed—no bullet hole, no blood, brains all intact—nothing like his physical body down below.

> GEORGE: What a rush, I'm dead . . . deceased. If I'd known it was this easy . . .

He calls to Dr. Pompous and the nurses below, but of course, no one can see or hear him.

> GEORGE: Hey, folks, I appreciate the concern, but it's not necessary. Cut . . . the movie's over. I'm outta here.

The words are no more out of George's mouth when the doors to the operating room burst open and the ever-anxious Sit Sliver comes running in on a full caffeine jag. He slides to a stop at the foot of the operating table—breathless.

> SIT: Oh, shit, am I too late? Is he . . .

Dr. Pompous puts the electroshock pads on George's chest.

> DOCTOR POMPOUS: Clear.

The voltage hits. George's body stiffens and bounces uncontrollably. All eyes shift to the EKG—Nothing!

> SIT: Doc, tell me, is he dead?

> DOCTOR POMPOUS: (barking orders) Get this man out of here *immediately*. Prepare another defibrillation.

Two nurses grab Sit.

SIT: Let me warn you. I watch karate movies.

DOCTOR POMPOUS: Clear.

Again the voltage surges through George's physical body. And again all eyes shift to the EKG. A blip comes on the screen, then another, followed by a steady succession. Sit breaks free of the nurses and rushes back to Dr. Pompous.

SIT: What does that mean?

DOCTOR POMPOUS: That he isn't dead. All right, everybody, back to work, and get this maniac out of here.

Three very determined nurses grab Sit, wrestle him to the floor and drag him out. He goes kicking and screaming.

GEORGE: Good try ol' buddy.

George's subtle-body floats down from the ceiling and sits in half-lotus on the chest of his physical body. He leans over and takes a look inside his head.

GEORGE: Yuk! If I had known it looked like that in there . . .

Yet again the doors of the operating room fly open and Sit comes running back in. He makes a beeline for Dr. Pompous.

SIT: Wait, wait. The name is Sit . . . Sit Sliver. Here's my card . . . agent, personal friend and confidant to my good buddy George, here.

GEORGE: You lying son-of-a-bitch. What are you up to?

SIT: He just disappeared. Everyone thought he was dead.

DOCTOR POMPOUS: Well, he's going to be dead for sure if you don't get out of here, Mr. Slither.

SIT: No, Sliver . . . like a piece of wood in your finger. It's right here on my card, see . . .

The card slips from Sit's hand and falls into the gaping hole in George's skull.

SIT: Oh shit! Sorry.

DOCTOR POMPOUS: (screaming) OUT!

The nurses do their best to extricate Sit, but he has come for answers and he will not be denied. He attaches himself to the operating table with an iron grip.

Meanwhile, George's subtle-body floats back up above the fray to the ceiling where he watches in total disbelief at the insane goings-on below; the nurses pulling on Sit and Sit pulling on the operating table as Dr. Pompous—singing at the top of his lungs—attempts to operate on his moving patient.

SIT: I got to know, Doc. You think you can save him?

GEORGE: I don't want to be saved, you scumbag . . . you slime of the earth. You never returned my calls. For two years, all I got was your voicemail telling me you were in a meeting.

SIT: Doc, this is a matter of life and death.

DOCTOR POMPOUS: I'm painfully aware of that Mr. Finger. Now will you get the hell out of here?

SIT: No, the name is Sliver . . . Sit Sliver. But the important thing is George's career is at stake.

GEORGE: Ahhhhh, now the plot thickens. What's the angle, you little shit?

DOCTOR POMPOUS: You don't seem to grasp the seriousness of the situation.

SIT: (turning aggressive) No, Doc, I don't think *you* understand the seriousness of the situation. Hollywood has been calling ever since they heard George resurfaced . . . the tabloids, the gossip hounds, the talk shows. My phone has been ringing off the hook.

GEORGE: Ah, now it all becomes clear. Eat your heart out, you bullshit artist. I'm outta here.

SIT: (cozying up to Dr. Pompous) You can't let him die, Doc. I know he's got one last great performance in him. I smell Oscar here. You can do it, Doc. I hear you're the best. There's fame and fortune in it for you, book and movie deals, talk shows, your own doctor TV reality show. We're talking major seven figures here.

DOCTOR POMPOUS: (repulsed) Are you totally out of your fucking mind? This man will be lucky if he's a vegetable. He's already died twice. Now will you PLEASE leave!

SIT: Dead twice? Officially dead? (Sit can't believe
what he's hearing. It's all he can do to contain
himself.) Doc, baby, you're the greatest.

Sit pulls out his cellular and punches in a number. He does a
little jig while waiting for the party to answer.

SIT: Doc, do you know what this means?
Hollywood's going to eat this up. I can smell the big
time . . . death, resurrection. I tell you this could be
the biggest comeback story since . . . (The party on
the other end answers.) Hello, this is Sit Sliver . . .
no not shiver, Sliver. I'm calling for C.B. . . . Ah,
C.B., it's you. Sit, here . . . Yes, I'm with him right
now. You won't believe this. He's alive . . . and get
this, he's been dead twice. I mean, officially on the
other side, a goner, deader than a doornail, kicked
the bucket. I tell you it's the comeback story of all
comeback stories. Back from the dead, there's
millions in it . . . What? No, not Sid, Sit, as in not
standing.

CUT TO: A LITTLE LATER. HOSPITAL CORRIDOR. FAST MOVING SHOT.

Sit is doing all he can to keep up with C.B.—C.B. Blown, that is,
head of Blown Pictures. He's a short, imposing, bulldog of a man
in his 60's—power suit, power cigar, power walk, power
sunglasses, power hairpiece. This is a man who is used to giving
orders, not taking them, except from the dominatrix he visits
once a week who makes him crawl naked on all fours barking
and begging for forgiveness.

SIT: So, C.B., get this. It couldn't be more perfect if
we wrote the script. (Sit takes out his memo pad and
checks off the items.) There were reports that George

was in India looking for God, right? Then, he next
shows up in New York, making pornos . . . growing
psychedelic mushrooms in California . . . dating a
high society patron of the arts in Beverly Hills, in and
out of the loony bin no one knows how many times,
for . . . and get this, C.B., this is my favorite . . . for
insisting he was an extraterrestrial from some place
called the Pleiades. Now I looked it up and there is a
star system about four hundred million light years
from here called the Pleiades. Could this be any more
timely? We are talking commercial here, C.B.,
something for the whole family . . . God, sex, drugs,
murder, madness. I see a kind of mystery, sci-fi, new
age, psychedelic, resurrection, romantic, X-rated-
kinda-flick. I mean, C.B., this can't help but be socko
boffo at the box office.

C.B. BLOWN: Can they save him?

SIT: Well, that's the glitch, C.B.

CUT TO: INTERIOR. OPERATING ROOM. C.B. and Sit
come barging in.

GEORGE: No, I don't believe this.

C.B.: So, what's the storyline here, Doc? Can we
save him?

DOCTOR POMPOUS: Who the hell are you?

C.B.: I make movies.

DOCTOR POMPOUS: Well, isn't that nice! I
save lives.

C.B.: I immortalize them.

SIT: This is C.B. Blown, head of Blown Pictures. He made George a star twenty years ago.

DOCTOR POMPOUS: I don't care if he made Jesus Christ a star. This is not a casting office. I want you two lunatics out of here now . . . NOW!

SIT: (whispering in Dr. Pompous' ear) What's the name of the new fifty-million-dollar wing to the hospital? If you get the right answer, you win the grand prize.

DOCTOR POMPOUS: (finally getting it) Oh, shit . . . he's not *thee* Blown! No, tell me it's not that Blown.

SIT: (taking great delight in tightening the screws) Believe me doc, it's that Blown.

DOCTOR POMPOUS: Oh, my God!

SIT: Congratulations, you've just won an all-expense paid transfer to the county hospital.

DOCTOR POMPOUS: (kissing ass to the max) Oh, Mr. Blown, I didn't recognize you, what with all the blood and brains and everything . . . I . . .

C.B.: Can it, Doc. You think you can save my boy, here?

GEORGE: "My boy" . . . I don't believe what I'm hearing.

DOCTOR POMPOUS: To tell you the truth, Mr. Blown . . .

C.B.: Call me C.B.

DOCTOR POMPOUS: (becoming chummy) Well, Mr. C.B., we're doing everything we can, but it doesn't look good.

C.B.: Doc, I'm not ashamed to admit it, I love this boy. Not only was he a superlative actor but he was, I might say, a special human being, which may not be financially rewarding, but what are things of the flesh anyway?

GEORGE: I can't believe this. Please, someone, tell me I didn't write this. The only thing missing is the Three Stooges.

DOCTOR POMPOUS: Oh, I couldn't agree more, Mr. C.B., but I'm afraid there is too much damage. Best we just let him go in peace.

GEORGE: I don't care how I go, just please let me out of this B-movie piece of shit.

C.B. takes Dr. Pompous aside. As he speaks, he pulls out a roll of thousands and peels them off like slices of liverwurst.

C.B.: I'm not thinking of just myself, or even the millions to be made from exploiting the hell out of this has-been. I'm thinking of the fans who've been wondering all these years whatever happened to . . . to . . . ahhh, what's-his-name here?

DOCTOR POMPOUS: (pocketing a handful of thousand dollar bills) Well, he may not be able to speak.

C.B.: (peeling off more bills) No problem . . . we'll dub.

DOCTOR POMPOUS: (pocketing the money) He probably won't be able to walk.

C.B.: (peeling more bills) We'll use a double. It's done all the time.

DOCTOR POMPOUS: He'll just be a shell of his former self. We'll have to pump him full of drugs. There will be tubes sticking out of him every which way. He won't know what's happening, where he's from, who he is . . . nothing.

C.B.: Who does, Doc? Who really does?

DOCTOR POMPOUS: I mean . . . he won't have a past, future, not a clue who he is. As far as he'll know, he might as well be an alien. Nothing on this planet will make any sense to him. You'll have to give him a whole new identity.

C.B.: Doc, this is Hollywood. That's what we do best. People come here from all over the world to be who they aren't. You just glue him back together. We'll convince him of who he is.

C.B. hands Dr. Pompous the last of his roll of thousands and walks him back to the operating table.

GEORGE: Well, that's it. That's absolutely the last fucking straw. I mean, how stupid can it get? I no longer want to have any part of this moronic movie. I want my name off the script, the credits . . . off anything that even remotely associates me with this Disaster . . . . It's humiliating.

This film has nothing whatsoever to do with what I wrote. I take no responsibility for the morass of imbecilic, illogical, brainless drivel that it has deteriorated into . . . It's an embarrassment. What can I say? I'm sorry . . . I'm truly sorry to bail on you after you've come all this way with me, but it's clear there's no saving this absurd, celluloid fiasco.

It just got away from me somewhere along the line. I don't get it. I mean, I thought everything was going along fine. I liked the scenes with Marie and Daisy . . . and Sit . . . the Spaceman . . . the kid scenes in Iowa. I especially liked the scenes with Lee and Teen George, and Tiny and Susie. Then, somewhere in the scene before last, it turned borderline stupid with that whole Christ rap. But with this last scene, it has totally become ridiculous. What can I say? I had such hopes for this film. It was my last chance to make it in Hollywood after my acting career fizzled out.

You see, I think of myself as a serious artist, with taste, and . . . and discretion. I set out to write a thought-provoking movie . . . something that would illuminate the spiritual Self vis-à-vis madness, as seen from the point of view of one—this one, certified in such aberrant behavior. To be engulfed in ecstasy . . . to give up the illusion of separateness to . . . to rub elbows with my enemies . . . to lay down in green pastures . . . to become, a nobody . . . a nothing . . . to dissolve away . . . to become that which I suspect I am—THAT is sanity. Madness is to think I am who

I appear to be—this ego-encapsulated bag of bones
and flesh. But to say this, is madness, I know, so I
keep these thoughts pretty hush-hush so I don't end
up back in the loony bin like my Aunt Pinky . . . But
then I think, "Why not say it?" After all, there's no
saving this film, that's for sure . . . so what's to hide? I
mean, I've been hinting about it, joking about it . . .
talking around about it. Maybe it's time to just say it
straight out so there will be no misunderstanding.
Yeah, it's time to come clean. All right, here goes.
Here's the thing that's driving me crazy . . . the thing
I've been trying to deal with. Here it is in a nutshell
. . . I'm dying. There it is . . . there you have it. The
cat is officially out of the bag. And I've been dying for
some time. I haven't told anyone, but there it is.
Actually, I'm glad to finally get it off my chest.
Confession is always good for the soul. Father,
forgive me for I have sinned. It's all an act . . . every
single infinitesimal part of it . . . an act. Hell, I
wanted an Academy Award as much as the next
actor, so I could prove I really fooled you the best at
this business of being who I pretend to be—that is,
this part I'm playing. And believe me . . . I *am*
playing a part. But *the envelope* will never open for me.
Instead, I must be content to pretend to be who I am
for an audience of one . . . who, by the way, got up
and walked out on my last performance never to be
seen or heard from again. When she left...Marie that
is, it all fell apart . . . me, who I thought I was, who I
thought I didn't think I was. We all crumbled like
broken crystal in a pile of sharp edges. The only
thing that remained was the vacant feeling in the
area that my heart used to occupy.

But recently there seems to be movement in the
void. Signs of an honest-to-goodness heart being
detected, growing out of the shambles of her

departure. Marie leaving, together with this dying
business and the film falling apart like it is, has made
it abundantly clear, even to me, that a new
production is needed . . . something lighter, more . . .
visual, less words, more silence, more witnessing, less
judging, less trying to figure it out . . . more simple,
less complicated, less fear, more trusting, more
enjoying, less desiring, more stopping, more Being,
less doing, more surrendering, and more and more
and more—less. Let it settle itself, more . . . I know,
"He who hesitates is lost" was always your
comeback, but I no longer see a contradiction in our
points of view. For to "Let it settle itself" necessitates
that there be no hesitation . . . for the slightest
hesitation to let IT settle Itself . . . and all is lost.

ANESTHESIOLOGIST: We're losing him.

GEORGE: Okay, that's my cue. Got to go,
everybody. I love you all. I bow down to each and
every one of you. If you want to know the truth, this
entire screenplay has been my roundabout way of
saying, goodbye . . . toodle-oo, farewell, it's been nice
to know you. Actually, it's been magnificent,
glorious, wondrous. You all have touched me more
than I can ever say. As far as these pages are
concerned, do with them what you will. I may be
dying, but I'm not totally out of it. I know my
screenplay is overwritten, filled with typos, self-
indulgent and in need of a hell of a lot of editing. Oh,
I admit to a clever turn of a phrase once in awhile,
some imaginative twists and turns but according to
Hollywood's standards of scriptwriting—totally
unprofessional, obtuse, plotless, non-commercial, and
way too long to ever be made into a "real Hollywood

movie." But there's no time to do a rewrite at this
late hour and besides who cares? I certainly don't.
So please, start the music, roll the end credits and, for
God sake, let's get on with this dying business. Okay,
rock 'n' rollers, here we go . . . executing final
countdown sequence for blast off.

ANESTHESIOLOGIST: We are *really* losing him
this time.

GEORGE: T-minus twenty seconds and counting—
nineteen, eighteen . . .

ANESTHESIOLOGIST: Someone better do
something quick or he's going to be history.

C.B. grabs Sit by the collar.

C.B.: (with a threatening growl) Think of
something.

Sit frantically tries to come up with a plan. Then, as if by divine
intervention, he zeros in on the wholesome-looking nurse with
the well-endowed chest and is immediately reminded of
George's interest in *unwholesome* sexual matters . . . Eureka!

Sit divulges his devious little plot to C.B. who immediately gives
the green light.

Not wasting a second, Sit pulls Nurse Wholesome aside and
whispers something in her ear. Whatever Sit says doesn't go
down well with the shapely blond. Emphasizing her
dissatisfaction, Nurse Wholesome winds up and slugs Sit,
sending him sprawling across the floor.

NURSE WHOLESOME: (hands planted on her hips) Just what kind of a girl do you think I am anyway?

C.B. pulls out a fresh roll of thousands, peels off a few and shoves them in Nurse Wholesome's hand. She counts the wad with increasing delight. Then batting her baby blues, she coos . . .

Oh, *that* kind of girl. Why didn't you say so?

Without a moment's hesitation, Nurse Wholesome whips off her surgical mask and shakes her hair loose, letting it fall, all blonde and gorgeous, to the small of her back.

GEORGE: What the hell is going on down there? Will you have a little respect? I'm trying to die here.

C.B. snaps a command to Sit and they boost Nurse Wholesome onto the operating table where she strikes a curvaceous pose at the feet of George's physical—albeit, practically dead—body.

The CAMERA RISES UP to the ceiling where George's attempt at dying is interrupted by the sight of the luscious Nurse Wholesome below.

GEORGE: My, my, what do we have here? Let's have a hold at T-minus ten seconds while we check out this unanticipated development.

THE DOORS OF THE OPERATING ROOM FLING OPEN and Sit bursts in pushing a battered upright piano followed by the Script Girl stumbling behind with snare drum and bass and C.B. lugging his tuba. After some confusion the trio manages to set up at the foot of the operating table.

To put the finishing touches on his impromptu creation, Sit cues the stagehand in the rafters and the operating room FADES TO BLACK.

ZAP...When the lights come back up everyone: Dr. Pompous, the nurses, Sit, C.B., the Script Girl, are dressed to the nines in black tie and tails, all except Nurse Wholesome who stands, bathed in a pink spotlight, poised all sexy and primed for her musical cue.

Sensing that this is the moment he's been waiting for his whole life, Sit gives the downbeat and the fledgling "Blown Trio," playing their first ever gig, break into an out-of-tune, jumbled strip number...the Script Girl extra heavy on the drums . . . boom-ba, boom-boom, ba . . .

Although disgusted with the way the movie of his life is unfolding, George isn't quite offended enough to look away as Nurse Wholesome peels, slinks and otherwise slithers her way out of her uniform, revealing George's favorite—garters, panties, stockings and high, high heels. This is another example of just how stereotypical George really is.

Sit's devious little scheme seems to be having the desired effect, if the rising of the sheet over George's pelvic region is any indication.

> GEORGE: Well, maybe I had you all wrong, Sit. This is very thoughtful of you, a little going-away present. Thank you.

> ANESTHESIOLOGIST: We're getting an erection??? I mean . . . a reaction.

> SIT: Old dependable George.

With prurient anticipation, George's subtle-body starts drifting down from the ceiling.

> GEORGE: I don't believe this. I'm dying and I'm getting an erection. (He floats down only inches from Nurse Wholesome.) Oh, God! Look at those breasts. I must be dead and gone to heaven.

George reaches out for Nurse Wholesome's bosoms but only manages to come up with a hand full of nothing. By the time he realizes this is Sit's devious plot to draw him back into his physical body, it's too late.

George frantically starts flapping his arms in an attempt to rise back up. He looks like a giant cartoon bird trying to get airborne, but to no avail, and he comes crashing back into his mortal self.

> GEORGE: Oh, not back here again. Sit, you son-of-a-bitch. I should have known you were up to no good.

> SIT: (doing a jig) Gotcha, George, gotcha.

C.B. gives Sit a congratulatory slap on the back.

The thing is, George, in all good faith, *is* trying to die, but his good intentions are constantly being hijacked by his carnal obsession. In this case, THE FULL UP-VIEW of Nurse Wholesome's beauteous ass as she positions herself for George's most succulent view.

> GEORGE: Oh! There is no doubt about it. That *is* God!

As if to confirm George's conjecture—that God does indeed dwell in human form as a woman's ass—Nurse Wholesome ever-so-deliberately slides off her panties, revealing for George's perusal, the *whole* of his obsession.

George's erection is practically poking through the sheet—
SLICE.

DOCTOR POMPOUS: Oops!

The sheet collapses.

GEORGE: Oops! What's "oops"?

SIT: What happened?

DOCTOR POMPOUS: Sorry. Cut the wrong thing.

GEORGE: What does that mean? "*Cut* the wrong thing . . . "

C.B.: What wrong thing?

DOCTOR POMPOUS: You see here . . .
(pointing to a portion of what's left of George's brain.) this part controls, shall we say, certain male functions.

GEORGE: Will someone please explain what the hell is happening?

DOCTOR POMPOUS: It mainly controls his ability to . . . you know, get it . . .

SIT: Get it up . . . You mean, he won't be able to get it up?

DOCTOR POMPOUS: I'm afraid not.

SIT: No problem. This is a spiritual man, a monk, a man above the fray, a seeker of God. What use does he have of such earthly pleasures?

C.B.: Doc, I thought it was something important. We can't think of sex at a time like this. Carry on, I see no problem.

GEORGE: No problem . . . NO PROBLEM! All right, that's it. I'm really outta here this time. Resuming countdown. T-minus ten seconds and counting, mark . . . ten . . . nine . . .

ANESTHESIOLOGIST: We're losing him again.

CUT TO: GEORGE'S POINT OF VIEW OF NURSE WHOLESOME swiveling her luscious hips above him as she shamelessly descends over his face. But to George's credit, he is trying with every bit of will power he can muster to leave all of his obsessions behind and die.

GEORGE: This is very tempting folks . . . kinda the acid test, so to speak. Good try Sit, but all that's in the past now. I'm through with sex, careers, fashion, fortune, fame, movies, sex. What did I leave out . . . sex. Did I say sex?

George's resolve is being tested to the max as Nurse Wholesome lowers her sumptuous derriere onto George's face, devouring his so-called life, and coincidentally extinguishing our cinematic POINT OF VIEW.

Here in the BLACKNESS, A SEAMLESS TRANSITION unfolds and we find ourselves in A STARRY PANORAMA OF OUTER SPACE through which we are accelerating at warp speed ZOOMING through clusters of star fields headed for the ball of blazing light at the center of the approaching galaxy.

> GEORGE: (VOICEOVER) This dying business is a little more scary than I thought. I'd really like to slow things down a bit. I think I'm about to have a major anxiety attack. I'd <u>really</u> like to do this dying thing later...A timeout would really be nice... just a moment to get my bearings. A little diversion perhaps... A movie would be nice... Yeah, a movie would be really great... something light... a comedy. . .something real stupid and some pop-corn . . . butter please and a large Coke.

OPENING TITLE OVER APPROACHING GALAXY.

FANTASTICK STUDIOS INK
PRESENTS
HOW TO MAKE PERFECT MOVIES

> GEORGE: (VOICEOVER) Great timing. The movie's just beginning... I didn't miss a thing.

Nearing the center of the galaxy, we plunge over a horizon of light and are sucked into an enormous black hole where the gravitational pull is so intense not even desires can escape— BLACK.

SUPERIMPOSE FINAL TITLE:

A FILM BY GEORGE OOPS

SOUND OVER: HAMMERING AND BRICKS FALLING.

WE PULL BACK OUT OF THE BLACKNESS through the hole just opened in a brick wall.

The Excavator continues hammering until he figures the opening in the wall is sufficiently wide enough to fit through but as it turns out—not quite.

The Excavator's little miscalculation causes a minor cave-in when he tries to squeeze through, pinning him in the wall.

This is Voyeur George staring in the movie of his life, a usual stuck between scenes.

Voyeur George thrashes about in an attempt to break free but only manages to make his situation more intractable. Exhausted, he slumps forward hanging half in, half out of the brick wall.

> SPACEMAN GEORGE: (VOICEOVER) Oh, shit! I just realized that I've seen this movie before. I couldn't get through it the first time. No, pleasssssse don't make me watch this movie again.

The CAMERA SLOWLY MOVES CLOSER TO GEORGE: the DOLLY making a creaking sound as it rolls over the old floor.

Resigned to his fate, George slowly looks up into the camera.

Now it is commonly agreed, in the world of Hollywood dramatic filmmaking, that it is unacceptable to break the illusion and look directly in the camera, a strange thing for George to do, especially considering his obsession to keep his identity in doubt. But that is precisely what he has just done. Consequently, he has blown his cover and never again will be able to hide behind the audience's suspicion that he didn't know they were there.

George lunges out as far as he can in an attempt to grab hold of the camera lens to help extricate himself but he can't quite reach it.

The CAMERA INCHES A BIT CLOSER.

George stretches out, straining for every millimeter, and does, just manage to grip the edge of the lens and secure his hold. His hands loom huge around the WIDE ANGLE FRAME.

With a seemingly tight grip, George starts pulling, but instead of extricating himself from his predicament, he only manages to draw the camera closer to himself until his nose is smashed up against the lens. Then, in an imperceptible reversal—like a breath shifting from in to out—the CAMERA BEGINS MOVING BACK IN A SLOW STEADY RETREAT until George is stretched out to the max.

At this point the pressure on the bricks reaches critical mass and gives way, causing the CAMERA/DOLLY TO SLINGSHOT back across the bathroom, consequently releasing our hero from the wall in an explosion of bricks and plaster and the camera shoots out the bathroom door with George in tow to the ROARING SOUND OF A '57 CHEVY LAYING RUBBER.

FAST CUT TO: GEORGE'S GRANDPARENTS' HOUSE. THE CORRIDOR LEADING TO THE ATTIC—the one at the top of the stairs lined with all the monsters and demons who, if not in body, then in spirit, have accompanied George throughout his life in the guise of fear, doubt, nightmares, unworthiness, phobias and stage fright—to mention a few.

THE DOLLY STREAKS DOWN THE
PSYCHEDELICALLY ELONGATED CORRIDOR AT
ROCKET SPEED WITH GEORGE HANGING ON TO
THE CAMERA LENS FOR DEAR LIFE.

FAST CUT TO; INTERIOR. ATTIC. THE CAMERA and
its hanger-on-er EXPLODES through the door and PLOWS
through the attic SLAMMING into the opposite wall.

Everything comes to an abrupt halt. When the dust and plaster
clears, George is left smashed up against the lens starring out at
us in a frozen panic, wild-eyed, uncontrollably trembling and
seemingly not knowing who, what or where he is.

After a time, the camera EVERY SO SLOWLY tilts down and
deposits dear pathetic George on the floor—and out.

SOUND OVER: FOOTSTEPS COMING DOWN THE
HALL AND ENTERING THE ATTIC.

A big hulk of a man, dressed in white, kneels down beside
George and rolls him over. George looks up dazed, not having a
clue where he is.

> MAN: Hello, George.

> GEORGE: Is this . . . heaven? Am I dead?

> MAN: You look very much alive to me, George.
> How are we feeling?

> GEORGE: (sits up) Who are we?

> MAN: We're your friends, George.

The man refers to his muscle-bound partner who waits out in the corridor.

GEORGE: You know I'm not with the movie company, right? You must be the guys come to clean this place up.

MAN: No, we're not from a movie company, George. We're the Orderlies from the hospital. We've come to help you.

GEORGE: (It all comes back.) Of course, how silly of me . . . I used to play up here in the attic when I was a kid. Just came up to look around. I guess I fell asleep. I had this crazy dream about this . . . never mind. Thank God, you've come. Did you see my mother? She was in the garden.

ORDERLY #1: She's right here.

George's mother steps out from behind the player piano. George staggers to his feet.

GEORGE: Hello, mother. Now everything is going to be all right. These are nice men.

MOTHER: Yes, dear. They are very nice. I told them you wouldn't give them any trouble like you did last time, and they assured me that if you'll cooperate, they won't use that funny little jacket.

GEORGE: (whispering to Orderly # 1) Let me talk to her. (turning to his mother) I'm sorry, mother. I didn't want to do this. I had to call these nice men. Please forgive me, but I'll stay with you, I promise.

ORDERLY #2: (calling from the corridor) It's
time we were going, George.

GEORGE: Mother, are you ready to go now?

ORDERLY #1: (taking George's arm) Would you
please come with us, George?

GEORGE: What? Oh, you think I'm the one who's
. . . Oh! I see where the confusion is. No . . . I'm not
the one who's crazy. It's my mother. I'm the one
who called you.

MOTHER: Oh, my poor baby. Mother will stay
with you. Now, don't make it difficult for the nice
men.

Orderly #1 tightens his grip on George.

GEORGE: What the hell is going on here? She's
the crazy one, not me.

George breaks loose and backs out into the corridor. Orderly #2
stands at the other end holding up a straitjacket.

ORDERLY #2: George, either you come with us
peacefully-like or . . . remember last time?

George is definitely cornered. His eyes dart back and forth
between the two orderlies.

FLASH CUT TO: CLOSE. THE GRANDFATHER CLOCK
at the foot of the stairs. The second hand ticks off the final
seconds of the final hour . . . ten . . . nine . . . eight . . .

CUT BACK TO: THE HALLWAY. WRITER GEORGE has been replaced by his younger self—YOUNG GEORGE—age ten. The voice, however, coming out of Young George is that of his older self—Writer George.

> YOUNG GEORGE: You've got to believe me, I'm not insane. It's her. Don't you see what she's doing? She's turning it all around.

> MOTHER: I'm sorry, George. (She turns to Orderly #1.) I really can't watch this. It's more than a mother can bear . . . seeing her baby . . . (She wipes a well-timed tear from her cheek.) If it's all right, I'll wait downstairs.

> ORDERLY #1: I think that's best. This could get messy.

George's mother walks down the corridor. As she passes her son, she pats him on the head.

> MOTHER: My dear baby, I had such high hopes for you. But you've turned out be just like your father . . . a no-good fucking polecat.

George is left speechless as his mother totters the length of the corridor and down the stairs.

> ORDERLY #1: George, you've been such a disappointment to your sweet mother. Why don't you be a nice boy and come with us real peaceful like?

> YOUNG GEORGE: You're going to let her go? She's an actress, for Christ sake . . . Can't you see that? She's nuttier than a fucking fruitcake. She

was just pretending she didn't know I was there
watching through the crack in the bathroom door,
naked. Go ahead, ask her . . . ask her.

ORDERLY #1: Okay, George. Have it your way.

The Orderlies close in on Young George from both ends of the
corridor.

As they approach, they MUTATE into the BLACK AND
WHITE MOVIE MONSTERS of George's childhood—
Dracula and The Wolfman—the horror duo that always scared
the living shit out of Young George at the Saturday matinee and
who have been hiding out in the dark of the corridor all these
years, waiting for his inevitable return.

There's no doubt about it. This time the monsters have Young
George cornered for sure. This time there'll be no tear-assing
through the dark to the safety of the attic and slamming the door
behind him . . . as usual.

Young George reckons he has two options: one, be devoured
and have that be the end of it or, two, execute his long-delayed
plan—the one where he turns on his camera light and films the
monsters before they have a chance to fade away in the light of
the situation, proving to the knot-heads who run this madhouse,
once and for all, that he isn't insane. He decides to go for option
two.

CUT TO: VIDEO FLASHBACK

CLOSE. JACQUES. (continuing his aura reading of George)

JACQUES: Now I see in the auric pattern that you
are entering into what I would call the energy of
exactness. You will be very disturbing to people

because they've come to expect a certain kind of emotional leniency from you. Until now you've sponsored weakness in associations. But that will no longer be the case. This will cause you to lose some old friends that may not have had your best interest at heart. And I see that now is the time for this change.

END VIDEO FLASHBACK

CUT BACK TO: THE HALLWAY.

It's now or never. Summoning all of his courage, Young George puts his camera to his eye, snaps on the light and starts making "Perfect Movies."

Immediately the battle is on and George's soul is the prize. The monsters attack from both flanks simultaneously. Young George frantically PANS BACK AND FORTH from Dracula to the Wolfman, blasting them with his light. They become enraged that this pipsqueak would challenge their unquestioned authority of the dark.

Disregarding the light—and at the risk of being shown up for the B-movie actors that they really are—the monsters attack in a desperate do-or-die assault to save their washed-up careers. They bite and rip and tear at George's camera. The screen erupts in an insane disembodied flurry of claws, fangs, blood and overexposed, out-of-focus body parts.

But somehow—God only knows—when the battle is over, Young George is left standing, without a scratch.

WHAT YOUNG GEORGE SEES THROUGH HIS CAMERA: THE OVEREXPOSED MONSTERS cowering away in the darkness, their careers as bad guys all but over.

Young George is ecstatic. He has finally documented his fears. He's got it all in his camera—proof positive that evil exists and he isn't crazy. Now all he has to do is get his precious evidence to safety. He races back down the corridor to the attic and slams the door behind him.

INTERIOR. ATTIC. WRITER GEORGE HAS REPLACED HIS YOUNGER SELF.

He muscles the bureau and player piano in front of the door along with some boxes and trunks, straps on his father's old 20's football helmet and, arming himself with his trusty baseball bat in one hand and piano stool in the other, readies himself for what's next . . . and *what's next* are the Orderlies (no longer their monster selves) who come crashing through the door.

The Orderlies explode into the attic sending the player piano flying. On impact, the piano roll kicks in and out comes a ragtime ditty from the twenties: "Roll out the barrel, we'll have a barrel of fun . . ." A perfect musical accompaniment to the SPED-UP, MADCAP, ZANY, SILENT-MOVIE MAYHEM that ensues.

The Orderlies rush George with a full frontal attack. However, they misjudge the tenacity of their invigorated opponent. In a double move with a half twist, Writer George swings his bat at Orderly #2 as he simultaneously smashes Orderly #1 over the head with the piano stool, leaving both attackers sprawled on the floor. George-2, bad guys-0.

With his newfound confidence, George goes ballistic, hopping, hooting, hollering and smashing and bashing everything in sight. In a strange way, George is having the time of his life. He has faced his fears, met them head on, and is still here to tell the tale.

But the Orderlies have a different end in mind. They regroup and make another vicious assault, coming at George like mad bulls. The collision sends all three across the room smashing into a wall. On impact it collapses, revealing the true nature of our whereabouts: A MOTION PICTURE SOUND STAGE IN HOLLYWOOD.

The cornfields, the white puffy clouds, the picture-postcard day—it's all a painted backdrop that comes crumbling down, sending the camera crew and the Director running for cover.

Now that the illusion has finally been shattered, there is no stopping George. He's on a mission to demolish every last infinitesimal part of the misconception of his existence so there can be no misunderstanding whatsoever, that any of this life is, or ever was, real.

> WRITER GEORGE: (VOICEOVER in the PRESENT as he types) I was on a roll. I couldn't stop myself. Actually, I had no choice in the matter. I was just playing out my part, like actors do in the movies where the storyline is all worked out—storyboarded, rehearsed and edited. In fact, the script had been written years earlier, adapted from a novel long before destiny ever cast me in the part. By the time I got the script all the bugs had been worked out, my character decided on, my reaction in any given situation was inevitable, fated right there on the page.
>
> All I had to do was make it look convincing that I was making all these choices myself and pretending I didn't know how it was all going to turn out. But of course, I'd read the final draft of the script. I knew how it ended, and still the crazy thing was, even though I knew I was really in for a fucking ride, I wanted the part.

I knew my character would end up alone . . . no more pretty-breasted women to cuddle with, no more anticipated rendezvous, fast cars and first class jets, no more red carpets and adoring fans, no more six-figure bank accounts and easy lays, no more youth, career, or anyone who cares, and ultimately no more life. Although I must admit, I tried to convince the studio heads to change that.

I kept insisting that this was a Hollywood movie, for Christ sake. The audience doesn't want their hero to die. But in the end, I lost the battle. But in spite of that, in spite of everything, I couldn't pass up the role. It was as if it were written for me. Plus, whoever got the part was going to be a star, for sure. That I would end up dead, well . . . I'd just have to learn to live with that.

George revs up and makes a running leap at the opposite wall. It caves in like a house of cards, bringing down a rafter of lights that bursts into flames. In a flash, the fire spreads throughout the movie set. More lights fall and explode. The Iowa cornfields go up in a blaze. The crew runs every which way. In spite of Orderly #1 practically being decapitated by falling debris, he and Orderly #2 are more determined than ever to get this son-of-a-bitch.

The Orderlies spot George scrambling up a ladder to the catwalk and charge after him. There's no doubt about it, they've got him cornered. No way can he escape. With sadistic delight, the Director screams for his cameraman to shoulder his handheld camera and film George's inevitable capture.

What everyone miscalculates, however, is that this is George's moment and he will not be denied. He has found his courage and is screwing it to the sticking point.

WHAT THE CAMERAMAN SEES THROUGH HIS HAND-HELD CAMERA—George, up on the catwalk, silhouetted against an Iowa sunset painted backdrop.

Here, high above the maddening crowd and seemingly undaunted by the Orderlies scrambling up the ladder, George makes his dramatic farewell, playing out the final moments of his fifteen minutes of fame to the last second.

Shamelessly performing to the camera below, George takes a deep Shakespearian bow, as if to an audience of adoring fans, and timing his exit perfectly to escape the grasp of the pursuing Orderlies, nonchalantly grabs an overhead cable and with the *devil-may-care* attitude of the great swashbucklers of the silent movies, swings down through what's left of the inflamed attic set, and leaps, Douglas Fairbanks-style, through the window of the only remaining wall, disappearing in the flames of the Iowa cornfields.

END OF THE SPED-UP, MADCAP, ZANY, SILENT MOVIE MAYHEM

CUT TO: SOMEWHERE ELSE ON THE HOLLYWOOD SOUND STAGE.

The overhead sprinkler system is coming down like a torrential rainstorm.

George comes splashing through the water and ducks behind a row of painted New York City backdrops, and none too soon, as the enraged Orderlies run by. They are followed by the Director, his cameraman—shouldering his handheld movie camera—an aging studio cop, some disgruntled crew, a sound guy with his microphone on the end of a long pole, and tottering along behind everyone—George's mother.

George waits until the main band of vigilantes has past, then seeing his chance, he reaches out and in one fell swoop puts a hand over his mother's mouth and before she knows what's happening, pulls her into the shadows with him.

She struggles to break free but realizes soon enough any attempt to liberate herself from her son's grip is futile and goes limp in his arms.

George slowly takes his hand from his mother's mouth. In the presence of their mutual recognition, all suspicion that the other didn't know what the other suspected but was too ashamed to reveal melts away in an incestuous embrace. Unable to contain themselves, they slump to the floor, ending in a heap, soaked, devouring each other in kisses with the passion of lovers having been separated by years and wars. When they finally speak, it's all we can do to understand their garbled words.

> GEORGE: Come out, come out, whoever you are.

> MOTHER: Are you . . . sure?

> GEORGE: Yes . . . It's finished. I've blown my
> cover.

George caresses his mother's face, becoming more and more rough, grabbing handfuls of her fleshy cheeks and peeling them away until, emerging from under her aging prosthetics, George finally uncovers, Marie.

> MARIE: No doubts?

> GEORGE: None.

> MARIE: I don't think I could have kept it up
> much longer.

GEORGE: You absolutely had me convinced.

MARIE: Thank God. That makeup was killing me.

GEORGE: What an absolutely incredible performance.

MARIE: Then you believed me?

GEORGE: Believed you! There were times . . . I mean, I didn't know what was real and what wasn't real and, hell, I wrote the script. I couldn't detect a flaw in your performance. It was scary. You were brilliant, my dear. Absolutely brilliant.

MARIE: And tell me you got it all recorded.

GEORGE: Every delicious, awe-inspiring, moment. All we have to do is a little editing and book a flight to the Cannes Film Festival. Come on, let's get out of here while the getting is good.

MARIE: Where are we going?

GEORGE: Back.

MARIE: Back?

GEORGE: Yes. I got the word. The Mother Ship is coming to pick us up.

MARIE: George . . . I can't go.

GEORGE: What?

MARIE: I can't go.

GEORGE: No, we'll do the festival thing first, pick up all the awards. Then we'll get the hell out of here.

MARIE: It's not that . . . I'm . . . I'm not ready yet . . . I mean, there's a situation.

GEORGE: (the wind taken out of his sails) The yoga instructor?

MARIE: Yes, we're getting along so well, and . . . I think I'm really smitten. Do you understand?

GEORGE: Yeah . . . I guess I knew.

MARIE: I'm sorry, George.

GEORGE: Me too . . . I mean, we knew that someday it had to end, right? Hell, I mean, I'm old enough to be your father. I mean, after all, it was just a movie.

MARIE: . . . A *perfect* movie.

GEORGE: Yeah, well, all except the ending. But hey, you've got your life. I've got what's left of mine. I mean . . . are you sure?

MARIE: I'm sure. Don't be mad.

GEORGE: I'm not mad. I mean, at some point every actor has to take off the makeup and go home, right? It's just that . . . well, I mean, we've come so far. What if . . .

Marie lovingly puts her hand over George's mouth.

> MARIE: There will always be what-ifs, George.
> Best to just let it settle itself.

> GEORGE: (surprised) What about your famous
> warning . . . he who hesitates is lost—that always
> made me feel like I messed up?

> MARIE: Just a little something to keep you on
> your toes, Georgie.

> GEORGE: Well, that it did, for sure . . . So . . .

> MARIE: God, I hate goodbyes.

> GEORGE: Don't leave. Not yet.

> MARIE: Don't you understand? We have too
> many links with the past. You tell me all the time,
> 'Every writer, every morning, wipes the slate clean
> from which everything begins again, new,
> untouched by pasts and futures.'

> GEORGE: Me and my big mouth. All right . . .
> but one last dance.

> MARIE: All right . . . but something slow.

> GEORGE: . . . And close.

> MARIE: (she smiles) . . . And wet.

Marie moves into George's open arms—close. And tentatively,
like two love struck kids at a high school dance, move out from
the shadows into the downpour—for the moment the slate is

wiped clean *of what-ifs*. But only for a moment, as the sound of approaching voices reminds George of his many links with the past.

George spins Marie out in a kind of Astaire-Rogers, choreographed dance move, à la one of those 1950's MGM Technicolor musical numbers with full orchestra accompaniment. When she comes back in George's arms it's obvious, even to him, it's really over.

> GEORGE: Thanks for the dance.

> MARIE: Always a pleasure.

THE CAMERA MOVES IN FOR A BIG HOLLYWOOD CLOSE-UP AS THE TWO KISS.

SOUND OVER: The mob getting closer.

> MARIE: You've got to go, George. If they catch you, they'll take you back to the loony bin.

> GEORGE: But . . .

> MARIE: No buts . . . GO!

George reluctantly pulls himself from Marie and backs away.

> MARIE: (calling after him) We're just actors playing a part, right? Even now, none of this is real . . . right? Right, George?

> GEORGE: (calling back) We agreed. It's all real as far as the "I" can see. That was the deal. Just remember, don't stop acting until the director says, "Cut."

George gives a playful wink, turns and disappears in the smoke and rain.

CUT BACK TO: MARIE—CONFUSED. She calls after George.

> MARIE: What are you saying? Is this movie over
> or what?

George doesn't answer. He's long gone. Marie walks away in the opposite direction enveloped in the smoke mumbling to herself.

> MARIE: What am I suppose to do now . . .
> pretend like nothing happened?

CUT TO ANOTHER LOCATION ON THE SOUND STAGE.

WE ARE MOVING WITH GEORGE as he fumbles his way through the smoke and downpour. Eventually he finds himself in front of the painted backdrop of the strip joint across the street. Above, the purple pulsating neon light flashes on and off— *ABANDON ALL HOPE YE WHO ENTER HERE.*

Somewhere the sound of a woman screaming and moaning—in pleasure or pain, it's impossible for George to tell. It seems to be coming from the DILAPIDATED HOTEL MOVIE SET across the way.

Curious, George moves to the window and peeks in. It's Susie's room. In fact, Susie is in the bed on her back making a buck, just like back in the '50s. A teen boy is wedged between her legs. Susie, in her carefree style, is sucking on a joint and encouraging the teen with random "ooh's" and "ahh's" and occasional screams.

SOUND OVER: APPROACHING VOICES OF THE
SEARCH PARTY.

Figuring his best escape is through Susie's room, George raises
the window and climbs in. It's dark except for the purple
pulsating neon light flashing across the street.

GEORGE: Susie?

SUSIE: Is that you, George?

GEORGE: You remember me?

SUSIE: Of course I do. How could I forget you?
I've followed your movie career . . . Whatever
happened to you?

GEORGE: It's a long story. You'll have to read
the book.

SUSIE: Am I in it?

GEORGE: It's a surprise. You've got a special
part.

SUSIE: You look like you're in a bit of a hurry.

GEORGE: Yeah, well . . .

SUSIE: You always were in a hurry as I recall.
Want a hit? Slow you down a little.

GEORGE: Don't mind if I do.

George hunkers down on the floor next to Susie's bed. She offers
him the corner of the sheet to dry off.

GEORGE: It's so good to see you, Susie. Am I interrupting anything?

SUSIE: You're always welcome, George.

Susie offers George a joint. He takes it and sucks in a big one. The teen on top of Susie is totally oblivious of George and Susie's conversation.

GEORGE: God, Susie, you look great . . .just the same.

SUSIE: You too, George . . . just a little older. Hand me my bag there on the floor.

George hands it to her. Susie takes something out and drops it in George's hand—car keys.

GEORGE: What are these for?

SUSIE: The Chevy. They fell out of your friend's pants. Remember?

GEORGE: Not really. Remind me.

SUSIE: Your friend . . . what was his name?

GEORGE: You mean, Lee?

SUSIE: Yeah, him. Don't you remember he came back and called through the door to make sure you found the keys that fell out of his pocket?

GEORGE: Wow . . .that's right. I'd forgotten.

They pass the joint back and forth a couple of times before Susie
inquires . . .

SUSIE: So, George, did you ever remember who
you are?

GEORGE: Glimpses once in awhile, but . . .

SUSIE: What are you looking for, George?

GEORGE: Peace of mind.

SUSIE: Sorry to be the one who breaks the news
to you but there's no such thing.

GEORGE: No, don't tell me that after I've come
all this way.

SUSIE: I'm here to tell you, baby. It's the nature of
the mind to keep movin'. Peace ain't what the
mind's about. Best to just let it go.

GEORGE: What? Lose my mind? You kidding?
I'll go crazy.

SUSIE: You got it wrong, Georgie. What's driving
you crazy is *resisting* letting your mind go . . . not
your mind going. It's going with or without you.
You might as well stop resisting and enjoy the ride.

GEORGE: How do you know these things?

SUSIE: Just came to me one day.

GEORGE: What . . . like a revelation?

SUSIE: Just like. A-men.

George retrieves his video camera from his shoulder bag and puts it to his eye.

WHAT GEORGE SEES THROUGH HIS CAMERA: SUSIE IN CLOSE-UP. The Teen Boy is OUT OF FOCUS in the BACKGROUND, his head bobbing in and out of frame.

SUSIE: What are you doing, George?

GEORGE: I want to make sure I get this.

SUSIE: Gosh, if I'd known I was going to be in the movies . . . (She playfully primps her hair.) How do I look?

GEORGE: Just like a movie star.

SUSIE: Okay, so what do you want to hear?

GEORGE: How you know I won't go crazy if I lose my mind.

SUSIE: Okay. So this is how it went down. I had just done this trick, right? And I'm sitting here wondering what it's all about . . . life, ya know? And I'm cry'n and feeling sorry for myself and I hear someone calling my name . . . real nice and gentle . . . 'Susie' . . . 'Susie' . . . sounding just like my daddy when I was a little girl. And I look up . . . and lo and behold, it's Christ. Jesus in the flesh. (Susie points to the black velvet painting of Christ on the cross above her bed.) And he climbs down off the cross just as real as you and me, and I'm not stoned or noth'n, and he says he's thirsty as all get

out and do I have anything to drink. So I pop a
couple of cold brews and we sit here on the bed
together . . . no fool'n around or noth'n . . .
although I tell you, I'da been up for it, but him
being Christ and all, I figured it wasn't cool. And
the thing is, I'm naked, not a stitch, and he holds
me in his arms so tender, not com'n on or noth'n,
and we're drinking our brews, just enjoying hang'n
out, you know, talk'n about what movies we've
seen and stuff. He loves the movies by the way . . .
but he thought all the ones they did of him were
pretty hokey. Finally he says, 'It's all a dream,
Susie.' And I say, 'What is?' And he says, 'All of it
. . . birth, death, and all what's in-between . . . you,
me, it's all a dream.' Then he says, 'Susie, it's time
you woke up.' And I ask him, how? And he says,
'There is no *"how"* . . . drop the *"how."* The *"how"*
is the problem. There's only *"Now."* There is no
"how".' Then he says, 'Do you have faith?' And I
say, 'Yes, Lord." And in that instant, dear George,
I woke up to who I am . . . just like in the morning
when you wake up out of a dream and know
nothing was real.

GEORGE: You're saying that life is just a dream?

SUSIE: Every frame of it, baby. Sh-Boom, Sh-
Boom.

JACQUES: (VOICEOVER) You will be inclined
to believe on first thought that this is just too far
out . . .

CUT TO: VIDEO FLASHBACK

GEORGE'S VIDEO OF JACQUES. TIGHT CLOSE-UP. Eyes closed, cognizing George's future.

> JACQUES: But due to the changes that have been occurring, by this tripping through your consciousness . . . it causes you to release a lot of this mental stubbornness . . . suddenly there is a flexibility that floats through the pattern. It's like opening your eyes for the first time . . . a clarifying realization . . . the removal of the dream state.

END VIDEO FLASHBACK

CUT BACK TO: SUSIE'S ROOM.

> GEORGE: But that's just it. I can't seem to tell the difference between waking and dreaming anymore . . . where one leaves off and the other begins.

> SUSIE: (taking another hit) Figure it's all a dream, George. Then you'll be safe. Figure none of this is no more real than those movies you make in your head that never make it to the screen. It's just a light and shadow show, baby.

> GEORGE: Okay, so how do I get out of the dream?

> SUSIE: There's no getting *out*. There's only waking up *in* it.

> GEORGE: Okay! So how do I wake up?

> SUSIE: You want to know how, George. There is no *how*, there's only *Now*.

CUT BACK TO: VIDEO FLASHBACK

JACQUES continues with George's aura reading.

> JACQUES: The key to this is, you need more love
> for Self to stabilize the awareness that you are
> moving into. Once you have that, then it seems
> there is no limitation. This unusual idea, as
> farfetched as it may sound, will force you into a
> recognition of Self, totally different than you have
> ever experienced, and manifesting in total
> fulfillment.

END VIDEO FLASHBACK

CUT BACK TO: GEORGE'S VIDEO POINT OF VIEW OF
SUSIE.

> GEORGE: There must be something I can do
> though.

> SUSIE: No, George, sorry. It happens on Its own,
> but if you insist, there's something you can play
> around with . . . a little something to keep you off
> the streets.

> GEORGE: What?

> SUSIE: Go in. Go in as deep as you can.

The Teen Boy takes Susie's spiritual advice to George as a cue
for him and increases the intensity of his youthful fervor.

> GEORGE: Susie, are you talking to me or him?

Susie is having difficulty answering George, divided as she is between his questions and her professional duties.

> SUSIE: I'm telling you. Just let it all go. (The Teen Boy reacts with a timely thrust.) That's it baby . . . give it to mama.

> GEORGE: (trying to keep Susie on track) Let what go?

Suddenly the Teen Boy stops.

> TEEN BOY: What's happening? Everything is going black.

> GEORGE: What are you talking about, Susie? Let go of what?

> TEEN BOY: I feel like I'm losing my mind.

> SUSIE: Good . . . let it go, baby.

> GEORGE: But if my mind goes, I go.

> SUSIE: And I go and you go and e-go . . . we all go.

> TEEN BOY: Oh no, little bits of my mind are drifting off. I can see them floating away.

> SUSIE: Don't pay any attention. Just keep going in . . . deeper.

SOUND OVER: ANGRY VOICES IN THE HALL OUTSIDE SUSIE'S DOOR.

GEORGE: Shit, they've found me!

TEEN BOY: (panicking) Oh God, everything is disappearing.

Knowing he has to get the hell out of there, George reluctantly backs away to the window but keeps his video camera running in hopes of getting some last minute instructions of what to do from Suzie.

SOUND OVER: FISTS BANGING ON SUSIE'S DOOR.

GEORGE: Susie, what should I do?

THE ORDERLIES: (SOUND OVER) You should give yourself up. We know you're in there.

The Teen Boy pulls away.

TEEN BOY: I think I'll do this next time.

Susie yanks him back down.

SUSIE: This *is* next time, sweetie. Don't stop now. We're just about to the good part.

SOUND OF: SUSIE'S DOOR BEING BROKEN DOWN.

TEEN BOY: Oh, God, I'm disappearing. I can't find myself anywhere. I'm losing my mind, I know it.

GEORGE: (raising the window) Please, Susie . . . tell me, what should I do?

SUSIE: Let it go . . .

GEORGE: Let what go?

SUSIE: Your mind.

TEEN BOY: My mind? No . . . not my mind.

GEORGE: But I'll die if I do.

SUSIE: That's the whole idea, baby . . . die!

George climbs out of the window and makes a quick ZOOM BACK INTO THE ROOM for a last shot of Susie but she's blocked by the Teen Boy who rises up into his video frame.

George ZOOMS IN CLOSER to make sure he's seeing what he can't believe he's seeing—himself. The Teen Boy is him, Teen George, looking back at himself from all those years ago, desperately trying to gather up his departing mind from the ravages of reefer madness.

George flashes on the stoned possibility that his entire existence has been nothing more than reefer madness—and that the span of his life—since he was with Susie, back when he was a teen—is nothing more than a breath between tokes, a hallucinatory projection of a nonexistent life that he has only imagined all these years to be. And that in "reality," Lee is still waiting for him downstairs in the Chevy to take him home to his fretting mother.

George is shaken from his self-induced mind-fuck by THE SOUND OF SUSIE'S DOOR CRASHING DOWN. Making a hasty retreat, George stuffs his camera in his shoulder bag and hightails it through the smoke and water.

He's put a fair distance between himself and the loonies chasing him when he hears a familiar voice up ahead. He slides to a stop.

VOICE: George . . . George, over here.

CUT TO: WHAT GEORGE SEES THROUGH THE
SMOKE—TEEN LEE, LEANING OVER THE HOOD OF
HIS '57 CHEVY.

Aware that his grasp on reality is a bit shaky, to say the least,
George approaches his vision cautiously. On closer inspection—
bizarre as it may be—the Chevy appears to be parked in front of
a REAR PROJECTION SCREEN.

[NOTE: A rear projection screen is a fifties version of a *green
screen*—a translucent movie screen on which film is projected
from the back and viewed on the front surface. Most commonly,
this technique is used in interior car scenes where the projection
of the passing street is seen out the rear window creating the
illusion the car is moving. This cinema trick is usually enhanced
by members of the crew rocking the car from side to side.]

GEORGE: Lee, is that really you?

LEE: Who did you expect, Alfred E. Newman?
Did you get the keys?

GEORGE: Keys?

LEE: Didn't you hear me? I knocked on Susie's
door and told you the keys to the Chevy fell out of
my pants.

GEORGE: Keys? Oh, right, the keys. (He searches
through his pockets.) This is unbelievable, you
being here.

LEE: George, I didn't have the keys to the car.
How was I supposed to go anywhere?

GEORGE: But you don't understand how weird
this is.

George tosses the keys to Lee. He unlocks the Chevy and gets in.
George just stands there, dumbfounded.

GEORGE: . . . Unfuckingbelievable!

LEE: You said that. Now get in.

GEORGE: But Lee, this is a movie set. This isn't a
real car.

LEE: George, you're taking this movie thing too
far. So you got a little stoned. Come back to reality.
It's two in the morning and I'm going to have hell
to pay when I get home. Now get in and let's get
out of here.

GEORGE: Don't I look different . . . older?

LEE: Yeah, sure. You got laid. You look real
mature. Come on, lets get out of here.

Reluctantly, George decides to go along with this latest wrinkle
in his questionable reality and gets in the Chevy.

LEE: So what happened?

GEORGE: You'll never believe it.

Lee turns the key but the Chevy won't start.

George looks in the rearview mirror. He sees himself as Teen
George. But we see him as just crazy middle-aged George.

GEORGE: What the fuck is happening?

LEE: I don't know. It just won't start. It must be
that cheap carburetor I put in.

What does start up, however, is the REAR PROJECTOR.

Like magic, out the back window of the Chevy, the rear
projection screen lights up with the street scene of downtown Los
Angeles where Lee parked his Chevy in 1957, down the block
from Susie's dilapidated hotel, out of which comes running the
Orderlies, the Director, the cameraman, the sound guy, the
studio cop, some firemen and half a dozen very pissed off
members of the film crew.

One of the Orderlies spots the Chevy.

GEORGE: Oh, no. They've found us. Come on,
start it.

LEE: I'm trying. (He looks in the rearview mirror.)
Shit, are they all after you?

GEORGE: I think it's safe to say they are.

LEE: What did you do?

GEORGE: You don't want to know. For Christ
sake, just start the car!

Lee pumps the gas hard and turns the key. VA-
ROOOOOOOM. The Chevy kicks in. The Orderlies have just
about reached the back bumper when Lee throws the Chevy in
gear and peels out.

Not about to give up the chase, the frenzied little group runs back to Susie's hotel where the Orderlies' ambulance is parked, pile in, and with sirens blaring and lights flashing, hang a U-ie and come tearing down the street after the Chevy.

[NOTE: all of this has been seen on the rear projection screen out the back window of the Chevy. But now we . . .]

CUT TO: A REAL L.A. STREET. HIGH ANGLE. NIGHT. First the Chevy, then the ambulance comes racing down the street and slides around the corner.

CUT BACK TO: THE MOVIE SET. INTERIOR. CHEVY. LEE AND GEORGE The ambulance can be seen out the back window on the REAR PROJECTION SCREEN.

> LEE: What the hell did you do to piss off all these people?

> GEORGE: It was all a setup. Susie isn't really who she appears to be.

> LEE: You're saying, Susie isn't a hooker?

> GEORGE: No way. Well maybe she's a hooker on the side, but that's not who she really is.

> LEE: Then who is she?

> GEORGE: I don't know exactly but she wasn't talking like any hooker. I think she's from somewhere else.

As George says the words *somewhere else,* he all but disappears in the OVEREXPOSED HEADLIGHTS of an oncoming semi-truck.

FLASHBACK: IOWA. INTERIOR '47 FORD. Young George (age nine) and his father are moving along a country dirt road, dust kicking high in the evening sun. Young George is looking at the world strobe by through his toilet-roll camera.

YOUNG GEORGE: Sometimes, when I look through my camera, I can't find me anywhere.

FATHER: Then where you are?

YOUNG GEORGE: I don't know . . . somewhere else though.

FATHER: And where is somewhere else?

YOUNG GEORGE: I don't know . . . it's like it's in back of everything out front . . . It's back there. (He points in back of his head.)

FATHER: You definitely have your mother's fuck-up imagination.

The CAMERA MAKES A FAST MOVE into Young George, ZOOMING down the length of his toilet-roll camera, into the center of his eye and on through, emerging "in back of everything that's out front" of what he thinks is there. We only linger here a brief moment before the screen erupts in a blaze of OVEREXPOSED LIGHT as simultaneously the headlights of the passing truck sweep across Writer George's face and in a flash we are back in the Chevy.

George is left staring off into space appearing in a frozen stupor.

LEE: George, talk to me, good buddy. What's up?

GEORGE: (struggling to get the words out) The somewhere-else place . . . I'd forgotten.

LEE: I give up. What are we talking about?

GEORGE: All these years . . . I'd forgotten all about it. That's what Susie meant when she said to 'go deeper.'

LEE: Yeah, she told me the same thing.

GEORGE: No, I'm not joking around here. It's nothing like that. Marie was saying the same thing as Suzie.

LEE: Are you having some kind of mental breakdown, George? Tiny told me about you smoking weed and thinking that it was a Salem cigarette.

GEORGE: No, Lee. It's all coming clear . . . the clearer I'm not me gets clearer.

LEE: Oh, well, thanks . . . that clears everything up.

GEORGE: (elated) It's just like Christ said.

LEE: How did Christ get into this?

GEORGE: Don't you see? He's always been in it. He *is It*.

LEE: George, I got to tell you as a buddy, you're not acting normal.

GEORGE: Normal . . . what could be more normal? Christ talked to Susie. He told her this was all a dream and that it was time for her to wake up.

LEE: Wake up?

GEORGE: Yeah. To who she really is. Lee, I've got a feeling that none of this is what it appears to be.

LEE: Yeah? Well, tell it to those guys who are about to drive up our ass.

George takes a quick look around. The ambulance (on the rear projection screen) is right on their tail. The mad little group inside can be seen yelling and screaming for the Chevy to pull over.

GEORGE: I got to get out of here, Lee.

LEE: Duhhh, man.

GEORGE: No, I mean really out of here. Where are we?

LEE: Earth, George. A group of colonies in North America. L.A., 1957, Eisenhower, Elvis, Wheaties Breakfast of Champions . . . Does any of this ring a bell?

GEORGE: I've got to get to New York. All the info for takeoff is in my Mac.

LEE: In your what?

GEORGE: My Apple.

LEE: You left something in an apple so you could take off?

GEORGE: My Macintosh . . . my Apple. It's a computer. It hasn't been invented yet.

LEE: (not wanting to push George over the edge anymore than he already is) Okay, good buddy. Take it easy. No problem. You want to go to New York to get something you left in an apple . . . we go to New York.

CUT TO: A REAL L.A. STREET LOCATION.

Lee does a nifty maneuver around some cars at an intersection and floors the Chevy putting major distance between them and the ambulance.

 The Chevy comes barreling around a corner and makes a fast turn into an alley. Lee slams on the brakes. He no more cuts the lights than the ambulance speeds past.

INTERIOR. CHEVY.

LEE: All right. Now, what the hell is going on?

GEORGE: Okay . . . Susie said that the Lord said that life is a dream . . . not *like* a dream but *is* a dream, and it was time for her to wake up.

LEE: You're high, right? Tiny got you stoned and you've got reefer madness.

GEORGE: (finally getting it) Of course, it's just like Marie said . . . 'You can't know it as long as

you have a *you* to know it.' We have to let our
minds go to know *it*.

LEE: Good buddy, you don't have to try to let
your mind go, it's already gone.

GEORGE: Come on, Lee, let's give it a try.

LEE: What?

GEORGE: Letting our minds go.

LEE: How?

GEORGE: Not *how* . . . *Now*.

LEE: I'm missing something here.

GEORGE: There isn't any "how." There's only
"Now."

LEE: Oh . . . so you're saying, Now . . . is how?

GEORGE: Exactly. That's where everyone always
gets messed up. They get lost in the *how* and miss
the *Now*. That's what Susie said Christ told her,
'There is no *how*. There's only *Now*.'

LEE: What?

GEORGE: Oh, hell, man. That's it. The "Now"
is the somewhere-else place. Finally the clues are
all coming together. Let's give it a try.

LEE: Give what a try?

GEORGE: Letting our minds go.

LEE: Thanks, but no thanks. Me and my mind are going to sit this one out.

GEORGE: Okay, but this could be pivotal. Wish me luck.

LEE: What? You're going to lose your mind right here in downtown L.A.? In an alley? In the middle of the night? George, it's two in the morning and I gotta get home.

Undaunted, George sits up, back straight, closes his eyes, takes a deep breath and begins repeating spontaneously with each inhalation, "There is no *how*" and with each exhalation, "There is only *Now*."

CUT TO: VIDEO FLASHBACK

JACQUES: (continuing his aura reading) Let me repeat. Make the effort to conceive the understanding that the length of your life is the Now.

END VIDEO FLASHBACK

CUT BACK TO: INTERIOR CHEVY.

LEE: George . . . George, come on. I got to get home. I've got a band rehearsal tomorrow.

But George has fallen silent and all but dropped his last *how* in favor of *Now*. Lee checks to see if his good buddy is still breathing . . . Just barely.

LEE: Okay, you've taken this too far, George.
You're spookin' me.

George doesn't answer. Lee hems and haws, then reluctantly decides to follow his good buddy into the Now. Taking a firm grip on the steering wheel, he closes his eyes and starts repeating, "There is no *how*, only *Now* . . . There is no how . . . only . . .

And here our two experimenters sit—still, so very still, and yet becoming even more still and more and more and . . .

WRITER GEORGE: (VOICEOVER in the PRESENT—mumbling along as he types) In the stillness, it came to me to put my attention on the only thing that seemed reasonable—the thought of the thought that precedes the thought, I AM. Hoping this was the clue I had been looking for, I cautiously approached the edge of my last thought and, disregarding my better judgment, leapt blindly into the abyss. In an instant, all things recognizable ceased. There was nothing. No sound. No picture. No *thing* at all—only the familiar absence of the presence of anything recognizable.

It was as though I had awakened in a universe with no dimension . . . everything was removed, including me. I couldn't find me anywhere. The only thing that remained was the vague awareness of *something else*. Then *wham!* the thought sneaks in . . . 'You've gone too far this time,' followed by a shockwave of doubt that rippled through the stillness, shattering it beyond repair. In an instant, a million, billion, trillion other thoughts came crashing in. Before I know it, I'm back and I've brought my whole fucking story along with me, a string of shit a million, billion light-years across. Everything was there, just as I had left it . . . birth, death, the sun, moon and stars, the good ol' times, downtown L.A., the alley, the

Chevy, Lee, me, everything . . . just as I'd left it . . . a moment ago . . . a lifetime ago, a merr-y-go, a merr-y-ego-ago, and round and round E-go-I-go, gently down the stream, merr-i-ly merr-i-ly merrily merrily . . . life is but a dream . . . life is but a . . .

Lee comes hurtling out of Now.

> LEE: Christ, hell . . . fucking shit! What was that all about?

> GEORGE: I don't know, but I think we're onto something.

> LEE: Yeah, like what?

> ETY: (VOICEOVER) Oh, if I could only find the word. I've been looking for it for weeks . . .

CUT TO: VIDEO FLASHBACK

INTERIOR. ETY'S BEDROOM. Ety has become much more comfortable talking into George's camera.

> ETY: Something that is the very first. It's actually a little bit before the first. It's the thing that created it. In Hebrew, it's Rashoni. (Then it dawns on her.) Firstness. That's it. Firstness. Does that word exist in English?

> GEORGE: It does now.

> ETY: Oh, I'm so happy. Firstness. (She writes it on her pages.) That's it, the real thing before the ONE starts.

END VIDEO FLASHBACK

CUT BACK TO: INTERIOR. CHEVY.

LEE: I felt like I was losing my mind. I mean, I could really see little bits of it actually drifting off.

GEORGE: I know. Me, too. But how could we know we lost our minds, if we didn't have a mind to know we lost it?

LEE: Run that by me again.

GEORGE: Look, there's got to be something else, a part . . . apart from my mind, to know I lost it.

LEE: Yeah, like what?

GEORGE: Like something not involved in the scene at all. Like a . . . a watcher. Of course . . . a *silent watcher*.

LEE: You're losing me here, George.

GEORGE: It's like . . . who I think I am, isn't who I am at all.

LEE: You're not?

GEORGE: No. It's like, who I am is whatever it is that's watching who I think I am . . . or something like that. More research is definitely needed.

LEE: Yeah, well . . . (He starts the Chevy.) you can leave me out.

SOUND OF APPROACHING SIREN. Lee and George spin around. The ambulance speeds by the alley.

THE SOUND OF SCREECHING BRAKES.

GEORGE: Shit, they've found us.

The ambulance comes roaring back up the street and turns into the alley.

Lee pops the clutch and peels out.

The ambulance can be seen out the back window [ON THE REAR PROJECTION SCREEN]. Lee is pushing the Chevy to the max as he shoots out of the alley and races down one side street after another, on and off freeways, over bridges, across deserts, over mountains, through forests, cornfields, dirt roads, two-lane blacktops, through the Lincoln tunnel.

Having lost the ambulance somewhere between L.A. and New York, the Chevy comes barreling around a corner and skids to a stop in front of Writer George's New York apartment, smack in the glare of the lights of a TIME PRIORITY COURIER DELIVERY VAN.

George is out of the Chevy before it comes to a stop and races around to Lee's side.

GEORGE: Wow! That was incredible. Come up and check out my Apple.

LEE: Thanks, good buddy, but I think I'll wait until it's invented. See you tomorrow at school.

GEORGE: Yeah, sure. Hey . . . don't I appear different somehow?

LEE: Come on, George. None of us are really who we appear to be now, are we?

GEORGE: What?

Lee starts to drive away, then slams on the brakes.

LEE: Oh, and, by the way, good buddy I've heard that when you start questioning the dream, waking isn't far off.

Lee gives a mischievous wink, hits the gas and lays rubber all the way down the block, leaving George dumbfounded.

GEORGE: What the hell???

VOICEOVER: . . . Mister . . . hey, Mister.

George spins around and is confronted by a Time Priority Courier driver (TPC), a hyperwhite, nerdy looking, affable kid with coke bottle glasses, overextended ears and braces.

TPC: You know a *George Oops* in this building? He doesn't answer the buzzer.

GEORGE: That's me.

TPC: I gotta package for you, if you would just sign here.

George signs and takes the package.

TPC: You wouldn't be the same George Oops who was in that movie *West Side Story*, would you?

GEORGE: The very same.

TPC: No shit!

GEORGE: No shit.

TPC: Hey, would you do me a favor and sign an
autograph for my mother? She's a real big fan . . .
Got your picture, the album. She must have seen
that movie a hundred times. My ol' man doesn't
even rate like you.

George scribbles his autograph on a scrap of paper, and
hurries up the front steps of his apartment house. The
Time Priority Courier calls after him.

TPC: So whatever happened to you?

George stops in his tracks. He's had it with this question and
tonight, for some reason, he's not willing to let it slide.

GEORGE: (his back still to the kid) So you really
want to know what happened to me? Huh, kid?

The Time Priority Courier rushes up the steps in back of
George.

TPC: Are you kidding? My mother would wet her
pants if she knew I was talking to you.

George takes a moment to get into character. When he turns
around, he's a portrait of a broken man—slumped shoulders,
voice trembling, on the verge of tears.

GEORGE: This is hard for me, kid but I've got to tell
someone. I hope your mother won't be too
disappointed but I've been in jail for the last twenty
years for killing a fan who wouldn't leave me alone. She

stalked me night and day, day and night. I couldn't get away. If I went to a restaurant . . . there she was. If I went skiing in Aspen . . . there she was. If I went to an orgy in Hollywood, there she was. One time, she came down the chimney as Santa Claus. Finally, I just couldn't take it any longer. I snapped. I went berserk and stabbed her to death with her own ballpoint pen . . . eighty-five times. Do you have any idea what someone looks like when they've been stabbed eighty-five times with a ballpoint pen? You don't want to know. It's a horrible sight . . . There's ink everywhere and, the thing is, it doesn't come out. You can wash it in cold water, use stain removers, beat it on rocks, but it won't come out. But that's another story. The thing is, I just broke out of jail. You can't tell anyone kid . . . except your mother.

> TPC: (hardly able to get the words out) You're . . . ahhh . . . kidding, right?

George goes psycho. He grabs the kid by his collar and brings him up nose-to-nose.

> GEORGE: Kidding . . . kidding??? Do I look like I'm kidding, kid? I've been twenty years behind bars. I don't know from kidding, kid. I'm on the lam. Do you think your mother would hide me out?

The Time Priority Courier tries to get away from this lunatic, but George hangs on.

> GEORGE: I'm begging you, kid. Ask your mother. For all those wet panties she got watching me in the movies thirty years ago.. Fuck, she owes me, kid.

TPC: Look missss . . . Mister Oops. I really don't
think I can help you.

GEORGE: Call me, George. And what's your
name?

TPC: Uhhh, Melvin.

GEORGE: Well, Melvin, hear me. They're after
me. If they take me back, I'll fry. Your mother's
my only hope. She's got to hide me out. I can't go
back to the big house, Melvin. You don't know
what it's like in there. Please . . . please, you got to
help me.

After much twisting and turning, Melvin manages to break loose
and hightails it to his truck. George runs over and jumps in the
dumpster by the curb.

GEORGE: That's right. Hurry, Melvin. We're
talking life and death here. Tell you're mother, I'll
be waiting right here in this dumpster. Hurry.

Melvin throws the van into gear and guns it. George jumps out
of the dumpster and runs down the street after the fleeing van,
screaming at the top of his lungs.

GEORGE: And tell your obsessed-fan mother to
get a fucking life!

George runs halfway down the block before he finally gives up
the act.

GEORGE: Well, that was rather good if I do say
so myself . . . rusty, but still a bit of the ol' actor in
there, after all.

INTERIOR. GEORGE'S APARTMENT HOUSE. ENTRANCE HALL.

George comes running in. He stops at the foot of the stairs and opens his package. It's a 16mm film can with an accompanying letter from Aunt Lucille. George moves under the bare bulb hanging from the ceiling and reads:

> Dear George . . . In going through the attic the other day, your Uncle Clarence found this old film. He was going to throw it out. Then I remembered you was always playing with your daddy's camera when you was a youngster and thought maybe it was your film and you might want it.

George pries open the old film can. Along with the reel of 16mm film, there's an envelope—postmarked 1954, brown with age. The return address is stamped with the Kodak trademark.

THE CAMERA MOVES IN CLOSE ON THE LETTER AS GEORGE READS:

Dear Customer:
We recently discovered the enclosed reel of film in our vaults titled *George's Birth*. It has been here for five years due to a misfiling. You sent said film to Kodak for development but due to the questionable nature of said film, Kodak elected not to send said film back. At the time, we sent you a letter stating Kodak's policy in relation to nudity and/or pornographic material which said film was judged to be, and therefore said film was to be destroyed. However, in the meantime, our lawyers have advised us that we could not legally destroy said film. We are therefore returning said film. If, however, any further film is sent to Kodak of the pornographic nature of said film for development, we will take legal action.

George unrolls a few feet of the film and holds it up to the light. He is overjoyed with what he sees. His whooping and hollering can be heard all the way up the stairs.

INTERIOR. GEORGE'S APARTMENT. He bursts in the door, throws the film can on the futon and disappears into the closet.

He emerges a few moments later carrying his 16mm Bell and Howell movie projector—the one from the attic when he was a kid—balances it on a stack of books next to the floor-futon, threads the film from Aunt Lucille, then scrambles back into the closet, reappearing with his whole battered spaceman outfit.

He dumps everything on the futon, strips down to his boxers, climbs into his beat-up silver spacesuit, zips up, sticks on the phony beard, slips on the wig of dreadlocks, straps on the oxygen backpack, grabs his space helmet and heads to the computer where he types in: **How to Leave This Mundane Existence.**

While waiting for the connection, George scarfs down what's left of his cold Thai takeout and is about to crack open his fortune cookie when he hears a familiar voice.

> FAMILIAR VOICE: . . . Mother Ship emergency line.

> GEORGE: (elated) Is that you, Zarvox?

> ZARVOX: A rose by any other name . . .

> GEORGE: Oh, great. It's me . . . George . . . your ol' pal. It's so good to hear your voice. How have you been?

ZARVOX: Only small win-dow for transmission.
No time to dilly-dally. En-ter pass-word.

GEORGE: Password, password. (trying to remain
calm) Shit! I knew I'd forgotten something vital to
the whole outcome. Okay . . . think . . . think.
Password, password . . . Shit! I can't remember.

ZARVOX: Must be all those drugs you took. . .
de-stro-y-ed your brain.

GEORGE: Come on, Zarvox. We've spun
through the universe for eons together. It's me,
George, your ol' buddy, your ol' pal.

ZARVOX: Un-able to make ex-cep-tion. You may
not be who you app-ear to be. Must be careful of
im-pos-tors getting on the Mo-ther-Ship.

George bangs his fist down on the table in frustration
inadvertently smashing his fortune cookie—CRUNCH. And
there, as fate would have it, stuck to his sweaty fist, is his fortune.

THE CAMERA MOVES IN CLOSE ON THE LITTLE
STRIP OF PAPER. IT READS: *The answer you're looking for is
LOVE FOR SELF.*

GEORGE: Are you still there, Zarvox?

ZARVOX: Trans-mi-ssion time running out.

GEORGE: Okay, okay, I think I got it. Love . . .
love is the password. I think that's what I forgot.

ZARVOX: Sorry. That does not match our files . . .
close but no cigar.

GEORGE: Oh, hell.

CUT TO: VIDEO FLASHBACK

JACQUES REPEATS HIS EARLIER DECREE THAT
GEORGE HAS FAILED TO PICK UP ON.

JACQUES: Okay, let me repeat this. The key . . .
the clue . . . is . . . you need more love for Self to
stabilize the awareness that you are moving into.
Once you have that . . . it seems there is no
limitation.

END VIDEO FLASHBACK

GEORGE: (checks out his fortune again) Okay . . .
okay, how about this . . . *love for Self?*

ZARVOX: Bingo. Pass-word ac-cept-ed.

GEORGE: (elated) Yes . . . thank you, Lord!

ZARVOX: State your re-quest. And George, try
to re-sist your pro-pen-sity to ram-ble.

GEORGE: Okay, here it is in a nutshell. Think
I've been recognized. Disguise wearing thin. Don't
know how much longer I can keep up pretense. All
pertinent information has been collected.
Respectfully request to be evacuated as soon as
possible as the more I believe I am who I appear to
be, the less likely I will be able to lift off . . . Succinct
enough?

ZARVOX: How Sur-pris-ing . Re-quest be-ing re-
layed to Mo-ther Ship for pro-cess-ing. Stand-by.

George has no patience . . .

> GEORGE: Zarvox, you're killing me here with this waiting.

Zarvox comes back on line.

> ZARVOX: Re-quest grant-ed. You are 'go' for
> liftoff. What is your des-tin-a-tion?

> SPACEMAN GEORGE: Destination? I thought I
> was returning to the Mother Ship.

> ZARVOX: Must con-fer with su-per-vi-sor.

> SPACEMAN GEORGE: How long is this going
> to take? I don't have . . .

> ZARVOX: Pa-tience, George, pa-tience. All will
> be re-vealed.

> SPACEMAN GEORGE: But . . . but . . .

ZARVOX'S VOICE FADES AWAY replaced by a small video
picture. Because of the static, video freezes, artifacts and
constant break-up, it's hard for George to make out the image.

> SPACEMAN GEORGE: No, it can't be. Is that
> you, Tiny?

> TINY: (sounding echoey and far away) How's it
> goin,' George? We've been looking forward to
> your return.

> SPACEMAN GEORGE: You're in on this too?

> TINY: From the get-go.

SPACEMAN GEORGE: When you got me stoned back when I was a kid . . . you knew then?

TINY: To know or not to know, that's a tricky question.

SPACEMAN GEORGE: How about Susie?

TINY: How about Susie? Ain't she a piece of work? The sister is outrageous, truly an alien of extraordinary abilities.

SPACEMAN GEORGE: I knew it. She's not from here. What about my good buddy, Lee?

TINY: Special agent. Kind of like a guardian angel.

SPACEMAN GEORGE: I knew something was up with him. This is incredible. I feel like everyone knows something I don't.

TINY: So, what's the hesitation, George? You know . . . *he who hesitates is lost.*

SPACEMAN GEORGE: That reminds me . . . Marie. What about Marie?

TINY: Part of the stealth force, Special Operations. Their expertise is surgical strikes. They leave the body-mind organism intact but obliterate the ego. It's the . . . take-no-prisoners approach . . . an attention-getter for those straying too far off the program, if you get my drift.

SPACEMAN GEORGE: Oh, I got the drift all right. I drifted right down to my knees. But it didn't do any good. I still can't seem to figure it out.

TINY: Nuth'n to figure out, my man.

SPACEMAN GEORGE: I feel like I've forgotten something, something vital to the whole outcome.

TINY: You're on the right track with this love business. Keep searching.

SPACEMAN GEORGE: Come on, Tiny. Give me a break . . . a hint, something concrete. I'm losing my mind here.

TINY: All right, George, calm down. Now follow me. This is real basic stuff. There are three places you can hang out. You are either sleeping . . . dreaming . . . or awake. You following me so far, George?

SPACEMAN GEORGE: I'm right with you . . . waking, dreaming or sleeping. Got it.

TINY: Well, there's another one, a fourth . . . not too many people know about. It's that *somewhere-else place* you keep getting glimpses of. But it's nuth'n like the other three. Don't get them mixed up. In fact, it's the absence of the presence of the other three.

SPACEMAN GEORGE: You're losing me here, Tiny. Could you just bottom-line it for me? Tell it

to me like I'm the stupidest person that ever lived.
What is it?

TINY: All right, George, calm down. Now dig it.
What I can tell you is . . . you are not *of* the world.
You are not even *in* the world.

SOUND OVER: APPROACHING SIREN. Spaceman
George takes a fast look out the window.

WHAT HE SEES: Melvin's Time Priority Courier van and the
ambulance coming full bore down the block. Spaceman George
shoots back to his computer.

SPACEMAN GEORGE: Tiny, if you could just
pick up the pace a little. I'm kinda in a hurry.
What were you saying?

TINY: The bottom line is, you are not *in* the
world, George, the world is *in you*. In other words,
life is but a dream, *Sh-Boom, Sh-Boom.*

SOUND OVER: VEHICLES SCREECHING TO A STOP
DOWN BELOW.

George takes another fast look out the window. All sorts of
wacky folks come tumbling out of the two vehicles. It looks like a
casting call for a Fellini film.

First, Melvin's mother unloads herself—a large rotund woman
in curlers clutching an autograph book. She's followed by a slew
of paparazzi reminiscent of a pack of jackals thirsting for the kill.
Then Melvin stumbles out followed in chaotic succession by the
Orderlies, the Director, his cameraman, the soundman, the
studio cop, and various and sundry outraged members of the
film crew. To top it off, a buttload of "reporters" from the

tabloid gutter press come screeching to a stop in their over-sized gas guzzling multipurpose off road vehicle accompanied by C.B. Blown, Sit and Nurse Wholesome, who is, apropos to nothing, clad in a skimpy, to non-existent, camouflage bikini.

SPACEMAN GEORGE: Look, Tiny, can you just get me back to the Mother Ship? I got these people after me. They want to take me back to the loony bin and fry my brains.

TINY: George, the Mother Ship is here. It's been here all along.

SPACEMAN GEORGE: No.

TINY: Yes.

SPACEMAN GEORGE: Then why don't I get it? I mean, really get it, permanent . . . like everybody else?

CUT TO: VIDEO FLASHBACK

GEORGE'S VIDEO OF JACQUES. He's still in a trance, reading George's aura.

JACQUES: You are so very stubborn, George. Once you get an idea locked in your head, a million tons of TNT wouldn't dislodge it. But I see, in spite of yourself, you're opening up to a fantastic realization. You are being directed to a spiritual pattern that is completely contradictory to who you think you are.

END VIDEO FLASHBACK

CUT BACK TO: SPACEMAN GEORGE AND TINY.

> SPACEMAN GEORGE: Will you please tell me who the hell this guy is who keeps cutting into my life?

> TINY: He's assigned to the . . .

> SPACEMAN GEORGE: The nut cases, right?

> TINY: Let's say, the more resistant cases.

> SPACEMAN GEORGE: Look, Tiny, do you think I'm ever going to get *it?*

> TINY: Eventually.

SOUND OVER: The mad horde clamoring up the stairs.

> SPACEMAN GEORGE: (panicking) I don't have *eventually.*

> TINY: Okay, then you might be interested in the *Never Mind* program.

> SPACEMAN GEORGE: How long does it take?

> TINY: No time at all.

> SPACEMAN GEORGE: Now you're talking.

> TINY: It can be dangerous, though.

Because he's so engrossed in his conversation with Tiny, George is unaware the room is filling with smoke.

SPACEMAN GEORGE: How dangerous?

TINY: If you don't totally surrender every last iota
of who you think you are, you could end up back
here in a karmic rebirth loop lasting for eons before
your number ever comes up again.

As the two continue their conversation, the **CAMERA
SLOWLY DOLLIES AROUND GEORGE** eventually
revealing that the wall in back of him is missing, and that
George's apartment is really a MOVIE SET on the Hollywood
sound stage. To make matters worse, in the distance, creeping
through the smoke, is George's deranged band of pursuers,
looking like cartoon characters all huddled together, skulking
onto the set behind George, who is totally oblivious of his
impending ambush.

SPACEMAN GEORGE: Okay, Tiny, let's say I
surrender every last iota. Then what?

TINY: You're outta here.

SPACEMAN GEORGE: Really out of here, like
gone? Vapor trails?

TINY: Outta here for good. Gone, as if you never
was.

SPACEMAN GEORGE: Excellent. Let's go for . . .
Tiny and George's conversation is brought to an abrupt halt
with the Director screaming through his megaphone
"ROLLLLLLL CAMERA!"

The lights on the news cameras flood on. George is lit up like a
deer in the headlights. Before he can make a run for it, the
Orderlies grab him and throw him to the floor. The paparazzi

rush in flashing away in a mad feeding frenzy. Even with the overwhelming odds, it takes everyone piling on George to restrain him. In the middle of the pandemonium, Melvin's mother barrels headlong into the fray, unleashing her massive bosoms in Spaceman George's face, demanding he autograph them.

George's capture is finalized when Sit burrows in through the chaos and joyously provides the Orderlies with a straitjacket.

THE CAMERA MOVES IN THROUGH THE TRIUMPHANT MOB TO A CLOSE-UP OF SPACEMAN GEORGE—bound and gagged with duct tape. He looks totally and pathetically out of his mind—but not in a good way.

The Orderlies grab Spaceman George by his heels and, accompanied by the clamoring horde, victoriously drag George off the movie set, disappearing in the smoke.

There is a moment of silence, then the SOUND OF TYPING FADES UP.

The CAMERA PANS BACK into the smoke filled room.

There, at his computer, is Writer George, naked, barely visible through the smoke, silhouetted in the purple pulsating light from the neon sign across the street, typing as fast as his misspelling will allow.

Writer George has finally figured out the last scene of his screenplay and will not be deterred no matter what. Yelling, screaming, smoke, sirens, downpours, the couple fucking in the next apartment, reefer madness—nothing will stop Writer George now until he has written the last page of his screenplay and it's printed out.

THE CAMERA MOVES THROUGH THE SMOKE, ACROSS THE ROOM, INTO THE COMPUTER SCREEN AND PANS ALONG WITH THE WORDS AS WRITER GEORGE TYPES:

CUT TO: THE FINAL SCENE. MENTAL INSTITUTION. MOVING SHOT. Spaceman George is being dragged by his heels down the corridor.

AND WE DO . . .

CUT TO: MENTAL INSTITUTION. CORRIDOR. SPACEMAN GEORGE'S UPSIDE-DOWN POINT OF VIEW AS HE'S BEING DRAGGED ALONG.

Microphones and video cameras are thrust in Spaceman George's upside-down face. The frantic Press falls over themselves trying to keep up, shouting a relentless barrage of dimwitted questions: *How does it feel being a has-been? Did you really discover Sharon Tate? Is it true you only enter buildings from the East?*

Sit can be seen jumping up above the fray frantically waving a copy of *Daily Variety*. The headline reads: OOPS PIC SOCKO BOFFO BOX—UNDERGROUND GOES MAINSTREAM.

C.B. is beside himself with excitement. He and his new starlet Nurse Wholesome are throwing out copies of TIME magazine like Frisbees. The picture on the cover is Spaceman George, gagged and bound in a straitjacket, with the caption: OOPS! HE'S BACK.

CUT TO: The *HE WHO HESITATES IS LOST* GAME SHOW.

The doors in the back of the theater burst open and the Orderlies drag in Spaceman George. The audience rises in a standing ovation, lining the aisles as Spaceman George and his jubilant entourage make their way to the stage where . . . Dr. Julia J. Olson waits to perform the final insult.

The Orderlies pick up Spaceman George, slam him into a wooden chair and lash him down.

Dr. Olson forces her way through the media frenzy to the center of the stage and raises her hands. Without saying a word, everyone, including Melvin's mother, falls silent.

In a grand gesture, Orderly #1 hands Dr. Julia J. the dreaded discombobulator. She takes the offering with solemnity and, as if coronating a king, raises it above Spaceman George. With an offstage drum roll, she lowers the dreaded device onto Spaceman George's head.

Everything appearing ready, Dr. Julia J. gives Orderly #2 a nod, and with vicious delight, he rips the duct tape from Spaceman George's mouth, taking a fair amount of his epidermis with it.

> SPACEMAN GEORGE: (screaming) No, please
> don't fry my brains! I'll never get back to the
> Mother Ship.

> DR. OLSON: Now, George, calm down. We're all
> your friends here. Besides, it's Showtime.
> A VOICE: (booms over the PA) Okay, everyone,
> five seconds to air. Let's pull it together . . . Five,
> four, three, two and . . .

> ANNOUNCER: Welcome back to *He Who
> Hesitates Is Lost*, the game show that asks the
> question, who are you if not who you think you
> are? And now, here's your host, the ever popular
> psychiatrist to the stars, known affectionately as the

terrorist of the psychic world, Dr. Julia J. Olson.
And now . . . Heere's Julia. J.

The applause signs flash.

> DR. OLSON: Ladies and gentlemen, please
> welcome back Spaceman George. He has chosen
> to leave it all behind, to give up searching for who
> he is, and go for the very tricky *Never Mind* package.
> Let's hear it for Spaceman George.

The audience goes wild, stomping, hollering and whistling.

> DR. OLSON: Are you ready, George?

The audience falls silent in anticipation.

> SPACEMAN GEORGE: Remind me . . . if I
> make it through . . . give up . . . what happens?

> DR. OLSON: You will be realized in *It*.

> SPACEMAN GEORGE: *It?*

> DR. OLSON: Yes, *It*, the one and only, the
> original, bona fide, universal, omnipresent, God of
> Gods, Light of Lights, It-ness consciousness. In
> other words, you'll be outta here, nowhere to be
> found, over and done with, end of story.

> SPACEMAN GEORGE: (resigned) Okay, let's go
> for it.

> DR. OLSON: Are you sure? There's no going
> back, no changing our minds.

SPACEMAN GEORGE: For God's sake, let's do it. Put me out of my misery, one way or the other.

DR. OLSON: Okay, then here goes, George. Just answer a few easy questions and you'll be outta here.

A huge grandfather clock is rolled out on the stage—an enlarged replica of the one at the bottom of the stairs at Young George's grandparents' house.

The hands on the huge clock are at 11:57. Melvin has the honor of giving the pendulum a swing and—the ticking begins.

DR. OLSON: This should only take a couple of minutes.

SPACEMAN GEORGE: What if it takes longer?

DR. OLSON: You don't want to know.

SPACEMAN GEORGE: The monsters and demons?

DR. OLSON: George, we're wasting time.

SPACEMAN GEORGE: Go . . . go.

DR. OLSON: First question. Your name . . . What is your name?

SPACEMAN GEORGE: My name. You know my name, it's . . .

Before Spaceman George can answer we . . .

CUT BACK TO: WRITER GEORGE'S APARTMENT. Writer George is still where we left him, sitting naked at his computer, frantically typing this last scene.

THE CAMERA MAKES A FAST MOVE INTO THE COMPUTER. A JOB APPLICATION FORM IS DISPLAYED.

On the top line—under FIRST AND LAST NAME— **GEORGE OOPS** is boldly printed.

Writer George hits the DELETE BUTTON.

The name George Oops vanishes. In its place, Writer George types in: **NOBODY**. A flash of electricity shoots across the screen. As it does we . . .

CUT BACK TO: THE GAME SHOW. CLOSE ON SPACEMAN GEORGE.

The electrical charge surges through Spaceman George. Sparks shoot out from under the discombobulator. Spaceman George's body jerks and stiffens. At the back of the stage, the voltage meter on the giant electric shock machine bounces into the red. Spaceman George goes limp.

> DR. OLSON: George, George. Are you still with us?

No response. The audience goes silent.

CUT TO: VIDEO FLASHBACK

JACQUES. RELENTLESSLY CONTINUING HIS AURA READING.

JACQUES: It's the beginning of a very powerful force. You'll experience a current of contradiction . . . a spiritual pattern which is totally contradictory to who you think you are. These conflicts will so improve your awareness that all of a sudden the blinders are removed from your eyes.

END VIDEO FLASHBACK

Nurse Wholesome comes running out from the wings carrying a bucket of ice water and throws it in Spaceman George's face. The shock brings him hurtling back to consciousness. The audience gives a collective sigh of relief.

DR. OLSON: You were saying?

SPACEMAN GEORGE: (dazed) I was? What was I saying?

DR. OLSON: Your name. You were about to say your name, for the record. What is your name?

SPACEMAN GEORGE: My name is . . . hmmm, that's strange. I don't seem to remember . . . just a minute. . . (George sings in hopes of remembering.) *Happy birthday to you . . . Happy birthday to you . . . Happy birthday dear . . . dear . . . (He waits for his name to pop forth but nothing shows up.)* I do have a name. Everybody has a name. I mean, if I didn't have a name, I'd be . . . I don't know, I'd be . . . a nobody.

The audience bursts into applause.

DR. OLSON: Oh George, this is so exciting.

SPACEMAN GEORGE: I don't get it. Why all
the . . ?

DR. OLSON: No time for chitchatting, George.
The seconds are ticking away. Let's move on. Next
question. What do you do?

SPACEMAN GEORGE: What is it with these
questions? You go to the movies, don't you? I'm in
the movies. Everybody knows that I'm an act . . .

Before Spaceman George can get the word "actor" out of his
mouth we . . .

CUT BACK TO: WRITER GEORGE at his computer.
CLOSE on the second line of the application form. Next to
OCCUPATION it reads: **ACTOR**.

Writer George DELETES the word ACTOR and types in:
NOTHING. Again there is an electrical surge, and again we. . .

CUT BACK TO: *THE HE WHO HESITATES IS LOST*
GAME SHOW.

As before, Spaceman George stiffens and passes out from the
electrical shock. And again Nurse Wholesome drenches
Spaceman George with a bucket of ice water.

DR OLSON: Tell us, George. What is it that you
do?

Spaceman George's eyes flutter open. Although dazed, he seems
calmer somehow, more accepting of his fate.

CUT TO: VIDEO FLASHBACK

JACQUES. CONTINUING HIS AURA READING OF
GEORGE.

> JACQUES: It will take a little while for you to
> conceive of the fact that what has been is of no
> value and, what you anticipate to be, is of less
> value. But how you function within the freedom of
> Self . . . at this Moment . . . Now . . . is the most
> valuable place your attention can be.

END VIDEO FLASHBACK

CUT BACK TO: THE GAME SHOW.

> SPACEMAN GEORGE: Well . . . let's see. I do . . .
> What do I do, actually? Not too much, really. Come
> to think of it, I don't do anything. Everything just sort
> of . . . settles itself.

Dr. Olson becomes giddy with anticipation. The applause signs
flash. The audience goes berserk. Spaceman George is totally
bewildered at the audience's response.

> SPACEMAN GEORGE: Why is everyone . . ?

> DR. OLSON: Oh, this is so thrilling. I had no
> idea it would be so much fun playing doctor.

> SPACEMAN GEORGE: You mean, you're not
> an actual, bona fide doctor?

> DR. OLSON: Oh, come on, George, get real.
> This is Hollywood. Nothing is what it appears to
> be.

SPACEMAN GEORGE: But there must be something that's real here.

DR. OLSON: Oh, poor dear. You really are from Iowa, aren't you.

SPACEMAN GEORGE: But . . .

DR. OLSON: No time for *buts*. The seconds are ticking away. Now I want you to inquire deeply into this next question. It's crucial to the whole outcome. Are you sure you were born?

SPACEMAN GEORGE: What kind of stupid question is that? Of course I was born. How the hell do you think I got here? I can prove it. I was born in . . .

Before he can get the words out we . . .

CUT BACK TO: WRITER GEORGE'S COMPUTER. CLOSE ON THE THIRD LINE OF THE APPLICATION FORM.

Under the question, PLACE OF BIRTH it reads in bold type: **AVOCA, IOWA**.

Writer George hits the DELETE BUTTON and George's birth vanishes. In its place, Writer George types in: **NO ITEMS FOUND**.

CUT BACK TO: THE GAME SHOW.

Again, the electrical current surges through Spaceman George and he passes out. And again, Nurse Wholesome revives him with a bucket of ice water.

DR. OLSON: Come, come, George. Tell us. What's your proof? You were born where?

SPACEMAN GEORGE: I . . . I was, born . . . I was???

There's uproarious laughter and applause from the audience.

SPACEMAN GEORGE: I don't get it. Why is everyone so . . ?

DR. OLSON: Please, George, stay focused. You're almost there. Now, here's the final question. It's the biggie. Listen carefully. Who are you when not being who you think you are?

The audience collectively leans forward in their seats as an offstage drumroll adds to the tension.

SPACEMAN GEORGE: Who am I?

DR. OLSON: Yes. Who . . . are . . . you?

SPACEMAN GEORGE: I don't get it. I'm me. Who else could I be?

DR. OLSON: And who is me?

SPACEMAN GEORGE: Me . . . here. This me...this bag of bones and flesh sitting here.

DR. OLSON: Is that who you really think you are?

SPACEMAN GEORGE: Well, not just. I'm other things, too.

DR. OLSON: For instance?

SPACEMAN GEORGE: Well, for instance, I've got a mind and a brain . . . molecules, atoms, thoughts, ideas, feelings. . . and . . . and, I mean . . . I'm what you see. I'm me.

DR. OLSON: Be careful, George. Is that your final answer? You're a . . . *me?*

SPACEMAN GEORGE: Just a minute…let's see here. If I'm not me then I've got to be . . . now I've got it . . . No, I'm not that either . . . Oh, I know, I . . . am . . .

DR. OLSON: Yes, George?

SPACEMAN GEORGE: (rethinking) No, I'm not that either. Let's see . . . Okay, now I've really got it, I am . . .

DR. OLSON: Come on, George. Not much time left.

SPACEMAN GEORGE: (panicking) Shit, I knew I forgot something vital to the whole outcome. Who the hell am I? I am . . . I am . . .

CUT BACK TO: WRITER GEORGE'S APARTMENT. POINT OF VIEW FROM INSIDE THE COMPUTER, FRAMED ON THE BACKSIDE OF THE SCREEN—on which George repeatedly types:

who am I? . . .who am I? . . . who am I? . . . who am I? . . . Who am I? . . .who am I? . . . who am I? . . . who am I? . . . Who am I? . . .who am I? . . .

who am I? . . . who am I? . . . Who am I? . . .who am I? . . . who am I? . . . who am I? . . .

SOUND OVER: INNER VOICE . . .

INNER VOICE: Come on, George. Will you just fucking say it so we can get the hell out of here.

SPACEMAN GEORGE: Who's that?

INNER VOICE: It's me. Who the hell else do you think would be in here? I tell you, George, if you fuck up again and we have to come back here, I'm through.

SPACEMAN GEORGE: But I don't know. I really don't know who I am. I'm confused.

INNER VOICE: Oh, bullshit. Look at your life. It doesn't get any more obvious than this. All that crap you've been going through, searching for God, enlightenment, bliss . . . excuses, always putting it off. It's always 'next time' with you. Well, this *is* next time. It's here, right, now. You've got a chance to clean up your miserable life and you're still hesitating.

SPACEMAN GEORGE: But . . .

INNER VOICE: No but's. Just do it and let's get the hell out of here.

SPACEMAN GEORGE: Oh, I don't know. I . . .

INNER VOICE: Come on, George. Everybody thinks they are somebody they aren't. Even Christ had to admit it.

SPACEMAN GEORGE: Really?

INNER VOICE: Sure. You know when he was up there on the cross screaming, 'Father, why did you forsake me?'

SPACEMAN GEORGE: Yeah.

INNER VOICE: The Father didn't forsake him. For a moment he just bought into the part he was playing . . . you know, some victim guy nailed to a cross playing the messiah, everybody praising him and everything. After a while you start believing it yourself . . . it's a co-dependent thing. But after he saw the truth and dropped the mistaken identity, the dying thing was a snap.

SPACEMAN GEORGE: How do you know these things?

INNER VOICE: I'm your inner Self, all wise and knowing. Damn it, George. End this fucking endless movie and let's get out of here.

SPACEMAN GEORGE: Okay, but if . . .

INNER VOICE: Just do it, George.

SPACEMAN GEORGE: With and E or an O?

INNER VOICE: What the hell are you talking about?

SPACEMAN GEORGE: You can spell it both ways, with an E or an O

INNER VOICE: It's your call, George. I don't
care if you spell it with an E or an O or in
Mongolian . . . just fucking do it and let's get out of
here.

SPACEMAN GEORGE: I think I prefer the more
classic version with an O . . . on the other hand . . .

INNER VOICE: Okay! That's fucking it. I'm
outta here.

SPACEMAN GEORGE: Okay, okay . . . I'll do it.
Here goes.

CUT TO: WRITER GEORGE'S COMPUTER SCREEN.
CLOSE ON THE FOURTH LINE OF THE APPLICATION
FORM WHERE NEXT TO **IDENTITY** IT READS:

A SPECIAL SOMEBODY.

Writer George hits the DELETE BUTTON. And in place of 'A
SPECIAL SOMEBODY,' types: **IMPOSTOR**—with an O,
instantaneously igniting a humongous blast from God knows
where . . . the other side of the universe, setting off a chain
reaction echoing through an endless string of George's reluctant
incarnations, where, in each he has pretended, acted, conned,
faked, and generally scammed his way through one lifetime after
the other—but no more. Not this time. The good ol' times _is_
over, ending here and now with a karmic bullet that has
George's name on it, exploding through time, finding its mark
right on target, in the back of Impostor George's head, the force
propelling him crashing half-faced through the computer screen
of 'Who am I's' splattering a good portion of his brains over the
lens.

CUT BACK TO: *HE WHO HESITATES IS LOST* GAME SHOW.

Spaceman George sits slumped in his chair, head fallen forward, sparks flying out from under the discombobulator.

Nurse Wholesome does her ice water routine again, but no response this time. She douses Spaceman George with a second bucket and a third, but sadly, still, no reaction. The audience sits in hushed silence.

> DR. OLSON: Is there a doctor in the house?

Dr. Pompous rushes forward and checks Spaceman George's vital signs. After some probing and poking, Dr. Pompous confirms that Spaceman George is still among the living—but just barely.

Dr. Olson all but shoves the microphone in Spaceman George's mouth.

> DR. OLSON: George, if you can hear me, what is your final answer? Who are you when not being who you think you are?

Just as the grandfather clock strikes the final hour, Spaceman George's trembling voice booms out over the PA . . .

> SPACEMAN GEORGE: I don't have a clue! I . . . I . . . I can't find me anywhere.

Dr. Olson can hardly contain herself. She is almost giddy ˙ with excitement.

> DR. OLSON: It gives me great personal pleasure to announce that Spaceman George has left his mind

behind, along with the good ol' times, the best of times, and I might add . . . just in the nick of time.
Consequently, Spaceman George is officially and totally (The audience joins in.) OUT . . . OF . . . HERERERE! (Dr. Olson adds) Next stop . . . the Mother Ship.

The audience leaps out of their seats in an uproarious ovation. The place comes unglued: cameras flash, balloons drop from the rafters, confetti falls like snow, the corks pop and the champagne flows. The party has begun.

At the back of the theater, the doors fly open and Susie and Tiny make a grand entrance leading hundreds of gospel singers down the aisles to the stage singing, "*Row, row, row your boat, gently down the stream, merrily, merrily, merrily, merrily, life is but a dream, life is but a dream . . .*"

The audience joins in with voices rising to a deafening pitch as the classic children's song turns into this wild, hand-clapping, funky, kick-ass gospel rendition. The joint is absolutely jumping.

To top it off, Teen Lee bops out on stage, dressed in a purple tuxedo, toting a tenor sax. He's accompanied by five Black dudes in sharkskin suits with greased-back hair—The Chords— the group direct from the Fifties who had the original crossover rhythm and blues hit, *Sh-Boom, Sh-Boom.*

Lee gives the guys the downbeat and in counterpoint to everyone else singing *Row, row, row your boat,* the Chords, with Lee on sax, wail in with *Sh-Boom, Sh-Boom, life is but a dream,* the perfect musical accompaniment for Spaceman George's sendoff.

C.B. and Sit eagerly squeeze in on either side of Spaceman George for a final photo op. Before the paparazzi can flash away, Spaceman George's head falls forward and his body goes limp. The room goes silent.

Doctor Pompous rushes in, puts his stethoscope to Spaceman George's chest and desperately searches for a sign of life, but alas, there is none, and the good doctor sadly announces the departure of Spaceman George.

C.B. is outraged that he has missed getting a final photo op with his star, but Sit to the rescue one last time—he's got this emergency covered. He yanks up Spaceman George's head, and lashes it to the back of the chair with his tie. Without losing a beat, he takes his ballpoint pen and, with the artistic skill of an amoeba, draws two gawking eyeballs on George's closed lids. And for a final stroke of genius, Sit shoves his pen in Spaceman George's mouth, lengthwise, pushing out his cheeks, so as to shape a pathetically distorted smile.

C.B. is righteously impressed, so much so, that he proclaims to the celebratory masses that Sit is the new Head of Production of Blown Studios. Sit's life is now complete.

The Director screams through his megaphone for his cameraman to move in for a CLOSE-UP of the two moguls as the paparazzi flash away.

Not to be left out, Nurse Wholesome dances into the frame with a happy Melvin squeezed between her breasts, and cozies up between C.B. and Sit.

Not to be left out, Melvin's mother bulldozes her way into the photo all but crushing poor Sit in her ?. This starts a minor stampede of cast and crew squeezing into the photo—Dr. Julia J., The Director, the Orderlies, Susie, Tiny, Young George and Joyce, George's Father, The Chords, Lee, Grandma and Grandpa, Pastor Clarence, the Super, Teen Lee, Dr. Pompous. It's a packed frame.

To complete the picture, Daisy cartwheels out on stage, ending with an Olympic back flip onto Spaceman George's lap.

At this point, all sense of decorum has broken down. Even members of the now drunken audience are forcing their way into the photo.

Spaceman George's demise has done nothing to dampen the raucous celebration. On the contrary, his departure seems to have added to the festivities.

In an attempt to bring some semblance of dignity to George's passing, Dr. Julia J. directs the Orderlies to prepare Spaceman George for his return to the Mother Ship.

The Orderlies untie Spaceman George and replace the dreaded discombobulator with his mirrored-visor space helmet and lock it down. Noticeably shaken, the two lift Spaceman George above the cheering crowd and tearfully deliver their one-time nemesis to the joyous assembly, who in turn, pass him hand over hand, above their heads, downstage to the camera.

Dr. Julia J. now directs everyone's attention to the back of the stage where, on her cue, the curtains part and Marie—again playing the part of George's mother—(also known as the Slut in the next apartment, also known as the Actress) totters out on stage carrying a lengthy object wrapped in velvet.

The crowd respectfully parts as "George's mother" makes her way downstage where Spaceman George is held aloft. Playing the moment for all it's worth, she beckons Sit to approach. He eagerly comes forward and goes down on bended knee.

With an actress's dramatic sense of timing, George's mother unfurls her velvet parcel and holds its contents up to the camera for all to see. It's Young George's baseball bat, the one he used to beat off the monsters and demons when he was a kid. George's mother lovingly bequeaths the bat to Sit, with all the regal dignity of a queen knighting her subject.

Sit accepts the bat with bowed head as if being knighted by Excalibur. After a silent moment he rises and, with as much humility as he can muster, comes downstage to the camera.

With pride bursting and tears streaming, Sir Sit lines up on the lens and, like a baseball player going for a home run, takes a savage swing, smashing the lens of the camera to smithereens. Our POINT OF VIEW immediately goes OUT OF FOCUS.

We are now looking through an empty optical tube where, at the other end, the blurry image of Spaceman George can be seen held aloft.

With voices raised in ecstatic celebration of *life is but a dream, Sh-Boom, Sh-Boom,* Spaceman George is slid headfirst up to the camera. From our POINT OF VIEW it appears George is being stuffed into the opening that was the camera lens.

THE PICTURE GOES BLACK.

• • •

SOUND OVER BLACK: A WOMAN SCREAMING AND MOANING—IN ECSTASY OR PAIN—IT'S IMPOSSIBLE TO TELL.

AFTER A MOMENT THE CAMERA PULLS OUT of a dark and mysterious passageway. We realize soon enough we are emerging from between a woman's legs giving birth. Infant George is the one trying to get out.

This is the scratched and faded 16mm black-and-white film that George's Aunt Lucille sent him. It's the footage George's father shot of Infant George being exhumed from one of those dark and foreboding places George has spent his life rummaging around in for clues as to who he is.

The CAMERA WIDENS OUT FURTHER revealing that Infant George's film debut is being projected on the wall of Writer George's apartment.

The CAMERA PANS BACK AROUND the smoke-filled room in search of the source of the projection. It's George's vintage 16mm Bell and Howell projector. It's still where George positioned it a few scenes back, next to the floor futon on a stack of books. However, no sign of Writer George.

The CAMERA MOVES into the flickering ray of light streaming through the smoke, and follows it back across the room to the chattering projector and into the lens, ending in a MACRO CLOSE-UP of the film running upside down as it passes through the film gate.

Here, front-row center, in our inverted, miniature movie theater, we watch between the sprocket holes as Infant George struggles to be born. It is, however, unclear whether Infant George is having trouble extricating himself from the mess he finds himself in, or, if he is trying to reverse the clutches of destiny and hightail it back to *somewhere-else*.

Either way, it is a moot point at this juncture, as eager hands squeeze in and yank Infant George from the anonymity of Being—being a *nobody*, a *nothing*—and thrust him into the spotlight of being a *somebody*, the pressure from which, as we have seen, has caused George to live his whole life acting as if he were who he appeared to be—that is, this impostor, this ego encapsulated bag of bones and flesh suspended between the belief of birth on the one end, and the fear of death on the other, and where, in limbo, betwixt and between, he has managed to eke out this momentary existence, it having at its core, no more reality than a dream.

At last, George has the celluloid proof positive that he has been searching for—that his existence is *"reel,"* if only at twenty-four frames a second. And it comes none too soon, as the end of his film runs out, leaving us with no picture, no sound—nothing—only a white screen as the last of George's proof of his existence flips through the projector . . . and gone.

> My mind reals off. What more is there to say? "Cut . . . Perfect! All is as it is and couldn't be other . . . Print it. That's a wrap!"

. . .

So now that the movie is over and the lights are coming up, any confusion as to what was real or imagined is hopefully Self-evident in the realization that there was nothing ever there in the first place but the play of light on a blank screen, and any reality alluded to was never anything more than the projection of the viewer's mistaken identity in a secret collusion with the Author's deliberate misdirection. . . and all just for the fun of it.

CPSIA information can be obtained at www.ICGtesting.com
Printed in the USA
LVOW131335101012

302263LV00001B/9/P

9 780615 175515